CW00394265

Cover art copyright © 2023 by Stefan Koidl

Edited by Brandon Applegate, bapplegate.com

Content warnings at the end of the book. Check the table of contents for page number.

Paperback ISBN: 979-8-9868771-0-5
Hardcover ISBN: 979-8-9868771-2-9

THE FIRST FIVE MINUTES OF THE APOCALYPSE

TALES FROM THE BEGINNING OF THE END

Edited by

BRANDON APPLEGATE

CONTENTS

EDITOR'S NOTE

Horror is for everyone, regardless of experience or trauma. For that reason, content warnings are located at the back of this book. If you don't feel you need them, that's great. If you do, please use them.

FOREWORD

THE WORLD IS ALWAYS ENDING

BRANDON APPLEGATE

We all have that event. The one where, years from now, we'll remember where we were, what we were doing, who we were with, what we were feeling. It's nearly cliché to talk about it. The Kennedy assassination, the moon landing, Woodstock, The Challenger explosion, the AIDS epidemic, the Oklahoma City bombing, Princess Diana's death, Columbine, 9/11, COVID lockdown, the January 6th insurrection—these are markers. Points on the maps of our lives. Moments where we are part of something bigger than ourselves, the collective whole.

Like many of my generation ("Elder Millennial" if you're wondering, I'll go ahead and take my cane now, thanks), mine is 9/11. I have two very distinct memories about the event. First is the memory of watching it happen. I was, of course, quite safe, sitting in a high school classroom in Texas. Mr. Mattingly wheeled in a massive tube TV on one of those black steel carts with the VCR underneath. He was a soft-spoken man for the most part, and we weren't kind to him. It was a rare event when he could shake us from our shouting and talking and laughter in homeroom. We walked all over the poor guy. But something about the squeak of the wheels on the cart, the way our teacher cleared his throat, the look on his face; it silenced us. He told us what was happening, and that it was important. He told us we needed to see it. He turned on the TV to scenes of billowing smoke and senseless death, walked to his desk at the back of the classroom and put his head in his hands.

We watched the end of the world in silence.

Of course, the world didn't actually end that day. We're still here. You're reading this. The Earth is whole, more or less, and still capable of nurturing and sustaining life. But that is the grand scale. And while it wasn't the biblical apocalypse, it was the end of a great deal of other things. It was the end of total safety. The first successful attack on sovereign American soil by a foreign power since World War II. The truth came out. We'd been living a lie. The ever-popular "It-Can't-Happen-Here" lie.

The second memory I have of the event is less concrete, though still distinct. It's the memory of the aftershock. Because that's the thing about events like this one: it feels like everything that follows is connected. Moments like that are dividers. There is life before and there is life after. Even though Columbine happened a couple years before 9/11, it seemed like the towers falling is what made everyone paranoid. Like it was the second hammer swing that drove the nail the rest of the way into the coffin of our innocence. A kid I rode the bus with was expelled for keeping a list of peers he didn't like. I remember the police dogs rummaging through the contents of his locker that had been dumped in the middle of the hallway. He wasn't going to do anything, but they weren't taking chances.

I went to New York my senior year, and I made a point to visit Ground Zero, which was, at that time, still a dirt pit. I don't even know why I went. It didn't happen to me. It wasn't my experience.

But it did, and it was.

The experience of life for most of us after that is a state of constant crisis. We watch the wars, the shootings, the mass deaths, the stripping of human rights with such detached cynicism. It's almost not even a choice. If a sound oscillates at a high enough frequency it becomes a single hum. A terrible, maddening hum of spilled blood and hate. It's easier to lump it all together into buckets of tragedy and feel about it like it's an issue and not an individual thing. If I gave every heinous event its due of emotion, I don't know how I would survive.

How else do you process this much evil? How else do you process this much pain and grief and suffering? You can deny the idea that anything can be done about it, or that anything is happening in general, which seems to be a favorite method of about half of the population. You can turn to religion or science or philosophy to try to understand it, try to sort it, categorize it, label it, set it on a table and examine it so you feel better.

Personally, I turn to the thing that I've always turned to. Horror, both books and movies, is like a roller coaster for your mind. Maybe one reason I like horror fiction so much is not because it's scary, but because it's so damned *sad*. It's a way to experience intense emotions at a safe distance—to practice for what you know is coming. And as my high school band director always said, "what you do in practice, you'll do on the field."

Is it any wonder that the years following 2001 saw so many zombie movies and books that we got completely sick of the undead? Is it surprising that there's been a resurgence in the genre after 2016? Do the rabid hordes climbing over walls and pressing at doors and windows remind you of anything? Apocalypse fiction always comes in the wake of insanity. I cynically poked fun at religion and science for trying to categorize and examine tragedy a couple of paragraphs ago, but we are just as guilty on the artsy side of things. I guess what I like more about this method is that it's turned inward. It's turned not toward the what and the why, the attempt to explain, but toward the spirit. How do we cope? What does it say about us? In a moment where everything could end, what really matters?

This book seems to present a common consensus. Whether it's a mother running through gunfire and toxic waste to have a few more seconds with her son, or if the end becomes an opportunity for revenge, reconciliation, even revolution, or someone who lived their whole life for someone else realizes at the last second that all they want is a moment to themselves—in all these stories the thing that ends up mattering is not the how or the why. Some of them don't even tell you how the end came about. What each of these stories focuses on, the thing that matters when everything else stops, is people. Each other. Ourselves. Our families. Our neighbors. Our friends. That the bombs are dropping is just an excuse to be our truest selves. And that person can be inspiring. Or terrifying. It's a concept we're all familiar with.

Because, whether on the smallest of scales or the largest, the world is *always* ending. And at the end of everything, what truly matters isn't the explanations. Humans will always be both the worst and best versions of ourselves. That part of it will never end. What truly matters is who we are, who we become, and what we learn.

Brandon Applegate
Hutto, TX
May 17, 2023

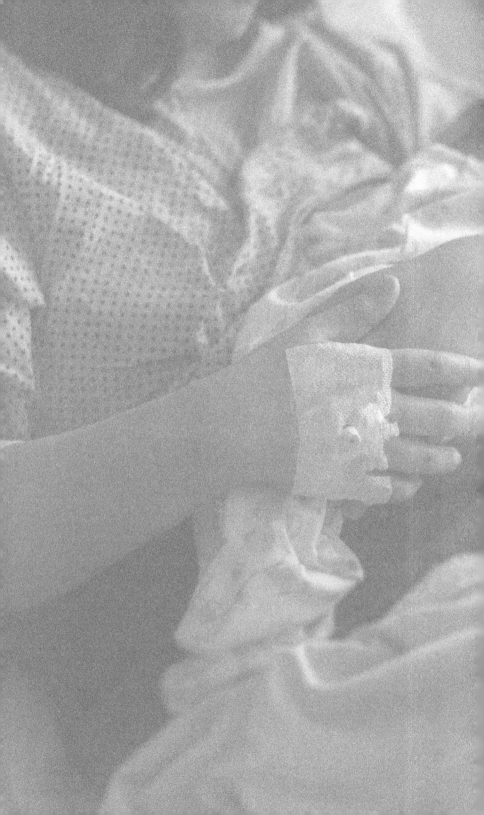

COMING EARTHSIDE

TARYN MARTINEZ

The woman next door won't stop screaming.

"I wish she'd shut up," Amaya says. Other than the monotone beeps of the heart rate and blood pressure monitors and the murmuring voices from the podcast she's streaming, there's nothing else to listen to in the Lenox Hill high-risk maternity wing. Her birth plan specified no television. It also specified *quiet*.

Luther shifts in the chair next to her bed, strokes her arm with his fingertips, just like they practiced.

"Try not to focus on that," he says. "Do you need anything? Ice chips? Maybe some white noise?"

"No, I—" She bites the sentence off midway to release a low groan. Luther grips her hand, lets her squeeze as hard as she needs to as the contraction ripples through her body. Her shoulders instinctively hunch over and tense up. He taps them both as a reminder to relax.

"And breathe out," he says. He's watching the clock.

Amaya dutifully hisses her breath out as the contraction ebbs. They're coming faster now. Harder, too. She tries to ease the muscles in her arms and back and feels the tightness lingering there. They took Lamaze classes together, even met with a midwife friend-of-a-friend for advice; Luther seems to have internalized the lessons a bit more than she has. Probably because she's the one whose cervix is stuck at 6 millimeters dilated.

"Just under a minute," he says. He sets the timer on his phone, then gets distracted by some notification or other and starts thumbing the screen. His brow furrows.

Amaya closes her eyes. She's lost the thread of conversation in her podcast but doesn't mind because the room is suddenly, blessedly silent. She knows her body is tiring. It's only been eight hours—eight hours since her water broke in their bed and they rushed here in the back of an Uber, Luther alternating between demanding the driver go faster and demanding he go slower, and her sitting, knees clamped, on a towel so they wouldn't be charged with a cleaning fee; eight hours since the L&D nurse took her blood pressure and realized she was, suddenly, preeclamptic and hooked her up to a thicket of monitors and drips and her low-intervention, low-stress, natural birth plan went out the window. Eight hours since the screaming in the next room began.

"Where's Dr. Liu?" Amaya asks. "I feel like more things need to be happening. Right? Like, *something* should be happening."

"She said you're progressing, remember? And your blood pressure was stable. She was just here a little while ago. Your next blood pressure check is at 2."

2 meaning 2 am. Time moves differently here. It's almost midnight, but the lights in the hallways are as bright as always. Nurses come in energetically, awake, at both regular and irregular intervals. It's never quiet or still, but there are long stretches of nothing.

The woman next door's scream crescendos to a new pitch. She and Luther look at each other.

"Ugh," Amaya says. "This sucks."

"At least you've got a private room."

"Yeah, with my own private horror movie soundtrack."

Luther's phone dings again and he turns off the screen hurriedly, then reaches for hers. At her questioning look, he chuckles, "Just wanted to see what episode you were listening to."

"Honestly, you can turn it off. It's not like I can focus anyway."

The crest of another contraction hits, then, from where it had been building. Amaya's body curls instinctively around her stomach, like it's trying to protect itself from pain coming from the outside. But this pain is hers and only she can bear it. The muscles in her calves, shoulders, neck all tighten. The cramping of her abdomen is a fist squeezing without end. Amaya clamps her eyes shut, bares her teeth. She thinks of the ocean. She visualizes waves moving up the beach, dampening the sand before retreating. The image dissolves against the fresh bright pain, which is all she can truly think of, her thoughts one unbroken strand of *ow ow ow ow*—

"That was the longest one yet," says Luther. He rubs her legs, her swollen feet. "I think it might be time, baby. I'll try to flag down a nurse."

As the pain fades and her mind returns, she realizes her phone is gone from the side table. Amaya eases up onto her elbows. It's not on the floor, at least not where she can see.

"Hey, have you seen my phone?" She calls to Luther, but he's already out the door. She wants to get up, too, but she's been warned against doing anything that might increase her blood pressure, and that seems to include just about everything. She wouldn't get too far with the number of machines she's hooked up to, either. Amaya breathes in, breathes out.

There's a gap of silence before the woman next door cries out again, a staccato burst that leads into a wail. Amaya shifts onto her side and considers putting a pillow over her head. Instead, she slides it between her bent knees to open up her hips. Another contraction is approaching, she feels, and thinks, *soon.* Soon their beautiful boy will be here, really here, not just a fuzzy image on a sonogram or kicks to her uterus. They'll be able to touch his perfect face and hold his perfect body, and everything will change: no more waddling to the bathroom every 20 minutes, sure, and no more heartburn or lower back pain; there will exist a new being who has never existed before and who will never exist again, an equal mix of

Amaya and Luther Jean-Baptiste, an act of seemingly-miraculous creation.

Amaya jolts awake. A glint of light reflecting from the blood pressure machine strikes her eyes, making her dizzy as she struggles to place herself. More voices join the screaming from next door, shouting authoritative, demanding words like *gorked* and *code* and *dystocia*. There is the loud screech of metal-on-metal, a slam, pounding feet. The lights in the hallway buzz, then flicker. An alarm somewhere clangs once, twice, before cutting off.

"What the hell—"

Luther is back in the chair next to her bed. He's returned without a nurse. His eyebrows pinch with worry, and the skin under his eyes is purpled.

"What's going on?"

"I'm not sure," he says. "Next door. There's something wrong."

Amaya glares at him. "Did you take my phone?"

It's already in his hands, along with his own. He puts them both face-down on his legs and rubs his face, his eyes.

"There's stuff on the news, weird stuff... I just didn't want you to worry. It's not good for your blood pressure."

She's about to snap at him that she can make her own choices, thank you, when a contraction blindsides her. Amaya gasps for breath; the pain presses up from her abdomen into her chest and down to her pelvis and through her back and it's all she can focus on. She grabs Luther's hand as hard as she can but barely feels it. The contraction goes on and on, never ebbing, and through slitted eyes she watches the green line of her heart rate spike. She turns inward, counting the seconds and losing count as the pain makes her mind fog.

When Amaya resurfaces, the sheets behind her back are sticky with sweat. Luther's hands place a straw in her mouth and a damp cloth on her forehead, and with those sweet simple gestures she's forgiven him.

The ghost of the last contraction hasn't left her yet. The pressure is still there, gathering itself.

"I think this is the real deal," she tells Luther. "I need Dr. Liu." Dr. Liu will help her, because Dr. Liu is a professional who has delivered hundreds, probably thousands, of babies as routinely as Amaya checks her email.

"I don't think she's coming," Luther says slowly. "Just trust me on this. We can do this—*you* can do this—but we're doing it alone."

"But the nurses…" Amaya trails off as she realizes there's no more noise from the room next door, or from the nurses' desk outside her room. The silence is so foreign it almost has its own sound. She understands that the nurses are gone.

The blood pressure monitor blares. Luther presses a button that turns it off.

"Please tell me what's going on," Amaya says. The contraction she was waiting for builds and expands. She groans long and loud into the silence. Her back arches, falls. Luther waits until she is done panting and hissing, responds: "There's a storm coming. A big one. People are hunkering down."

Luther's lying—he fidgets with the band of his wristwatch, like he always does when he feels uncomfortable—but she's already moving past the question, focusing on her own ability to survive this labor without her doctor.

The light glints into her eyes again, and she pushes the blood pressure machine farther away, but it's too late. A migraine pulses at the edge of her consciousness, in time with the throb of her womb. The nurse said that was a symptom of preeclampsia. Amaya massages her temples. They're hot to the touch.

"Can you close the curtains?" She says weakly. "It's getting really bright out. My head's splitting."

Luther pats her arm, then gets up and just stands in front of the windows. Staring. He seems to feel her eyes on him and draws the curtains tightly shut. The light outlines the cheap blue fabric like neon signage.

"Wait, why is it so bright out?" Her phone is back in Luther's pocket, but she knows she didn't sleep through her 2 am blood pressure check. She tries to sit up; the movement causes a pulse of pain to spear through her abdomen and she slumps back down.

"It's nothing," he says. "The storm."

Next door, a new scream cuts through the silence, thin, high, unmistakable: a baby's. The woman is silent; must be exhausted or, Amaya wonders, sedated.

Another contraction hits her, furiously. Even in the grip of the pain, Amaya feels something wet spilling out of her. She writhes, groans, kicks the sheets—anything to give her body something else to do besides experience this. There's a new depth to the pain. A pause for a few seconds, barely enough for a lungful of air, then another one grips her. She screams. Luther panics—he runs first to the foot of the bed, then to the bathroom to wash his hands, then back to the bathroom to grab as many towels as he can, which he packs under and around her. He drags the chair over to support him as he crouches between her legs.

Everything happens both slowly and quickly now. Where earlier the hours slipped by easily on a tide of discomfort, anticipation, and boredom, time distorts—each second feels as slow as a taffy pull and yet, when she looks up, the light framing the window must mean it's near dawn. How is her body causing itself this much pain? Her scream is so loud it seems to split into multiple overlapping tones from three different throats—a soprano, a contralto, a baritone—as it echoes down the empty halls. She grinds her teeth back together, catches her lip and tastes blood. There is no quiet left here; her scream underscores, supports, intertwines with the baby's next door, and what must be the mother's, implacable, everywhere.

And the light. In the brief intervals between contractions, when Amaya has the strength to open her eyes, she sees that the sky is pure white now, burning, painful. The edges of the curtains are smoking. Where the light touches her blood pressure monitor, the machine goes haywire, issuing a high whine as it dies. The heart monitor, too, goes dark.

Luther makes as if to stand, to go to the window again.

"Don't look," she begs Luther, her mind barely aware of anything other than the wave of pain carrying her, and yet her animal body hyper-alert and terrified of the voices screaming that one endless note, of the unceasing, unflickering light.

Because the sound and the light are the same, she realizes. The sound is one voice made up of many more than just her and the other baby and its mother. It's sibilant and low like a long exhalation, gaining volume and brass, and the light is intensifying, too, a white beyond all color, each of them heralding the other. She can almost make out words in the sound and the light. If only the pain would stop, maybe she could. Luther hears it too. Her eyes roll upwards.

"Amaya!" Luther shouts. He claps his hands forcefully, then spreads her legs wider. "You can do this. Focus. Breathe!"

The darkness behind her eyes is tinged red. Pain blooms—no, radiates, like the sun, as hot and implacable as the sun—from her vagina, and a noise unlike any she's ever made rips up and out from deep in her abdomen. The pain is unending. Part of her brain marvels that this is real, this is 2023 and she's here, flat on her back with her legs up, at the mercy of nature and the body and random chance, exactly like every other woman throughout time.

The other part of her is insensible with pain, consumed by it totally, wanting to cut herself off from her own body like a fox worrying off its own leg in a trap. She feels nothing beyond the burning pain, even as tears and sweat streak down her face.

"Keep going, baby! Push!" Luther's encouragement is so far away; she can barely hear anything through the fearsome pounding of blood in her ears and the screams. It's her, yes, she's screaming now too, but also the chorus of many voices in one rises in pitch with the light that rises outside the window, holding that same long note.

"I see the head! Push!"

She forgets to breathe, bears down with all of her strength, the tension building until it snaps like a rubber band with a rush of wetness across her lower body. Amaya blacks out for one second, two, three. She wakes, gasping, stars bursting across her vision.

The pressure eases. It leaves behind a hollowed-out ache like a missing tooth. Relief mixed with exhaustion. Luther cradles the newborn—their newborn, their child—in his hands, which look impossibly large around the baby's small body. Something dark and slick slides from her vaginal canal and falls with a wet plop to the floor.

The light is pouring in through the blackened rags of the curtains. It touches the sheet twisted around her bloodied sweat-streaked legs and burns them. It burns her legs too. Her entire body aches as raw as an exposed nerve, but even then she yanks them up and out of the way. The light hisses through the sheets, the blood-soaked bed. The chorus surges. The room is filling with light.

"Close your eyes," Luther begs her.

"I have to see him," Amaya says, and looks.

Luther's outline wavers, as if he is walking through a desert's heat. His face looks pale, wrong—the light. The light illuminates him from the inside; the paleness she sees is liquid and bone.

"He's...he's..."

The baby cries, and echoing his cry is the cry of the woman next door, and the doctors in the hallway, and Luther, and the millions of strangers outside of this hospital, and the polyphony of all of these voices crying out in ecstatic pain swells and peaks.

Amaya closes her eyes against the sounds, but just like the light with Luther, they're inside her; her bones vibrate with them. She doesn't need to look outside to know that the storm, whatever it really is, has arrived earthside along with the child.

"Let me see him, please."

Luther places their baby on her chest with hands that are dissolving into light. Light pours from his eyes and nose and mouth, so bright she looks away, and when she looks back up there is nothing left of him that isn't burnt or liquid.

But her son, her son--he's so radiant he puts the light to shame. Perfect face, perfect body; even slick from his journey, he's nothing less than miraculous.

"He's beautiful," Amaya weeps, as tears and aqueous humor drip down her cheeks from her melting eyes, as the light and the chorus and the cries of her newborn build into one long unending harmony, and everything changes.

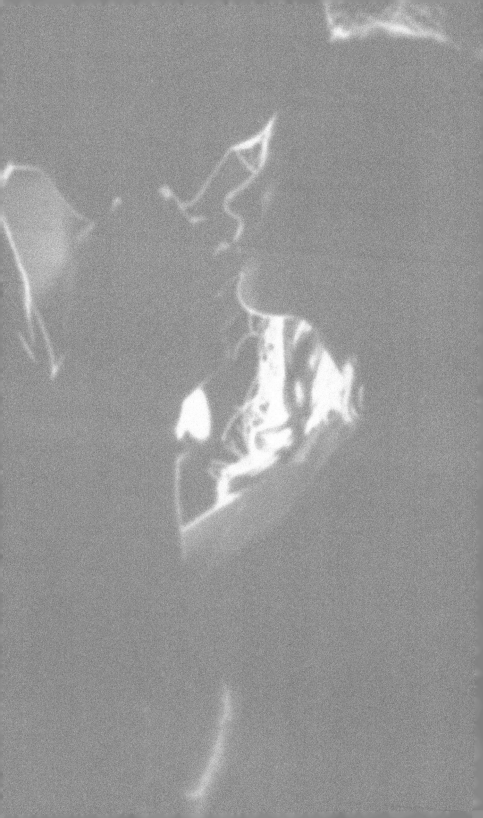

A EULOGY FOR THE FIFTH WORLD

CARSON WINTER

Trudy stared at her phone. "Kay hasn't called."

"No," said George, his voice cracking. "She hasn't."

She reached for his hand and wrapped her fingers over his own. They both looked out the window. "We knew that would happen though," she said. "I guess that's that."

"The kids," he said absently.

"I know." She placed her hand on his shoulder. "It isn't fair."

They leaned into each other, but did not cry. There were too many funerals and only so many tears. They weathered everything else up to this point—there was no use stopping now.

"They're gone," said George.

"Yes," said Trudy. "God help them."

"I can't believe it."

"We will be too," she said.

He rested his head on her shoulder. "How long?"

"An hour. Two, maybe?"

"Have you watched the news?"

"No, I've been avoiding it. What does it look like?"

"No one's filming it. No one's working today." He choked out a laugh, despite himself.

She laid back on the bed, looking up at the cross that hung above their pillows. "I don't know why I keep that up."

"Wanna chuck it? You can. You have time."

"What's the point?"

"I don't know."

George laid down beside her, wrapped her in his arms.

"Kay's dead," she said. "And the kids. That's everyone we know now."

"Everyone."

She looked to the window, narrowing her eyes as if hoping to see something on the horizon. "What should we do?"

"We can't do much, I guess. Get drunk? Scream? Play our music too loud? Fuck?"

"We could do all of that, I guess. We have time."

"You want to?"

"If it's our last chance, we might as well."

"How long has it been?"

"Too long. Or maybe long enough."

"We used to do it a lot."

"When we were kids."

"When we were kids." She thought about that, the way George pinned her arms up above her head, kissing her hungrily. They'd been together thirty-nine years. "We had good times, didn't we?"

George shook his head and smiled a wolfish grin. "I was insatiable." He looked at Trudy and leaned over to her ear and whispered, "Maybe I still am."

She laughed, closed her eyes, maybe too tightly. "Maybe I am too."

"Two hours?"

"Maybe."

"Should I pour some wine? The good stuff?"

"Yes, please. Let's have some. Let's have lots." She slotted her fingers together and marveled at their age. "This is good. This is what young people would do, right? I mean, this is what we would do if we were still young. We'd ring in the end times while making love. That's the type of thing I could see us saying, back then."

George called from the next room. "What was that?"

"Nothing, nothing."

When George came in, he had two glasses, a bottle of malbec, and a corkscrew.

"You want to drink it here?" she asked.

"I just thought, because the bed."

Trudy stood up from the bed. "No, this is the last time, ever. We can do it anywhere we want, within reason."

"The bed is comfortable."

"It's not exciting though. We can always come back."

"Where do you wanna go?"

She thought for a moment. "Let's go outside, on the veranda. One last drink, outside in the afternoon."

He motioned upward. "The whole sun thing doesn't turn you off?"

"It's beautiful still, I think. Doesn't it symbolize rebirth anyways?"

"That's what they say."

"That deserves a toast, then. Can we toast to rebirth?"

"Not ours," he said with a dry laugh.

She sighed. Shook her head. Stood on unsteady feet. "We better get going."

"Right."

She walked out ahead of him, climbed down the stairs and waited patiently as he caught up. Her eyes closed tight as she opened the door. She thought, for a moment, she might see something. But when she opened her eyes, it was all the same. The same world she'd always known, the same sun above.

"I'm coming, I'm coming," said George. "Right behind you."

He set the wine bottle down on the table, along with the glasses and corkscrew, and eased into his chair. Trudy looked up at the sun.

"No reason not to kick the bottle today."

"Nope, let's try to empty it," she said.

He raised a glass. "To rebirth?"

She turned to him and offered a limp smile. "To the sixth world."

"May they be better off than us."

The wine filled her mouth, a hint of bitter, dark fruit. She drank longer and deeper than she had for years. Across from her, George took a comparatively short sip.

"You know," he said. "I thought this would be worse."

"The wine?"

"No."

She shifted in her seat. "It's still pretty bad. Kay, the grandkids, all of our friends..."

"Yes, but that's just time zones. In another one, two hours, we'll be with them again."

"It is sad though."

"It is," he agreed. "I guess I shouldn't have made it seem like it wasn't."

"No, no. I know what you meant." The air was silent. "It's serene. I wasn't expecting it to be serene."

They drank, savoring the wine. The sun licked at their skin with a warm, dry tongue. Their posture was loose, uninhibited.

Trudy said, "If this is the fifth world, what do you think the others were like?"

"I'm not sure," said George. "I'm not sure I even want to think about it."

"Oh, don't be like that. Let's talk about it. If this is the fifth world, what were the others like? It's a game. A thought experiment."

He thought for a long moment. "Do you think each world improves upon the last in some way?"

"I don't know. I think it may be like that, but I don't know what that would look like. Who knows what is so good about this world that was so bad in the last?"

"Well, let's start at the first world," he said, reaching out to caress her hand. "What sort of world do you think that was?"

"A quiet one," she said, returning the touch.

"Too quiet?"

"Yes. It was too quiet. Nothing happened at all. It was very boring."

"But who lived there? There's only a new sun if someone dies, right? That's what they say, anyways. Someone had to live there and someone had to kill them."

She rolled her head back, feeling the sun on her face. George's touch crept up her arm, massaging her shoulders, working his way back down to her wrists. Wine sloshed in her stomach.

"I think there was one quiet girl, a child, and she must have lived in a small village—the first village. This was back a long time ago, where there was no one else. The whole world was one tribe. It was a quiet world. She ran out into the jungle and tripped and fell, breaking her leg. She could not scream for help, not effectively, because she was so quiet. No one at the village knew where she was. No one. Until her father went looking for this quiet girl and found her. She was shivering, bone-thin, and her ankle was twisted around. The poor thing was just so scared. Her father knew she wouldn't make it, but he did not want to live in a world where that was true. So, he killed her, and so ended the first world."

He lifted her hand to his lips. "Sad," he said.

"I know. But all stories about the end of the world are sad. Tell me about the second world."

George let go of her hand and stretched. He poured more wine. "The second world..." He thought for a moment. "The second world was larger than the first. There were more people. They were a very advanced civilization. We mirror them in some ways. They valued the same things we do. They looked like us. They fought like us. They lived in large cities."

Trudy unbuttoned the top of his shirt. "They can't be exactly like us, can they?"

He smiled. "No, of course not. The one thing that was different was that they could... *fly*. Yes, fly. They were all buzzing around the sky and eventually, over many thousands of years, they realized they could just keep going." He motioned to the sky, as Trudy pressed her lips against his neck. "Up there. They could go on forever, if they wanted. And so, as the world became more populated, more people began to fly away. They left earth until there was just one man. A father who loved his sons. And because there was no one left, he was so lonely that he felt like someone should do something. That no one should be so lonely. So, he did what he had to do to bring everyone back. Alone, on earth, he killed himself, so that a new sun would rise." He swallowed and Trudy pulled her head back from his neck. She rubbed at the mark.

"Think anyone will notice?"

George laughed at that. He drank more of his wine. She drank more of hers. They kissed outside, under their current sun.

"And now?" he whispered into her ear. "What about the third world? We're over the hill now. We're almost to the present."

His voice sent chills down her spine. Her cheeks flushed.

George stood from his chair, and kneeled in front of her. His hands nimbly undoing her shirt buttons, from the top down.

"The third world was very bad," she said, giggling. "There was a return to normalcy, a return to order. No more flying people." George's lips found their way to her navel. She gasped. "The third world was a world of hiding. People hid from each other constantly, because there was so little—oh, George—trust."

George stared up at her, smiling. He tugged at the clasp of her waistband. "Go on."

"No one trusted each other, so they would often do horrible things. Really bad things. Really, really, really..."

George's tongue teased at the elastic band of her underwear, with his hands, he reached up and eased her pants down, sliding them off easily.

"People would steal, they would kill. They would fight. Oh God! How they would fight. Whenever one would get near another, some horrible thing would happen. That's why they would hide."

He reached behind her, working his fingers in the band of her underwear, pulling them off her. George kissed gently at the soft flesh between her thighs. "What happened next?" he said, between mouthfuls of her flesh.

"One day, a great monster appeared. A very large, very scary monster. And it began reaching its hands into the earth and pulling out the hiding people."

George looked up from between his wife's legs. "They were living underground? Like moles?"

"Yes," she said with a laugh. "They were like mole people. All in separate little holes. Growing like carrots. And the monster came through and picked them, one by one, and chomped them to bits."

George's tongue lapped gently at her clitoris, darting back and forth, as she let out a long shivering moan.

"George, really. That's..."

"You have a story to finish," he said.

The sun felt good on her face. "Well, these mole people dug a hole. A tunnel, so that they could put aside their differences long enough to defeat this monster. Jesus, George! They—they spoke for many nights, back and forth. They held councils. Yes! Councils. But at the end, they were at an impasse. They were tired of being plucked from the ground and eaten. But they also knew that they could not stand to be in a tunnel with each other much longer. They had no choice. Oh—oh—oh. They decided that they would all climb out of their holes, together."

George's mouth glistened. "Poor bastards." He buried his face into her.

Her mouth opened, her legs kicked out. "Oh no," she said. "No, not yet." She ran her hands through his hair and pushed his head back. "You've got to tell me about the fourth world now. The one before this one."

She got out of the chair and pushed George onto his back. She removed the rest of her clothing, the sun catching every crevice her age lent her. Trudy felt free, pure. Exposed to no one but the sky. She ran a hand across his groin and felt him grow beneath her. "Hasn't changed a bit," she said.

George shook his head. "I took a pill," he admitted.

"You did?"

"I never told you."

"You could've," she said, rubbing it back and forth. "We're old, after all."

"Well, you know how it is..."

"I don't mind."

"...with us guys."

"Shh," she said, unzipping him. "Tell me about the fourth world."

"After all the mole people were eaten, their sacrifice gave birth to a new sun."

"Mmhmm."

"So, now the new sun rose over the horizon and a new world began. In the wake of the corpses that littered the earth, plants grew. Tall trees, and, and, and—"

Trudy sucked on him, slowly, using her tongue to draw lines across his heavy veins.

"The earth was green again, and it was so beautiful. The corpses disappeared with time, dissolving into rich soil. The new people of this world were not like the last world at all. They were very kind. They loved each other so much. They loved each other more than anyone could imagine." He closed his eyes and groaned as Trudy continued to work him up and down. "And they had children that they loved. They had children that they loved more than anything in the world. But as time went on, and age crept upon them... Oh, my... As they aged, and they saw the people they loved die, they became more bitter. But they never stopped loving each other. Not even for one second. They could never do that. Not ever. What happens next is—"

"Oh, does that feel nice?" She grinned.

He looked down at her. "I feel like a teenager."

"Enjoy it while it lasts."

"I am," he said. "I am."

"Are you going to finish?"

"Keep going and find out."

"The story," she said, as she stuck her tongue out, licking his length.

He leaned back. "God. If you insist." He cleared his throat. "These people loved each other too much. They felt everything too much. When one died, it was as if a part of them was torn out. Stomped on. And they got tired of it, eventually, they realized life hurt too much. It just did. There was nothing they could do about it."

"What did they do?"

"They realized that their pain had limits, and that to end suffering, they would need to transcend it. So they chose a mother, a lover like themselves, and asked her to do the unthinkable. She did not want to do it, but until she did, the sun would keep rising and setting on the same world, and it was not a world they wanted to live in. In the shadows of a great overgrown forest, in the silence, she resolved to never let her children know the same sorrow, and when the sun set, it was the last time."

Trudy climbed on top of him, kissing him. Tears touched the corners of her eyes. "You're a big softie."

"Not right now," he said.

She eased him inside of her, rocking gently back and forth. "No," she cooed. "Not right now."

Trudy looked at the man beneath her, her hands rested on his chest for support as she moved her hips back and forth. His eyes were half closed, but every once in a while, even in the wake of pleasure, he'd open his eyes and squint into the sky. She did too. The sun felt warm on her back but it wasn't as warm as it was minutes ago. It would get colder still.

George reached up toward her breasts, caressing her nipples, as she rode him. After a moment, he rolled over, taking her beneath him.

Trudy gasped as he held her arms above her head, kissing her deeply. She bit into his shoulder as he pumped into her.

"Now, tell me," he said, panting. "Tell me the story of the fifth world—our world."

She moaned. "Oh, George. No. No. I don't think I can."

"Let's do it together."

"It was a good world," she started. "Sometimes."

"It was decent," he said, his lips next to her ears.

"There was beauty in it."

"Yes."

"There was so much of everything!"

"Yes!"

"And yet... oh, keep going. Please, George, please."

He said, "But there was sadness too. Great... sadness. War. But also children. Lovers, there were still lovers."

"Yes," she said, clawing into his back. "There were lovers and they had a child."

"A beautiful girl."

"And she grew up into a beautiful woman."

"Headstrong, smart. Successful."

"And she got married to a nice man."

He thrust deeper into her.

"They had children. Great children."

"They were happy, I think. I hope. I think they were happier than most. But what about her parents?"

He stopped and they both stared into each other's eyes. The sky was pink. Trudy reached out to touch his cheek. "On the eve of their last sunset, they loved each other."

They kissed.

"Yes," he said. "They did."

When they finished, they stared at the sky, the pink and orange hues of a drowning sun.

"But why did it have to end?" he asked.

"I don't know," she said. "I wish I knew."

"That's all it takes, I guess. One person."

"Or many."

"Or many."

They reached out to each other, breathing softly, and softer and softer still. Cool air kissed their faces as the fifth world came and went.

ESTRANGEMENTS

D. MATTHEW URBAN

Garrett stepped into the living room, saw his children sitting cross-legged on the rug in front of the television, and screamed. Jessica and Tim's faces were gone, their skulls wrapped in a vile substance like greasy, pinkish-gray leather. Holes pocked the moist surface of the covering—purulent holes where dark flecks floated in pale jelly, narrow holes that flexed and shuddered obscenely, gaping holes housing coarse red worms that squirmed and writhed over shards of upthrust bone. Staring at the things that had been his children, now hideous, faceless freaks, Garrett howled in shock and terror.

"Oh my God, honey, what is it? What's wrong?"

Garrett spun toward his husband's voice. Terry stood in the doorway of the kitchen, an oven mitt on one hand and a spatula in the other. Concern and confusion shone from his wide, startled eyes.

"The kids, they're..."—turning back toward the children, Garrett felt his throat and chest clench, choking his words. He pressed a hand to his sternum and breathed slowly, in and out, until the knot around his heart loosened.

Jessica and Tim looked up at him, open-mouthed. They were the same beautiful children he'd tucked into bed last night, with the same adorable faces, now slack with surprise. Tim's lip quivered.

"What's wrong, daddy?" Jessica said.

"I thought I saw..." Garrett shivered at the thought of those terrible not-faces. Banishing the image with a shake of his head, he smiled sheepishly. "Sorry if I scared you, kids. My eyes were playing tricks on me. Must still be half-asleep."

"Then you'd better come in here and get yourself some coffee," Terry said, grinning and beckoning with his mitted hand as he receded into the kitchen.

Leaning next to the sink, Garrett sipped his coffee and watched Terry arrange cinnamon toast, scrambled eggs and bacon on the row of plates beside the stove. Now that his momentary fright—waking dream? hallucination?—had passed, Garrett savored the elements of the family's Saturday morning ritual. The kids in the living room watching videos, Terry in the kitchen preparing breakfast, himself taking it easy and making a list of the chores he'd tackle in the afternoon. Go to the farmer's market, mow the lawn, take out the trash. Everything in its place, as deliciously familiar as the 15-year-old indie rock songs drifting from Terry's phone on the counter.

The buzz of a text message interrupted the music. Terry glanced at his phone, frowned.

"Bad news?" Garrett said.

"Not sure." Terry slid the last strips of bacon onto a plate. "It's my sister. Vague as usual. She just says, *Are you seeing this?*"

Garrett chuckled. Typical Laura. "Well, are you?"

"Beats me. Grab the kids' plates, will you, honey?"

"Sure thing. Just one more sip." He swigged the last of his coffee. A plate in each hand, Terry leaned in, kissed him on the cheek and left the kitchen.

The clang of shattering ceramic brought Garrett to the doorway. Terry stood frozen in the living room, halfway to the breakfast table, chunks of porcelain mixed with heaps of food at his feet. His empty hands hovered waist-high in front of him as he trembled and made choking, whimpering sounds. On the other side of the room, Jessica and Tim stood staring at their second terrified parent of the morning.

Garrett hurried over, careful to keep his bare feet clear of the fragments of plate. Thinking of his own weird vision, he assumed Terry would be looking at the children, perhaps seeing those same revolting, hole-ridden swaths, but instead Terry was gazing at his own hands, his eyes full of fear and incredulity.

"What the fuck are those things?" Terry whispered. His fingers flexed and quivered. "What are they doing?"

Garrett put what he hoped was a reassuring hand on Terry's shoulder. "What things? You mean your hands?"

"Those aren't my hands. Those are…they're…"

"Baby, look at me." Garrett rubbed his thumb gently against Terry's neck. "Just look at me for a second."

It seemed to take a tremendous effort for Terry to pull his gaze away from his hands. His whole body quaked and strained. When he finally raised his eyes to meet Garrett's, his pupils were so dilated it was like staring into two black pits. Garrett thought he saw something move at the bottom of those pits, something that twitched and glimmered, and for a moment he wondered if he might be seeing Terry's brain, its pale whorls cringing in horror.

Terry blinked. His pupils contracted. His glance flicked back to his hands, and the tension seemed to drain out of him as he heaved a tremendous sigh. "What the hell is going on?" he murmured.

Wrapping an arm around Terry's shoulders, Garrett steered him to the breakfast table, swerving to avoid the shards and scraps that littered the floor. Tim and Jessica had vanished from the living room; retreated to their bedroom, Garrett supposed, to wait for their parents to start acting normal again.

Terry slid into a chair and slumped forward, shaking his head. Garrett placed a hand lightly in the middle of his husband's back.

"What did you see?" Garrett said.

"Monsters," Terry said. "Two monsters floating in front of me. Pale and slimy-looking, with thick, veiny bodies and little hairs sprouting out. They had five heads apiece, with long, jointed necks. Each head had one big pink eye, and all of the eyes were staring up at me."

"Anything else you remember?"

"One of the necks had a metal collar around it, the kind you might hitch a chain to. Like the thing had escaped from a dungeon."

Garrett slid his palm up Terry's back, along his shoulder, down his left arm. Lifting Terry's hand, he held it out over the table and ran his thumb along the fingers, over the pink fingernails. He tapped his thumbnail on the wedding band that gleamed on Terry's finger like a silver collar.

"Oh my fucking God," Terry said, a shudder of revulsion shaking his voice. "I could have sworn…"

"It's okay," Garrett said. "Just a trick of your eyes. One of those weird things."

Terry twisted in the chair, looked into Garrett's face. "What about you, honey? What did you see?"

Closing his eyes, Garrett saw them again—the greasy not-faces, the disgusting holes, the things glinting and squirming in the hollows. Something in the memory shifted, some subtle change of light, and suddenly he realized what he'd been looking at, what had made him scream with terror. Skin, eyes, noses, mouths, tongues…

"The kids," he said. "I saw the kids, but it didn't look like them. It looked like…"

"Monsters," Terry said.

They stared at one another, saying nothing. In the quiet, Garrett heard music drifting faintly from the kitchen, Terry's phone still playing the jagged guitars and swooping synths of their youth. The music faded for a moment, heralding the arrival of a text message. A few seconds later, it faded again, then again.

Terry rose, crossed the living room. As he passed through the doorway into the kitchen, Garrett glimpsed a shambling, misshapen creature, stiff tubes and knobs of flesh trailing from a central bulk wrapped in gauzy cloth as if bandaged to hide the scars of some mutilation. The grotesque beast slid into the mouth of a larger creature, disappeared down its gullet.

That's Terry, Garrett thought. *He's going into the kitchen.* But it didn't look like Terry.

The music fell silent. Garrett's breath rasped in his throat, his pulse hammered in his ears. His husband, their children, their house, their own bodies, the most familiar things in the world…was it some delusion, making them look monstrous? Or was it the familiarity itself falling away, revealing what was always underneath, unseen?

What the fuck was happening?

When Terry emerged from the kitchen, he looked like Terry again, but his expression filled Garrett with apprehension. He approached the breakfast table, his phone clutched in his hand. "More messages from Laura," he said.

Garrett took the phone, open to the messaging app. Collapsing into a chair, he read the texts from Terry's sister.

Are you seeing this?

Seriously bro this is crazy. Did you see the news?

The next message was a link to a story at a news site. The preview image showed a woman with blood running down the side of her face, a car overturned in the street behind her. Below the image, the headline read, *BREAKING: Deadly incidents around the world, trance-like states and acts of violence reported.*

Laura's messages continued. *Text me back Terry, or call or email, whatever. Something is seriously fucked up, we're getting scared. Love u*

If you see this don't bother texting back just go to the nearest hospital, they think it's some kind of medical thing infection or whatever and when they figure out a treatment hospital's where they'll have it so just go. Go now as soon as you see this go

ddnjfkdsbfgiabhsdif

FUCK GO NOW sdjnbkjdfs

gggggg

The chunk of charred bone flashed in Garrett's hand. He hurled the thing away with a yelp, and it clattered over the scales of the monstrous maw where he sat, coming to rest at the edge of a flat, scabbed tongue.

Terry's feet whispered on the floorboards. He picked up his phone where it lay next to the rug, the rug where Tim and Jessica had sat cross-legged in front of the television, watching videos. He gazed at Garrett, his eyes wary.

"We should get the kids out of here," Garrett said. "Go to the hospital, like Laura said. Get out of the house, at least. Maybe there's some kind of gas or toxin in here, some kind of leak, you know? Something that causes hallucinations?"

Terry frowned at his phone. "This news story she sent says it's happening all over the world. People not recognizing things, mistaking other people for...creatures. Attacking them."

"Attacking?" Garrett recalled what he thought he'd seen. Those wretched, faceless things, abominations that shouldn't live. If his vision hadn't gone back to normal, what would he have done? Would the horror of the sight have driven him to violence, repugnance forcing him to assault his own children?

No. I love them too much to ever hurt them. Some part of my mind would have known, would have stopped me.

The shambling bulk—*Terry*—Terry held out the phone toward Garrett. It showed the story from the link Laura had sent. A video was playing, a woman speaking. "I thought it was an animal," she said. Tears and blood streaked her face. "Some kind of deformed, vicious animal. It was coming at me, and I panicked. I grabbed the closest thing I could get my hands on, and I started hitting it. I just wanted it to go away, but it wouldn't go away, it kept coming, it was roaring and screaming at me, so I just kept hitting. And then it fell down, and I...I hit it some more and then...and then I saw..." The woman closed her eyes, covered her mouth with her hands. As she began to scream, the video ended.

Terry lowered the phone to his side. "'Acute agnosia,' they're calling it," he said. "No one knows why it's happening."

Garrett grimaced. "So we should all go to the hospital, to be there when they figure it out."

"I say we stay here," Terry said. "The hospital will be crowded. The more people, the more danger. Do you really want to put the kids in that kind of situation?"

"I'll keep the kids safe."

"And what if it comes back, this thing, this disease? You've already had a flash of it. How will you keep the kids safe if you don't know who they are?"

"I'll know. I'm sure of it. We'll go to the hospital, and then we'll—"

The words caught in Garrett's throat as Terry's eyes went wide. Terry's lips peeled back from his teeth, his hands rising, twisting into claws.

"Hey!" Garrett rushed to his husband, wrapped his arms around him and held him close. "Hey, baby, it's me. It's Garrett. It's going to be okay."

A rancid mass of flesh squirmed in his arms, snarling and squealing. A sticky membrane pressed against his cheek. He squeezed his eyes shut. *Terry, Terry, Terry...*

Terry relaxed against him, sobbing, his head on his shoulder. "Oh my God, oh my God..."

Garrett rubbed his hands along Terry's back, murmured in his ear. "You see? It's okay. We'll get through this." Still holding Terry tight, he maneuvered him to the breakfast table and down into a chair. "Now just sit here for a minute while I get the kids. We're going to the hospital."

The door to the kids' bedroom stood ajar. Garrett tapped a knuckle against the door, pushing it slowly open. The room was dark. "Jessica? Tim?" He flicked on the lights.

At first he thought the bedroom was empty. He swept his eyes across the unmade beds, the clothes and toys scattered around, wondering where the kids had gone. Then he saw them, huddled on the floor between the beds. Two lumps of misbegotten foulness, throbbing meat wrapped in slimy casings. Unnatural, unworthy of existence.

Your children. Your children.

"Daddy," one of the things—*Jessica*—said. "Daddy, I'm scared."

Garrett took a deep breath, struggling to master his own terror. "I know, sweetie. We're all scared. But we need to go to the hospital."

The other thing—*Tim*—widened its dark-flecked, pus-filled holes —*eyes, his eyes.* "Are you sick, daddy? Is papa sick? Is that why you've been shouting?"

"A lot of people are getting sick, and we need to go to the hospital so we'll be first in line to get the medicine."

As the things rose and approached him, Garrett saw them flickering back and forth, now his beloved children, now grotesque horrors. *Like that picture that's a duck one moment, a rabbit the next, depending on how you look at it.* He tried to force himself to see them as children, but he could feel his mind slipping, losing its grasp on their childness, their familiar humanity. He gritted his teeth with the effort of seeing them as they were, as he loved them. "Hurry," he said.

Terry was still sitting at the breakfast table, his arms rigid at his sides. "Come on, baby," Garrett called from the entryway. "We're going." Terry closed his eyes, pressed his hands over his ears.

Behind Garrett, one of the things made a chittering, hissing sound. He turned. "What did you say, sweetie?"

"I said, papa's sick, isn't he?" Tim whispered, his tongue's red worm writhing.

"Yes, he's sick. So the three of us will go to the hospital first, and once we've got the medicine, we'll come back for papa."

Garrett snatched the keys from the table in the entryway, led the kids outside and herded them into the car. For a moment, the five-year-old Honda was a chitinous beast, the children's devoured faces staring out in terror from its transparent belly, but Garrett wrestled his mind into seeing it as a car. He got in, turned the key in the ignition, began to back out into the street.

Jessica leaned forward in the backseat. "Papa!" she cried.

At the sound of her voice, Garrett braked instinctively and looked toward the house. The misshapen creature shambled from the front door to the driveway, flailing its tubes and swinging its bulbous knob from side to side. Even as Garrett screamed, he tried to recognize the thing, to remember the name he used to call it, but sheer, stark fear—fear for himself, fear for the children—overwhelmed him, loosened his mind's grip. The monster howled and squealed, waving jointed appendages that branched into gruesome, claw-tipped tentacles. A thing that should not, must not exist. Garrett put the car into drive.

The impact knocked the creature against the garage door. It slumped down, smearing dark ichor across the white surface. Garrett quickly reversed and surged forward again, crushing the thing against the sullied door. There was a squelch, a crack, a moan. When Garrett backed up, the tires crunched over the monster's vile limbs.

The children were screaming so loud, Garrett could hardly remember where they needed to go. *The hospital, the hospital.* He wrenched the car around and sped toward the edge of town, the medical center.

"Papa, papa!" Jessica shrieked.

"I told you, we'll come back for him once we've got the medicine," Garrett said.

"Why did you do that, daddy?" Tim wailed from the passenger seat.

"I had to...that thing...that, that monster..." A cloud seemed to gather over Garrett's mind. He had a good reason for what he'd done, he was sure of it, but he couldn't quite remember what the reason was. The children screaming so loud...he couldn't think...so loud...

Something hit him on the shoulder. It hit him again, harder. When he turned his head to see what it was, it hit him in the face.

"What are you?" Jessica screamed, her eyes shining with horror. "What did you do with our daddy?" She raised her arm, and Garrett saw the shoe in her hand a moment before it struck him in the eye.

Light exploded across Garrett's vision. He whipped his head

around to escape the next blow, but the movement sent his hands sliding left along the steering wheel, and the car went into a sharp turn. He'd been going too fast, he realized, rushing to get to the hospital, to get away from that thing whose name he couldn't remember, didn't want to remember. Still half-blind, he slammed on the brakes. The car skidded, spun off the road, rolled. Garrett felt his mind fly apart.

When he opened his eyes, he didn't know how much time had passed, couldn't remember where he was, where he'd come from or where he'd been going. Nothing felt familiar. He was sitting sideways, his face resting against a cold, flat surface. In front of him was another surface, cracked and shattered. He was in an enclosure, some type of cage or dungeon, and two shapeless creatures had been shut in with him. The creatures weren't moving. *Asleep*, he thought. He hoped so.

After a while, he managed to crawl forward through the broken surface and out of the cage. His body hurt, and he could tell that some parts of him were damaged, but he didn't know which parts, what they were called. He could stand, at least. He looked around. Shapes, colors. Nothing he recognized. He vaguely remembered he'd been going somewhere. He walked in what he thought was the right direction.

As he walked, the things around him changed. Unfamiliar things gave way to other, equally unfamiliar things. The only thing that stayed the same was the expanse overhead, the blue field with the white fleck floating across it. There was a name for that, he remembered, a fleck in a bright field. *Eye?* Yes.

He walked on, keeping his gaze fixed on the eye overhead, even though its bright stare hurt to look at. It was worth a little pain, he thought, to have something that stayed the same while everything else changed. When the pain grew too much, the stare too piercing, he closed his own eyes and walked in darkness.

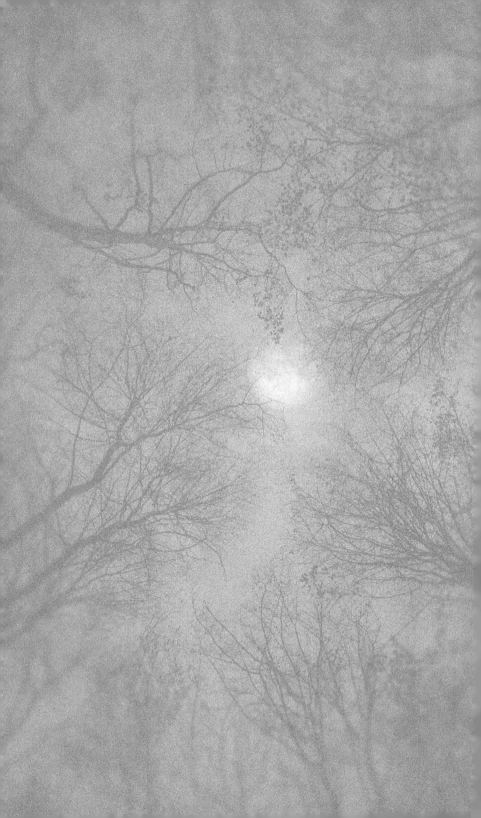

THE VIRIDESCENT DARK

SARA TANTLINGER

Ana had no rational reason to feel uncomfortable. Yet, unease filled her chest as if a boulder replaced her heart. The weight of anxiety might've made sense if the den had windows. At least then, she could tell herself the feeling stemmed from the paranoia of someone peeking through open blinds.

Maybe that's the problem, she thought. No windows. Her and her husband had turned the den into a library they both loved, but natural light would be a welcome visitor in the morning hours. Blake even built the wooden shelves himself, and together they'd spent countless hours arranging too many books in alphabetical order. The den was their curated place of idyllic happiness. Seclusion, books, and each other.

Still, Ana felt watched. Something lurked on the other side of the wall. Beyond the paneling waited a lively forest, full of summer wildlife and tangled fauna. The trees kept the small house hidden from the nearest road. A passerby would have to be pretty brave to take the turn off the main road and travel up their uneven driveway.

A gut feeling or intuition, some primal part of her brain recited a warning: *Do not go out there.*

She glanced at the clock on the wall, surprised it was almost midnight. Blake had already gone to bed. Their gray, short-haired cat, Walt Whisker, had followed him as usual, and Ana wished she had, too. She could go wake her husband, or crawl under the covers, but instead she picked up her phone. Nothing like an aimless social media scroll for distraction.

Missed calls and texts filled her lock screen. Her hand froze in the air as her heart sped up into a pounding rhythm. That many missed messages usually meant someone she loved was dead. She'd left the phone on silent for the past few hours while reading, and it seemed like everyone she'd ever met left a message.

"What the hell?"

The anxiety boulder in her chest shook. Fractured. Threatened to explode and send shards of rock to pierce her skeleton. With trembling fingers, she unlocked the phone, but couldn't bring herself to click on the voicemails or texts. Some thoughtless part of her gave into habit, opened up Instagram without really thinking. There was no reason why she should ignore the messages and open a stupid app instead, but she did. The action lacked explanation, just as she couldn't explain why she both needed and did not need to go outside. To see what lingered on the other side of the wall.

The same post displayed on her screen. Over and over. Photos and reels of a silver-green orb filled her feed. Similar pictures from different angles with varying levels of clarity. A blurry haze, tinted emerald, framed the bright orb. As Ana scrolled through the posts from a range of timestamps, realization pierced her like fangs sinking into her brain.

A familiar orb with craters, hovering in the darkness. What had happened to the moon to make it look so sick?

Within a few short hours, the green had expanded. A post from 9:00pm showed visible specks of green polka-dotting the moon. The most recent post, from a few minutes ago, presented the moon with nearly half its surface covered, like moss or a strange forest. The hellish haze glowed stronger, beaming an emerald aura down to

Earth. Ana zoomed in, spotted other hidden colors. Streaks of red and brown and black.

A numb panic took hold; the whole affair was too unbelievable for her mind to process. Captions and comments repeated similar sentiments of disbelief. People said goodbye to one another. They confessed secrets and sins. Shared dreams and wishes never to come true.

The rest were theories of what caused the moon to turn viridescent.

"What does it matter?" Ana whispered to the room. No explanation would stop whatever had come to plague the moon.

Despite her numbness, she almost laughed. The whole situation bordered on absurdity. Of course she'd learn about some freakish event through social media. It was more than an abnormality, though.

She'd read the article weeks ago and moved on, like everyone else. A scientist had gained brief internet fame for an eloquent piece stating a change to the moon would soon arrive. *The beginning of the end*, he had called it.

The end of the world. *Impossible.*

A kind of delirium consumed Ana. She set her phone down next to the book she'd abandoned, and walked toward the porch door. So many hours had been spent out there, sitting with Blake in the evenings. She'd read him a passage in a book she liked, and he'd recite a poem from memory for her. His warm voice would fill the night as she gazed at stars. They both worked hard to earn the beauty of those moments. How could it all disappear?

Fingers moved the lock to the left, unlatching the porch door. She moved robotically, muscle memory guiding her out onto the concrete. Her tomato plants and potted flowers glowed beneath the sickly haze, as if radiation lit the night. That's not what this was, though. Whatever the moon emitted—it was something new.

Strange dust clung to the porch furniture, lustrous against the off-white cushions. She stepped closer, an ache budding in her to reach out and touch the powder.

"Ana?" Blake's voice. The gentle sound of it nearly brought her to tears.

She stood still, halfway between the door and the sooty chair. "Stay inside."

"You should take your own advice."

"I think it's too late," she said, her eyes meeting his gaze once before she realized the dust had already fallen on her bare arms. It satisfied the curious ache, and she moved away from the small pile of green pollen collecting on the cushions. Her right pointer finger dabbed at the substance on her left arm, and she swabbed it around her skin like testing a swatch of eyeshadow.

"Stop," Blake said and took a step forward, but he lingered in the doorway, not venturing outside. "Ana, don't."

The fear in his tone, his concern... it broke her heart. She loved him more than anything in this life, but how could love save them?

"Please come back inside."

She drifted toward him and moved willingly when he put a gentle arm around her waist, guiding her toward the kitchen after he shut and locked the porch door. He was careful, she noticed, not to touch her skin, and had used the sleeve of his overshirt when he guided her away from the door.

Blake unbuttoned the overshirt and threw it in the trash. "We don't know what that stuff is."

She nodded and moved to wash off the dust from her arms and hands. Despite her scrubbing, a faint stain remained.

"Here," Blake had disappeared and returned with a new shirt and pants for her. She accepted the clothes, changed, threw the supposedly contaminated ones in the trash like he had done. Every movement felt like going through the motions. Ana had always prided herself on being in touch with her emotions, and with being able to honestly communicate with her husband. Now, she wasn't sure how she felt at all. Curious. Maybe sad. Maybe so hopeless she'd gone numb.

"Look at the windows." Blake's voice had gone even quieter.

Fear. She recognized that emotion clearly as she took in the mossy smears on the window. Green covered the glass. Where a speck started, it then stretched with wriggling tendrils, and quickly took over the surfaces around it. Like something sentient.

Ana looked away and focused on Blake instead. His big eyes. The wrinkled shirt. The waves in his hair and the freckles on his arms. All of these traits she loved. Perhaps it was selfish, but she didn't want the sick moon to take those things away.

"How long, do you think?"

He shook his head. "We don't know if this is the end, right? Maybe it's just a weird phenomenon."

She could tell he didn't believe his own words. Her thoughts went back to the Instagram comments. One had stuck with her, sewing itself into her memory with vicious stitches.

We should have listened to those scientists. They tried to warn us. Remember that article?

The article on something shifting within the moon hadn't been the only warning. There had been a few different teams of scientists in the spotlight not too long ago. Phycologists from both the freshwater and ocean studies of algae, and geologists, and others Ana couldn't remember the name of. She'd skimmed through the videos and articles, sure, but like so many others, she hadn't dug deep into the warnings.

"I couldn't sleep," Blake said and broke through her spiraling thoughts. "I kept having weird dreams, and then the cat started hissing. The bedroom was glowing. Freaky as hell."

Ana had to laugh. "Typical Walt Whisker, hissing even during the end times."

Blake cracked a smile, too.

"Now what?"

He held out his hand. "Come to bed."

She took up his offer and followed him to the bedroom where Walt crawled out from under the bed. The cat curled between them and purred with a sense of calm. His green eyes closed in contentment, and the long whiskers twitched. Ana relaxed on her side, trying not to think about the itching beneath her skin, but it felt like a thousand spiders danced there. Even in the horrible green blaze, Blake's face was a comfort.

She'd always associated the color with plants and forests. Soft moss and spring. Life. How could it bring the moon such sickness? Such death?

Blake held her with one arm, giving Walt Whisker enough room to shift and curl between them. "How did all of this happen so quickly?"

Ana scratched the purring feline behind the ears. Stroked his gray and white fur, then had to look away from the small nose and whiskers so her heart wouldn't catch in her throat.

"We'd been warned," she said, going back to her earlier thoughts of the news stories. One in particular covered the fact that over 400,000 pounds of man-made trash littered the moon. Something sprouted from the galactic garbage, the teams had said on the news. Something with life.

Oh. She'd forgotten. The memory came back with a punch, taking the breath from her.

"Algae," she murmured. "Do you remember? They said some perfect leakage of the space trash created an environment for an algae bloom. All it takes is the right condition, and something can sprout. Evolve."

How fast it multiplied, found a way to persevere even in harsh conditions. Once life began, it must have migrated across the moon's surface with stunning speed. Such a strange little organism...algae had adapted to live on ice, so why not the moon?

Everyone cared for a day, when the algae story first came out. The next day though, coverage was replaced with shinier and bloodier news across the country.

Ana didn't understand all of the science behind it, and there was little sense in trying to puzzle it out. She could lay here with Blake and Walt Whisker and ask a million questions about why and how; she could cast her wildest theories out into the universe and shout them to the sky above, but come morning, the end result would be the same. Either the planet would sustain, or it would not.

It was more than the destruction of the moon. That dust the algae created, like a plague of lime-tinted pollen, was already changing Earth. Whether it originated from space or dirt hardly seemed to matter. It was here, clinging to the windows and burning her skin. She didn't tell Blake about the itch, about how she wanted to take a hot knife to her arm and cut the flesh away.

"What are you thinking about?" He blinked those big eyes at her.

"We left a graveyard of trash on the moon, of course something would rise from that, you know? Something learned how to sustain itself."

"Even if that meant taking out all other life with it?"

"I guess we'll never know."

"Yeah," he said, a frown tugging his mouth down. "An explanation would have offered some comfort, I guess."

Ana reached for his hand, entwined their fingers. This was comfort, the feeling of his warm skin against hers.

Walt Whisker sat up, his spine arched and tail fluffed. An agitated *mrrow* filled the quiet home. A second later, windows rattled as the ground trembled. Ana had never felt an earthquake before, but maybe this was something different.

Blake held her close as panic sent her heart into overdrive.

"It's the end of the world and we're in bed," she whispered into the crook of his neck, breathing in the familiar cologne he had put on earlier in the day.

"I wouldn't want to be anywhere else." He kissed her head, and she shifted back to look him in the eyes again.

The power surged, killing the small lamplight and glow from the clock in the bedroom, which meant the Wi-Fi would be gone, too. Only the eerie luminosity from outside remained to bring light to the room.

"Did you respond to any texts or calls?"

Blake shook his head. "No. My phone was blown up with things I'd missed, but when I woke up, I went to find you first."

"I feel selfish, not answering when I had the chance," she confessed. Maybe she was the same as everyone on those comments she'd read earlier. Giving away their sadness and secrets as the world trembled on the brink of collapse. She doubted the phone would have service now.

"I don't think there's a textbook answer to this situation." Blake kissed her then, and all the terror in the world melted away, if for a mere moment.

Another earthquake. Sirens wailed from the far distance in town, but everything else was so quiet. The algae bloom grew thicker outside, completely obscuring the windows in mossy green. They didn't have neighbors. No one to go check on or anyone to come check on them.

Walt Whisker settled between them again, his gray tail with white flecks flicking left and right. Ears perked.

Ana caught her breath, willed her heart to calm, and then settled into their old routine. So many nights, before all the hell and haze, they would curl together like this. Walt would purr or meow at something only he could see, and then she'd say...

"Do you think Walt has a poem for us tonight?"

Blake blinked, then grinned at the question. The same question she'd ask any night when she wanted to hear him recite a poem. They did name their cat Walt Whisker in honor of the "Good Gray Poet", after all.

Blake hummed in thought and scooped Walt up closer to them. He leaned toward the purring creature. "Read us a poem, Walt," he said to the cat, as he always did during this game.

And when the next rumble came from outside, the windows shook so hard she was sure they'd break. They held up for now. Was that a small fissure in the window behind Blake, or her mind playing tricks?

There was barely a breeze, and not even a sound from animals outside. The quiet unsettled her most of all, and she returned her gaze to Blake, waiting for his words to cut the silence away.

"Does he have one about the moon?"

Blake paused for a moment. "Well, I can think of one, but it's not very happy."

"That's okay," she said.

Blake cleared his throat and hid his face behind the cat's head. Walt continued his purring, used to the weirdness of his humans, Ana was sure. She let herself pretend Walt Whisker was reading them a poem, one more time.

"Look down, fair moon and bathe this scene / Pour softly down night's nimbus floods, on faces ghastly, swollen, purple / On the dead, on their backs, with their arms toss'd wide / Pour down your unstinted nimbus, sacred moon."

Ana absorbed the words, picturing too clearly the mentioned faces. "That was an interesting one. I wonder what inspired it? I suppose the moon sees all in a way, life and death, all in the perspective of night."

"Maybe Whitman saw a moon that scared him once, too."

Ana huffed out a laugh. "If we live, I'll write a poem about the algae moon then."

Blake caressed her cheek. They both knew, there was no surviving this.

Ana closed her eyes and snuggled closer to him. She imagined herself outside, soaking in the green haze. Letting the algae dust her skin until it grew and bloomed into its strongest form. For a moment, temptation to tread back into the night surged in her thoughts. The itch in her arm grew, crawling up into her shoulders and then her chest. A prickle filled her lungs, making her breath come out in hitched waves.

The burn settled deep, from skull to torso to toe. It clung to something in her very cells, rewiring the atoms inside of her. The notion sounded insane even in her own mind, but she could *feel* it.

"I think it's blooming in me," she muttered, eyes closed. "The germination, it's delicious."

"What?"

"I see it painting my bones green. So many spores, twirling in my blood."

The ground shook once more, and she saw the shift of tectonic plates, too. Fractures opening around the world, inviting foreign dust to settle deep into the Earth's core. Would something new regrow from this, or would the planet simply swallow itself?

"It's okay," Blake whispered. "Shh, it's okay."

Glass shattered. Not in the bedroom, thankfully, but from somewhere downstairs. Even one broken window was bad enough. The bloom reached inside, Ana knew. It would stretch its algae fingers upstairs, then everywhere. All of those gentle cells rising into the air, covering them like a blanket.

"It's beautiful," Ana said and choked out a sob, tears flowed down and she opened her eyes. Blake looked back at her with an expression she couldn't believe was for her. An expression of terror. She moved closer and he flinched. During all of their years together, he had never flinched. Never recoiled.

"Blake?" She gripped his shirt, pulled him toward her. The cat scrambled away, hiding on the other side of Blake and hissing at the air where forest-green spores had come to dance in the emerald glow.

His shaking hand reached up, wiped away the tears on her face. Even in the hazy glimmer of the room, she could tell her tears were thick and green, like muck from a swamp. The liquid from her eyes settled on Blake's finger, and his skin absorbed it with parched enthusiasm.

"It's beautiful," she repeated. Her lips tingled, and she needed Blake near her. Touching her. She kissed him hard, and when she felt him relax into her body, she cried again with the joy of having him here with her.

Ana pulled away from the kiss. She'd left a trail of green dust behind on his quiet lips.

"I'm sorry," she said.

"It's okay," he whispered once again. "We're together, and it'll be okay."

She hoped he meant it.

The bloom skulked up the walls as the house shook once more. Glass splintered from the windows on both sides of the bedroom. Algae floated instead, drifting more like feathers than a solid form, but this was no ordinary organism. Algae birthed from the moon, intelligent and able to spread through hundreds of thousands of miles, from moon to Earth, in minutes.

Extraordinary, she thought. *Beautiful.*

Ana glanced outside through the broken window, and searched through the haze for the moon. No more silver shine, but the full moon still smoldered with radiant green. The streaks of red and brown, even black algae, made themselves more apparent than she'd seen earlier in those photos. It all swirled together from moon to Earth, space to soil. A communication she could only ever hope to understand.

Glass shards cut her feet, but she barely felt it, too transfixed on the universe changing before her eyes. Blake's left hand entwined with hers. In his right arm, he held Walt Whisker who was stained green, but otherwise meowed and stayed curled against Blake's side.

Ana turned toward her husband, beaming as he looked at her. His jade-tinted lips met hers. He pulled away and the glow beneath his pores grew stronger, bioluminescent. Pleasant spores fluttered in her belly when he squeezed her hand.

Blake closed his eyes. Ana knew what he would see there, just as she had—a universe evolving into viridescence.

He smiled. "It's beautiful."

THE HUNT

ALEX FOX

It's the birds Mark notices first. Flocks and strays steam overhead, a motley color palette, all moving eastward. His daughter points and there's wonder in her eyes as she tracks them through the cracks in the canopy.

"Daddy, look," Sadie whispers.

"Shh," he says. He studies a twelve-point buck through the rifle's sights. He and Sadie are well-hid downwind and he supposes it won't notice them until it hears the sharp, wet crack of the rifle. He shifts a bit and gestures mutely at his daughter. She inches forward on her belly and peers through the scope, closing one small eye. Though she's gone hunting with him before, this time it's different. This time she will pull the trigger. He's told her it's not a small thing, taking the life of another.

"You remember what I told you?" Mark breathes. He peers through his binoculars at the grazing buck. Maybe he will make her a hat rack with its antlers, a rug for her bedroom. None of it will go to waste, and it will all be in service to her.

"Chest," she whispers. "Opposite leg."

Mark smiles. "Whenever you're ready."

She inhales slowly. Exhales slowly. Small finger on the trigger.

Now, he thinks. The buck raises its head suddenly, sniffing madly at the air. Now, he thinks again, but it's her shot to take. He lowers the binoculars and watches the buck's blur of brown move through the wood. Sadie gasps and covers her head. The buck sails over them in a graceful leap. For a moment, Mark lies there, puzzled; why would it run towards the danger and not away? Unless it sensed something coming from the forest beyond. Like the birds.

So many birds the sky goes black. Birdshit falls like rain. Sadie giggles at first but then she whines. She takes off her ear-protection and pulls the hood of her camo-printed sweatshirt up.

"Gross. Daddy, what's happening?"

He can't answer because he doesn't know. The brush is too dense to get a clear sight of what startled the feathered hoards. Quickly, he stands, helps Sadie to her feet. He grabs the rifle, slings it around his shoulder. Keeps his pistol holstered for now. Something is wrong.

"We gotta move."

"Okay."

He takes her hand. They process back the way they came, following the buck's broken-brush trail. Sadie keeps getting tangled in the undergrowth but she voices no complaint. Perhaps she, too, senses the danger; or she sees the change on his face, feels his strong-gripped hand around hers, squeezing tighter than usual. They walk, and walk. Distant booms echo through the landscape.

"C'mere." Mark pauses to hoist her into his arms. She's eleven now, and tall at that, a bit too old and too big to be carried, but he wants her near.

She hugs him tight, warm breath on his neck. "What's going on?"

"I don't know," he says, honestly. "We'll have a better vantage point when we get to the truck."

They reach the marshland. Small critters ford the bogged lowlands in an unnatural procession; dark tendrils, flaring out across the mud-colored water. Mark sloshes alongside, peering over Sadie's shoulder. A distant, droning whir engulfs the landscape, an ever-present hum, like the ringing in one's ears after gunshot.

Once they reach dry ground he sets Sadie down, already fishing in his pocket for his brick of a phone. He kneels before her. "I don't know what's happening but I'm not going to let anything bad happen to you, okay?"

Her eyes glass with tears, and he can tell she's trying not to cry. She's always been a tough nut, always wanting to be like her daddy, and her daddy doesn't cry.

"Okay?"

Sadie nods. He takes her hand again, this time giving it a gentle squeeze. With his other hand he dials his wife, Teresa. Nothing. He's walked these woods half a dozen times and always had a few bars of service. A cold sweat breaks out beneath his flannel.

Onwards they walk, up and up until they crest the steep, barren hillside and blessedly, his pickup truck is still there. Sadie runs to it.

"Get in the back."

She asks no questions. She scrambles into the backseat. He lays the rifle down in the passenger seat, slams the keys into the ignition, turns on the truck. Half a tank.

Up here they can see all that lays westward. Mark exhales in disbelief. A great, hulking ship hovers, so large it swallows the horizon, blocking the sun with everything beneath in shadow. Beams of light shine down from the disc-like monolith, flickering, flaring; twisting columns of pale fire. He can hardly make sense of the ship's vastness. Some alien rider of death, the fifth horseman or perhaps their abominable evolution; a collective harbinger of the world's end. For a moment, he feels...lighter, weightless, a strange pull at his chest. He wants to drive towards the ship; he *will* drive towards it. He shifts the car into gear and the tires crunch atop the gravel as he makes for the western road. He must bathe in that holy fire, how warm it will feel. How pure.

"Daddy," Sadie says. Mark shakes his head, catches her face in the rear-view mirror. Gone is the glamor, the sensation. He turns the truck around.

"We're going somewhere safe," he says, like he knows there's somewhere safe.

Mark drives away from the tugging horizon. Thinking fast. Home is likely gone. Wife is likely gone. Everything westward lies beneath a thin haze of smoke, only the beams of light from this massive ship piercing the veil. Maybe she's not gone, maybe she's lying in wait, waiting for him, waiting for Sadie.

Sadie is all that matters. That's what Teresa would want, their child's safety. This graveled road should branch out to Highway 54, a remote road, all things considered, and then wind down into the valley. He swerves as another car crests the hill, speeding straight for the ship.

"What is that thing?" Sadie asks.

Mark casts a glance into the rearview mirror. Sadie's tear-streaked face stares back. "I don't know."

"What about momma?"

"We'll come back for her. But I know she'd want you safe first. We need to put that sonuvabitch in our rearview."

He gives the truck as much gas as he can without losing control, and fiddles with the radio. Static, then sudden channels catching, splicing together: "doom is upon us...the end....EMERGENCY–SEEK SHELTER...Baby can you hear this? Tonya Worsley? I'm at 41 Gestalt St...chhhh...DOOM is upon us...JUDGEMENT DAY..."

He shuts the radio off. Sadie is praying. Fingers clasped white-tight, loose strands from her ponytail framing her downturned face.

Mark's never been a religious man, not that he can remember. The only time he ever prayed was when Teresa was in labor with Sadie. Thirty-eight grueling hours at some ill-equipped rural hospital 'cause she came early. He prayed for her then, prayed for his yet unborn child and her bloodsoaked mother sheened in sweat. And by some miracle they both made it and Sadie was strong and weighed seven pounds, thirteen ounces and her mother held her with her face looking like the sun itself. Oh god, her mother. The most beautiful woman in the world, even then. Especially then. They both cried and they said they would go to mass for such a blessing, but babies aren't conducive to appointments, not even appointments with the Lord. And for one small moment, Mark wonders: is this my punishment? He had said, in that cold, barren waiting room: you can do anything to me, anything, take me away but let them live. And if you spare me, too, I shall sing your praises on high from this day until my last.

And he didn't.

Barreling through the trees as the road narrows, branches whipping and skittering across the car's windows. Mud road beneath unwieldy, pitted and pocked, not meant for such speed. Mark's teeth rattle in his skull. Just a bit more, just a bit more. The trees thin, the mud road ends, the paved road begins. A crash lies smoking in a charred heap in the far lane.

For a moment, when he turns the vehicle onto the road, the ship is visible. Squatting like a metal-forged god, so far at the end of the road, swelled in size like the moon when it rises. This is not the end of times but the beginning. He whips the truck around in a frenzied U-turn. He must see it, this ship, this god. He must feel the light emitting from it and though he sees no evidence of the beams now, he knows just a bit further down this highway lies an overlook and from there he can see it all, its fiery threads latched to the land like it is a marionette and it—this new god—the land's puppet-master.

"Where are you going, daddy?"

His daughter's voice is small compared to the new one in his head.

"Why are you driving towards the thing?" Her voice quavers. "I thought we wanted to go away from it—"

"Why would I want to do that?" he snarls. He feels like he's been cold all his life, cold as he was in the hospital's waiting room, and this ship is his offering, his blanket, his solace.

Sadie reaches out and covers his eyes. Instinctively, he slams on the brakes. Panting. That new voice—that insidious voice—cut off in his head.

"T-turn around," Sadie says. She squeezes her fingers tight so he cannot peak through, cupping them close; he doesn't want to peak.

Wants to get away. Blindly, slowly, he turns the truck around. Gives it a little gas, forward now, eastward. Away from the ship. How strange, he thinks, that she is unaffected. Sadie cracks her fingers open.

"Can you drive like this?"

"Not well," he says. "I think I'm alright as long as I can't see it. Just be ready. You might have to take the wheel depending where we get off. You remember how to drive a tractor?"

He angles the rearview mirror down, so he sees only her. Not the machined horseman skulking just beyond the backrow's headrest. She has stopped crying. Her face, small and set, nods.

"What's the plan?" she asks. Like she's been doing this her whole life, preparing for this moment, when she is no longer the child. When she must take upon herself the mantle of responsibility. Mark always suspected this would come during hunting or hiking, an issue with the farm equipment. Not during this. He feels an enormous gulf—he asks too much of her. But right now, she is all he has.

"The plan," he considers. "We drive down into the belly of the valley. Then we hunker down in the woods. Then we wait."

"I thought we were gonna go back for mom."

"We will," he says, firmly. As though speaking such things with authority might will them to life. "But not 'til we know it's safe for you."

Another car blares by, honking. Heading for the ship...the ship! He misses it, wishes to crane his head and catch a glimpse. No. No. Focus on your girl.

"Whatever happens," Mark says, voice high and thin with emotion. "Know that I love you. Your momma loves you."

"I know."

"You remember when I gave you that necklace?" Mark asks. He's been watching her in the rear-view, the way her face changes; the small registers of reality taking hold. She is clutching the whittled bone-pendant, and she opens her hand, and smiles down at it.

"Yeah."

"Did I ever tell you the story behind it?"

She shakes her head. No, she had been too young to hear; but she's no longer young, not now. This day has aged her, has forced her to come into the woman she was always meant to be.

"Well, I went on a solo hunting trip. I was young, then. You were a year old, and, it shames me to say, I needed a break. Bless your mother, she never got a break, and I—" his voice tightens. He took a lot of breaks that first year, most of which were met with Teresa's rightful scorn. "I went to Alaska. I had a caribou tag. I planned this trip, two weeks out in the brush, tracking and hunting. No food supplies other than a couple days' worth of jerky. A dangerous, stupid mission. I was young and dumb."

"Not like me," Sadie says with a grin.

Mark laughs. "No, not like you. If I had an ounce of your smarts I woulda stayed home. But I went out into the Denali preserve. Remote as remote can be and winter starts early up there. I was tracking, camping. Burying my own shit like a cat."

She gasps at the curse, and then laughs, eyes alight, like Mark has just let her in on some great, adult secret; speaking to her as he would his friends, his equals.

"That's what it was like. I didn't manage my energy well. Ate through my bag of jerky real quick and thought I'd be able to feed myself on the fish—good fishing out there, but they weren't biting for me. I was too headstrong to turn back. Thought it would make me less of a man." Speaking these truths out loud, he realizes how goddamn stupid it sounds. "So I kept pushing into the interior, thinking, if I just get a 'bou, it'll be worth it. I will have...proved something to myself."

Sadie looks up from the triangular pendant, brow arching. "And did you?"

"By the seventh day I was well-starved. I found a pair of shed antlers and took it as a sign. Started whittling them that night—bone's not the easiest to work with but in my starved state, that was my new mission. I stopped hunting, stopped tracking, all my thoughts were on you, and making you something. Proof... of my love, or dedication, I don't know. I was thinking of why I left you. Wondering why would I rather be out here with naught but my own thoughts, the gnawing of my stomach, the lonesomeness with only the squirrels' chatter to keep me company. It was both beautiful and terrible, being out there; beautiful for nature... the reflection it brought. And terrible knowing I had left you, on my own accord."

Sadie is silent. Mark's never been a feeling-man. Not externally; a weakness his own father beat out of him young. He's tried, but he's always been a man of action, not words. His love expressed through teaching, through passing down his grandpa's survivalist tricks, the farmer's codex tips. How to shoot a gun, how to identify plants, how to read the forest and handle the pigs, chickens, horses.

They drive down, down into the valley. It's getting dark and the truck's only got a bit of gas left, and he thinks it's better to save it. He pulls up to a dirt road well-hid in the brush, where the guard rail ends. He drives into the woods a-ways. He gets out, silent, too many truths of the heart worn on his sleeve. He ought not to be ashamed or embarrassed but these behaviors are well-ingrained. When he opens Sadie's door, she leaps into his arms, and gives him the strongest hug he's ever had. He hugs her back. He didn't realize he was crying, her shoulder damp with his tears. He sniffs.

"I wear it every day," she says.

"I know."

"I don't blame you. I don't remember you being gone. For all I remember, you were always there."

He smiles. He knows it's not true but he's glad that experience up North changed his flighty ways. He sets her down.

"It was something I needed," he says as she grabs her pack. He reaches over the bed of the truck and grabs his own gear, then gets the rifle, checks his pistol at his hip. "It was something I learned from."

He eyes the sky. Darker-grown, shadowed. So quiet here, all the animals fled, and the sense of dread swelling inside. Knowing the animals haven't stopped running, knowing they'll likely run 'til they die of exhaustion, and is he not an animal himself and is he making the right choice hunkering down here?

They make camp in a copse of oak and pine. Sadie squats to make a fire but he places a hand on her shoulder.

"No fire." He doesn't know who else wanders these woods, or if the smoke might alert the ship. He hasn't forgotten the ship, and though it is out of sight down here, he craves a glimpse still. He hopes his love for his daughter is enough to override that new, base instinct, if only for a little while longer.

He takes their camp chairs out of the truck. They sit, draping their sleeping bags over themselves, huddled shoulder-to-shoulder.

"You tired?" he asks.

She shakes her head.

"Me either." He doesn't know if he'll ever sleep again.

The woods are not so thick here. With the turning of autumn the canopy has lessened, the brush thinned, the trunks naked and gleaming in the strange, distilled light from the other side of the mountain. They can't hide forever.

A low rumbling coming in from the west. The air stirs. No birds left to flee. Sadie looks at him, wide-eyed.

"It's coming," she whispers. Quickly she rises, places her hands firmly across Mark's eyes. Her palms grow sweaty.

They hear it approach. Mark pulls his sleeping bag over his head, and places his hands over her own. He hears the ship, though he cannot see it, he sees it in his mind's eye. How many are there? Does it matter? Does it hunt him? Is it just passing by? What will he feel when that pure kiss of light touches him at last? Must he wait for it? Will he not seek it? It calls to him. He moves the sleeping bag, moves her hands away. She struggles to put them back. He rises. Sadie is crying. The pale beams of light sway in the woods like new-age specters. Overhead, the sky is gunmetal gray. The ship has come, and he will go to meet it; he must go to meet it.

"Daddy, no!" Sadie grabs him roughly, turns him. Claws at his sleeve, forces him to look at her. A brief flash of clarity.

"Sadie, it wants me, I can't...can't fight it, not forever. It's everywhere," he whispers, sagging at a tree trunk, keeping her brown eyes in focus. Folk always crooned about how much she looks like her mother; but he sees himself in her now, a perfect blend of Teresa and he. He hasn't even had the time to mourn the loss of his wife, for he knows she is gone; or perhaps she waits for him, where the lights dance. He catches glimpses in his peripherals, and it takes all his will to keep his gaze on Sadie.

Sadie kneels between his legs, sobbing. "I won't let it have you."

She's right. He can't give up, not yet. He must fight this thing with all he's got.

"Look away," he barks. "Turn around. Now!" Shaken, she obliges. His hand goes to his belt. He draws his knife. This might ruin her more than him disappearing into the unknowable, but he has to try, he has to, while he still has these bits of sanity, riling like snakes against the chains of the world-breakers.

"Don't look!" he shouts, hoarsely. Her back towards him, shivering and sobbing. The knifeblade shakes. He grips his wrist with his other hand to steady himself. No time left to think, not with the lights shuttering to and fro, calling to him. He drives the knife-tip into his right eye. He screams, blood wet and slick down his face, into his open mouth. A pain he has never felt—true fire, vision gone, body railing in disgust. Bile burns his throat. He drives the knife-tip into his left eye and it works as the best distraction from the pain in his right. Blinded now, and bloodied, but maybe now he won't have to leave her. She is old enough to grapple with this; she wasn't at the beginning of the day, but the world's end will force anyone to grow up, and fast. He gasps.

"Whiskey in the truck. Get it now, and a clean shirt from my pack. Please."

He hears her run off. The pain overloads his brain and he passes out for a few minutes. When she returns to him she screams so loud it causes him to rouse.

"It's okay, baby," he rasps. "Soak the shirt in the whiskey for me.

That's it, that's it." He takes the sodden shirt with shaking hands. He daubs his ruined eyes, hissing and drooling in pain, letting the alcohol seep and cleanse. He rips the shirt, makes a blindfold of it, so his daughter will not be forced to see the reality of their present situation on his face. He takes two generous gulps from the bottle.

Sadie seems to have screamed and cried herself out, though her breathing is still shaky.

"C'mere," he says, patting the ground. She settles down beside him. He places an arm over her shuddering shoulders.

"I know this is scary. I'm sorry. It was the only thing I could think of." His words are slightly slurred. Bad idea, to get buzzed during an apocalypse, but probably a worse idea to blind himself. He still feels the ship calling to him, but it's much subdued, knowing that he cannot glimpse its incongruous form, its heaven-light columns. "We'll figure it out, baby, it's okay, it's okay." It's not okay, but it's enough that he is with her still. He hugs her close, hook of his elbow crooked about her neck. Her whimpers have died down. "You'll have to be my eyes. Okay?"

"Yeah," she murmurs into his chest.

He has not given her a choice.

They sit in silence. They can't run, can't hide. Perhaps this act only bought a few more moments of solace, Mark can't be sure. But those are precious, at the end of the world.

"What's your favorite memory?" he asks, voice rasping in pain.

"Playing out back in the woods," she whispers, seemingly glad for the distraction. "Remember when we found that waterfall?"

"Of course," he says. He'll never forget her laughter overtop the rushing water, the fallen leaves like golden handprints swirling, sky-blue water veined between.

"And then momma came out and we all went swimming. It was cold."

Blood trickles out from beneath the cloth as he smiles.

"Daddy, you should see this," she whispers. "Now I understand. It's so... beautiful." She tries to rise; he holds her close. No, no, no; he hadn't considered this, she was so unaffected before and why now? Have the day's events forced her to this reckoning, he wonders, aged her in mind and sight and spirit so she is now prey? Or were they always going to have her, have us all?

She says, "The lights. They want me to join them. They want us…"

"Don't leave me, baby."

"Come on." She snakes out from under his arm. He reaches out, fumbling; grasps her hand. She tries to pull away, he holds her tight. "I need to go. I see momma. Momma! I'm coming…"

"Okay. Just… don't go alone. We'll go together." He pulls her staining form to his chest one last time. He smells her hair, her skin.

Pulses synced through their laced fingers, they walk.

RED ROVER, RED ROVER

TIFFANY MICHELLE BROWN

S helley cinched her fleece-lined bathrobe tight around her waist and braced for the cold. Though the local weatherman had predicted an end-of-winter thaw by noon, it was 1pm, and the sleepy cul-de-sac remained covered in a stubborn sheath of ice.

Chuck went on and on in her head about how she should wait until tomorrow to check the mail, because a slip on the pavement and a broken hip wouldn't be worth it. Blessedly, he was taking his customary afternoon nap, which meant Shelley could do what she damn well pleased.

She simply *had to* check the mail. Today's delivery might contain the postcard Mandy said she'd sent from Venice. If the mailbox held that slim yet sentimental piece of cardstock, the perilous trip down the drive and back would be worth it.

The air outside had teeth. Shelley shoved her hands in the pockets of her robe and began a careful shuffle down the drive. Within moments, her armpits had grown damp from the effort.

Don't lock your knees. Keep your stomach tight. No quick or overly confident movements. You can do this.

Her progress was slow but steady. She imagined the delicate loops of her daughter's cursive. The image warmed her heart, and though the heat remained localized in her chest, it was enough.

Just shy of the mailbox, a shock of color in Shelley's peripheral distracted her from her mission. She paused, curious, and turned her attention to the Owens' yard next door.

What she saw nearly laid her out on the ice.

Her neighbor, Mark Owens, lounged on a lawn chair in his frost-tipped lawn. He wore a scant yellow Speedo and, even more puzzling, a pair of floaties printed with cartoon characters. In brazen defiance of the inclement weather, Mark's skin did not pucker or shrivel. It was smooth, unbothered, and shined like fresh snow. The man's lips were painted a vibrant shade of red, a color that reminded Shelley of the dress Jessica Rabbit had worn in *Who Framed Roger Rabbit?*

What in the fresh hell was this?

Shelley had nothing against men wearing makeup. She'd lusted after many metalheads and punks in her youth—men with long hair, smoky eyeliner, and beautifully gender-bent clothing. That's how Chuck had lured her in. He'd swaggered over in ripped jeans and a too-tight leather vest, a bandana tied around his bicep and silver stars painted around his eyes.

But Mark? He was a homegrown, flannel shirt and classic Levi's-wearing kind of guy. She'd never seen the man don makeup. Not in photos from the past, not at Halloween, not as a joke. And Shelley wouldn't have pegged him as the type of man to wear a Speedo, not even in the tropics. The floaties were laughable, but in a joke-without-a-punchline kind of way. Add in the exceptionally cold weather, and the whole tableau was simply strange.

"Mark," Shelley called over, "what the hell are you doing? It's freezing out here."

Her neighbor turned and offered a huge, content smile. "Sunbathing."

Shelley scoffed and looked skyward. "What sun?"

"It's beautiful out. Nothing better than soaking up that natural Vitamin D. You should join me." Mark wiggled his hips, settling even deeper into the plastic slats of the lawn chair. His gaze shifted to his left, and he waggled his fingers as if trying to summon someone. "I'll have another mai tai, my man."

Oh God, is he hallucinating?

Shelley flexed her fingers, which had grown stiff and cold despite the warm lining of her bathrobe. She needed to do something or Mark would succumb to frostbite or pneumonia.

Shelley had planned on making her trip to the mailbox a quick one, so she'd left her cell phone on the kitchen counter. Without it, she had two options: go back inside and make the call, or head next door to check on Mark. Hopefully Mary would be home, and she and Shelley together could get him inside.

Shelley glanced over her shoulder to assess the feasibility of her first option. The front door of their Craftsman home seemed so far away. And once she felt the sweet reprieve of indoor heat, Shelley knew she wouldn't have it in her to venture out into the elements again. Mandy's postcard from Italy would sit in the box, unread, untouched. Shelley's heart clenched.

Besides, she was already out here, freezing, navigating the ice. The Owens' house wasn't far. She could pop over, sound the alarm, and help Mary get her husband indoors at least. If it was Chuck losing his damn mind on their front lawn, Mary would certainly appreciate a neighbor intervening.

And if she saved the day, Mandy's postcard would be there, waiting for her. The universe would see to it. A cosmic prize for Shelley being such a good person.

Shelley changed tack and slid sideways toward the large patch of frosted grass that lay between her house and the Owens'. As she moved, she kept her eyes on Mark, who periodically sipped air from a phantom glass. His red lips blazed amidst the dead grays and whites of winter, providing Shelley with a solid focal point, which helped her keep her balance.

When she reached the grass, Shelley picked up her pace, the threat of slipping no longer a concern. She was shivering now, her body rattling like a track as the five o'clock train rolled into the station. She would need a hot bath after this. The kind that turns your skin pink. A low-grade burn, but satisfying as all get out.

As she approached the chair, Mark squeezed a dollop of sunscreen into his palm and lathered up his arms. This close, Shelley could see that Mark's skin had begun to turn blue. And still, the man grinned, oblivious to the cold.

She shivered. How could he be enjoying this?

"Mark, this is madness. We need to get you in—"

The man's lips rippled, as if Shelley had thrown a stone into a red sea. She thought fleetingly of a murmuration she'd observed with Chuck over Lake Huron, starlings sweeping to and fro in coordinated swirls and spirals.

Shelley leaned closer, trying to figure out what exactly was on Chuck's mouth, because it certainly wasn't lipstick. The red color spun and pulsed.

It's a swarm.

The thought struck Shelley, unbidden and alarming. She shuffled closer, propelled by grotesque fascination. Up close, hundreds, maybe thousands, of wriggling orbs decorated her neighbor's lips.

Panic bled through Shelley, hot and jittery. She had no idea what had latched onto Mark's mouth, but her gut told her these odd, vibrating things were dangerous.

Run, Shelley thought, *run away.*

She took two desperate, unsteady steps before the attack. One moment she could see her Craftsman home, the place where she'd given birth to Mandy and raised her to be creative and kind; the next, she teetered through a seething, violent gale of red. Wind whipped Shelley's face as thousands of spherical bodies spun in a tornado around her. As they pressed closer and closer, claustrophobia clutched Shelley's psyche like a vice. She imagined drowning in a bucket of viscous blood. Impulsively, she opened her mouth to scream, and the red beings responded in kind, pouring down her throat.

* * *

SHELLEY SMEARED lipstick far outside her lip line. "Damn," she muttered, swiping at her skin first with her fingertips and then a wet paper towel. When she'd finished cleaning up and had perfected her pout, she adjusted the straps of her swimsuit coverup and left the bathroom.

Outside, the Caribbean sun kissed her shoulders. She removed her shoes and slinked through white sand, allowing the warm grains to tunnel between her toes. Chin tilted up to the sky, Shelley closed her eyes and soaked up the warmth.

Getting away had been such a good idea. She'd grown so weary of the deep-down chill of Michigan winters. Spontaneous sunburns were a welcome change.

Sinking into her beach chair, Shelley gazed out at the vast expanse of water before pulling a romance novel out of her canvas tote. She'd read no more than a hundred words before a beautiful hotel attendant, all green eyes and big muscles and a perfectly coiffed beard, approached and asked if she'd like a drink. Shelley ordered a margarita, rocks, extra salt on the rim.

The attendant turned to the man lounging on the beach chair next to Shelley, but she intervened. "Nothing for him. As you can see, he's indisposed." Shelley giggled.

"Very good, ma'am. I'll be back with your drink momentarily."

Her neighbor, Mark Owens, was there beside her, but he'd fallen asleep in the sun with his eyes wide open. Shelley couldn't fathom how he'd managed that, but perhaps he'd had one too many mai tais. He'd be in so much trouble with Mary when he stumbled back to their hotel room later, still under the influence of alcohol or fighting the onset of one hell of a hangover.

When her drink arrived, Shelley took a long pull of citrus and tequila. Her lipstick left a bright imprint on the rim. It was such a pretty shade.

She'd read two more pages in her book when an approaching

figure stole her attention. Shelley shielded her eyes from the sun, and the silhouette came into focus. Why, it was Marjorie Swissak, the young mother who lived down the block. How fortuitous that they'd decided to go on vacation, too. But she was dressed inappropriately, bundled up in a fur-lined goose-down coat that reached her knees. The woman had to be a walking sweatbox. Was this a new diet fad? A fashion statement?

Shelley waved and patted the seat next to her, but Marjorie frowned. There was something in her eyes that Shelley couldn't quite place. Fright? Discomfort? But how could that be, amid swaying palm trees and gentle waves and so much sunshine?

Shelley smiled, knowing her teeth would appear blindingly white and inviting in contrast to the bloody plume of her lipstick. "Marjorie, join me. You must be parched, all bundled up like that. Have a margarita. After all, it's such a lovely day."

NO MORE MEATLOAF MONDAY

ANGELA SYLVAINE

Miss Carter stood at the front of the classroom before the chalkboard on which she'd written several sentences about Dick and Jane and Sally. "Attention, Children."

Betty's desk sat in the row closest to the window-lined wall, and she smiled at the sound of excited screams from the kindergarteners outside—Georgie's voice rising above the rest, calling out "Marco."

Miss Carter smacked her desk with a ruler, and Betty focused straight ahead, hands clasped on her notebook and feet crossed at the ankles like a lady. She glared at the back of Tommy's head, watching as he pulled a peashooter from his pocket and loaded it with a disgusting chewed up wad of paper. Why did all boys like those silly things so much?

"Who can tell me the verb in this sentence?" Miss Carter asked, her eyes landing on Betty, who'd raised her hand. "Betty?"

She opened her mouth to respond, but the emergency siren cut her off. The speaker mounted in the back corner of the room gave a short blast, followed by another and another.

"Duck and cover!" Miss Carter shouted, and Betty's pulse spiked, as it always did during air raid drills, but no tears sneaked from her eyes like they had the first time. She was in first grade now, a big girl.

She slipped from her small, plastic chair to huddle under the desk, making sure to straighten her cardigan and tuck her bare legs beneath the skirt of her gingham dress before covering her head with her arms like Bert the Turtle taught them.

"Duck. Cover," Miss Carter said again, her voice rising frantically above the siren as she skittered across the room. "Hurry, children, this is not a drill."

Betty raised her head, bonking the underside of the metal tray that held her pencils, notebooks, and other school supplies. *Not a drill.*

She did exactly as she'd been taught not to and peered up at the windows, expecting to see fire and smoke, but the sky was clear blue dotted with cottony clouds. She strained to hear anything between the siren blasts, but only silence filled the gaps.

Miss Carter rushed past, pulling Tommy from his chair and shoving him under his desk. Tommy looked a lot like Georgie, same close-cut blond hair and round cheeks, but taller. The peashooter slipped from his hand and rolled to a stop at Betty's feet.

You look after your little brother, Betty, her mom had instructed that morning, as she did every morning before school. But Georgie knew what to do if he got trapped outside. Face the wall and huddle down, imagine you're Bert with a shell on your back. Duck and cover. Betty's eyes prickled and she pinched the skin at her wrist, focusing on that pain to stop the tears like her mom taught her.

Mom would be working on dinner. Meatloaf Monday. There were no desks at home to hide under, but the kitchen table worked, too. They'd practiced the air raid as a family last week, her mom and dad huddling them all together and hugging them close. Then Georgie tooted, and they all laughed so hard until her stomach hurt in a good way. Different from how it hurt now.

Miss Carter sprinted down the aisle toward the front of the room, slipped, and smacked her head on the floor. She moaned and sat up, leaving a red smear on the tile. Betty stared at the blood, told herself to be a good girl, to go help Miss Carter. Good people helped when someone was hurt. Betty's dad taught her that after they found their dog Lucky in the road, a smear just like that on the asphalt. He said someone, a bad person, had hit Lucky and driven away. And others had passed by and seen him and done nothing.

She made herself move, edging from beneath the shelter of her desk, but Miss Carter threw out one hand. "No, stay there," she slurred.

Betty shrunk back. Miss Carter crawled away, disappearing behind her desk, which was much larger than theirs and encased on three sides.

The siren cycled, and now classmates' cries filled the gaps. Betty clamped her mouth shut, swallowed down the sob that wanted to escape. She was a big girl, and her dad would come soon. He'd promised he would always take care of them, of her and mom and Georgie.

A sharp, ammonia smell wrinkled her nose, and she looked at Tommy huddled just a few feet away. He'd peed himself, the stuff staining his pants. But no one pointed or made fun like they did that time with Stinky Steven before him and his family moved away. Betty wondered where he was now, if he was under a desk somewhere, too.

The siren went silent, and Betty waited for the signal that they were safe. Three minutes of short blasts meant alert, and a one-minute-long blast meant all clear. She rocked in place, hands gripping her head, listening for the long blast to tell her it *was* a drill. Once it came, she'd go and find Georgie and they wouldn't even have to wait for dad, they'd run home and mom and dad would be there too, and everything would be fine.

A little squeak sounded, and Betty gasped. Pickles.

She looked up at the cage that sat on the counter beneath the windows. Pickles gripped the bars and squeaked again. It was Betty's week to feed and care for their classroom hamster, her job to keep him safe, but she'd forgotten. She'd left him there, scared and alone.

Betty crawled toward the counter and stood on wobbly legs. Pickles looked out at her with shiny, black eyes, clawing at the bars with his front feet. "It's okay, it's okay," she said, climbing the two-stepped wooden stool that sat against the cabinets.

She reached for the cage door and stopped, eyes locked on the window behind the cage, which sat open several inches. Outside, a yellow-brown cloud crept across the horizon, advancing toward them.

"Miss Carter," Betty said. "The window." She looked toward the front of the room, saw a hint of the brown fabric of her teacher's dress and one pale hand peeking through the gap between the desk and the floor.

"Miss Carter," Betty screamed. The hand didn't move, didn't twitch. She saw the red smear on the tile, like the red smear on the road. But Miss Carter said no, she said to stay back. It wasn't like Lucky; it wasn't like that.

BREATH COMING IN FAST PANTS, Betty climbed onto the counter. Pressing her face close to the gap, she shouted, "Georgie, are you out there? Are you okay?"

Nothing.

"Georgie, you answer me right now!"

No answer.

He's inside, Mr. Peterson brought them inside, that's all, she thought.

The dirty cloud crept closer, and a metal smell like from her dad's shop stung her nose. She gripped the windowsill, tried to close it, but the thing wouldn't budge.

"Help, me, someone," she cried, looking behind her at her classmates tucked beneath their desks, faces hidden. "We have to close the window."

They'd gone quiet, no more cries for their parents, no one bothering to answer her. Her lips and chin trembled. She pressed on the top of the window, trying to shove it down from above with all her strength. It wouldn't move. Exhaling a shaky breath, she tugged off her cardigan and shoved it into the gap, dirt from the sill marring the pristine, white fabric.

Pickles chattered in his cage.

"It's okay." The words scratched her throat, and she swallowed. "I'm coming."

Betty lowered her feet from the counter down to the stool, tugging at the hem of her skirt when it crept up to her waist, expecting some comment from Tommy about her underwear, but he said nothing.

She opened the cage door and reached inside. Pickles had let go of the bars, was lying in the wood chips lining the cage floor, panting. She scooped him up, holding him close to her chest as she jumped from the stool and returned to the shelter of her desk.

Pickles breathed too fast, his tiny chest rising and falling against her own. She stroked his soft, brown and white fur. "Shh, it's okay. I'll look after you."

Betty closed her eyes against the acrid air that stung her eyes, her nose, her throat. She wrapped her arms tight around Pickles and hunched over to press her forehead to her knees. "We're going to be okay," she whispered. "My dad will come, he promised."

And when he came, she'd get Georgie and hug him so tight too, and they'd go home to mom, and Pickles would come with them and live in Georgie's room. He'd like that.

Pickles scrabbled against her, and she held him tighter. "Shh, shh."

The siren blared to life again, giving a short, sharp blast, followed by another and another. Betty wasn't a big girl, after all. Tears leaked down her face, soaking her dress and soaking Pickles, who'd stopped moving, stopped struggling, gone completely still.

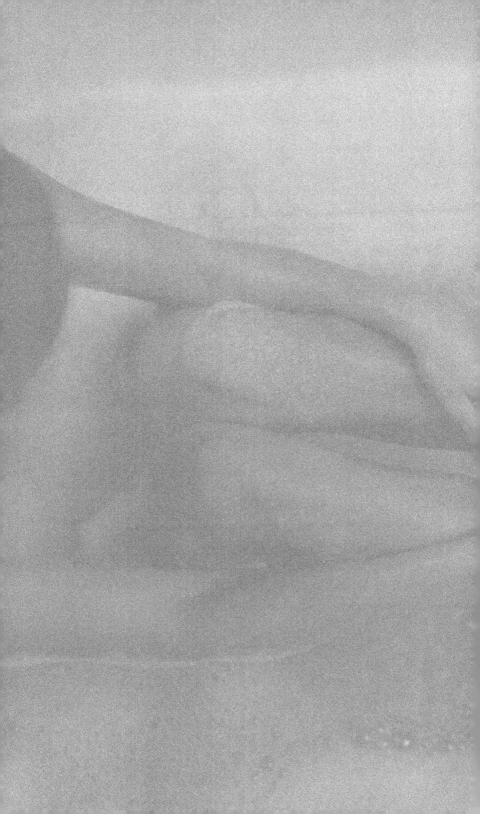

BONNIE'S ABLUTION

M. LOPES DA SILVA

Only a little time left.

Bonnie leaned against the wood of the bathroom door, thumbing through her iPod for the perfect playlist. She wanted something full of fun and love songs. Something light. It had been almost two years since she'd taken a hot bath. Her skin ached with nostalgic yearning for warm water tucked around her – that loving liquid quilt. Showers and grim sponge baths sprinkled with dry shampoos, yes: she'd taken plenty of those. But the kids never gave her enough time for baths, and Jeff was at work now, the commute a solid forty minutes even without the end of the world congesting the freeway; he wouldn't be home in time.

She checked her phone. Jeff had just texted her: *I love you. I've always loved you. Tell Alex and Nadine that I love them more than monkeys love bananas.*

Bonnie stared at the phone, then texted back: *You knew the world might end and you went to work anyway*

Three ellipsis dots formed beneath her text as Jeff constructed his response. She swiped back to her news feed. The scientific consensus was that Earth had been unlucky after all; the planet's gravitational pull was definitely yanking the meteorites off course, and they would hit the northern hemisphere in the next eight or nine minutes. Funny how everyone was back to trusting scientists these days, now that the sky was falling.

She didn't have a lot of time. Bonnie turned on the taps in the bath. She was relieved to see the water flow out, clear and steady. A wild element tamed by human pipes and gaskets. Bonnie dipped her fingers into the stream to check the temperature.

Bam! Bonnie jumped at the sound. It was the impact of a seven-year-old fist on wood.

"Moooom, please let us in!"

"Your father says he loves you more than monkeys love bananas," Bonnie said, her voice choking on the words, mangling them, mashing them into nothing.

"What? Let us in! The meter-ite is coming, mom!" Alex said.

Alex hadn't quite learned how to pronounce "meteorite" even though the word was constantly repeated around them these days. It was the kind of thing that Bonnie would usually think was cute. She *did* think it was cute, even now. Bonnie held her hand over her eyes, shutting out the light. At certain angles she'd get bad headaches, migraines really. She could feel one forming over her left eye socket. She'd been so proud when Alex had come out as non-binary earlier that year. Back then she'd been worried about their future and fitting in at school. That was when she'd thought that they would have a future.

"It's going to be okay. I love you, sweetie," Bonnie said. Alex made an inarticulate shriek: all vowels and anger.

The phone vibrated in Bonnie's hand. She glanced down to check the screen and saw that it was lit with Jeff's reply: *I'm sorry Bonnie we should have*

The screen went dark. She'd have to unlock her home screen to read the rest of his message. She looked at the bathtub, a quarter full. Bonnie tossed the phone into the toilet. The screen flashed a couple of times before going dark for good in the bottom of the porcelain bowl. How many minutes were left?

"Mommyyyyyyyyyyyyyy!" This wail was frantic, wild at the end with fear. It was the scream of Bonnie's two-year-old, Nadine.

"I love you, Nadine," Bonnie said, her voice quavering like her own mother's had when she'd been close to death. She stripped, remembering the hospital, how the white and beige plastics had converged on her mother's dying body. Bit by bit, piece by piece, they'd replaced parts of her meat with plastic and metal while her mind grew less interested in living. She couldn't go out and garden anymore, that was the worst part. With her shattered hip and her arthritis her mother couldn't continue to do the one thing that kept her going. That made life worth living.

"After I had you, and Mark left me, the garden was the one thing I had. Now what do I have to look forward to?" she'd said in the hospital. At the time the words had stung, venomous with Bonnie's own wounded ego, but now they made more sense than anything she'd ever read in any parenting book.

Bonnie peeled off her underwear, kicking them into her pile of stained, smelly sweats. She searched the shelves over the toilet, her motions growing increasingly frantic. She couldn't find the fancy bottle of bath oils that she'd been saving for a special occasion—but then she remembered Nadine had dumped that bottle onto a pile of her Squishmallows. Her bedroom had smelled like expensive musk and lilies for months. Bonnie settled for emptying the dregs of some generic body wash under the running tap. Cheap lavender fragrance fogged the mirror. The bubbles that formed were more air than foam, but they would have to do.

"Mom, come out, please! Mom!"

That was Alex again. Bonnie swiped at the tears that kept forming around the rims of her eyes and sat down in the bathtub. It wasn't hot enough yet. She yanked the hot water tap open, then jerked her toes away from the scalding sting that hit them with a gasp.

"Mom!"

"Alex, sweetie, why don't you two watch something on television for a minute?"

"No!" they shouted. "Come out here right now!"

"Mommy's taking a bath," she said.

The water lurched around in the tub. Toothbrushes and Legos danced on the bathroom sink. Bonnie gripped the porcelain edge of the tub and braced her other hand against the linoleum-tiled wall.

"Mommyyyyyyyyy!" both of her children screamed.

"It's just an earthquake!" she shouted. "Go watch T.V.! Now!"

The kids kept screaming. Bonnie turned and snagged the earbuds and iPod that she'd brought into the bathroom with her from the deflated sack of her sweatpants on the floor. She stuffed the earbuds into her ear canals. She hated the way the damn things felt, but with the sound turned up they blurred the screams into abstraction. Into pure bass rumble and a catchy rhythm.

Bonnie wept.

Piece by piece. Plastic sprouting from her mother's veins, blooming into IV bags. Her mother used to grow lavender. French and English. Desert and Fernleaf. Grosso and Lavenite. Bushes of blue and purple scratching up the perimeter of the backyard, blistering the flower pots. Bonnie couldn't remember the last time that Jeff had touched her with anything that felt like need or desire. He'd turned down so many of her advances, she'd taken a break from even attempting one. How long ago was the last time? Months? Years? It wasn't even important now. At least two years – Nadine was two and a half. So thirty months since she'd fucked another human being. Since she'd been held by someone interested in her pleasure. Fantastic.

She was a terrible mother. She'd tried so hard to be good. She'd childproofed and meal planned and sanitized and educated and comforted and created and healed and everyfuckingthinged else, but in the end all of that meant nothing: she was a terrible mother because she'd constantly neglected herself. Bonnie always shoved aside what she needed and wanted for the kids or for Jeff's convenience. Because she was the one who made it work, who made everything work out okay in the end. And that persistent neglect had eaten away at something inside of her, something crucial that she needed in order to love others. She could feel the ache of this mysterious organ's atrophy inside of herself; the pain fugitive but real.

Hot water danced up in the air, sloshing and spilling over the side of the tub. Sending lavender suds to soak the pile of her clothes on the floor. Bonnie wrapped the iPod in a towel to keep it dry. Alex was shouting something: Bonnie's little fighter. Their cries overwrote the melody playing in her earbuds, adding their own unblur-able, vibrant staccato. They wouldn't stop fucking shouting.

"Your father says he loves you more than monkeys love bananas!" Bonnie shouted back, so loud that her vocal cords itched after she'd done it.

Bonnie crammed her red-rimmed eyes shut. She turned up the volume on her iPod so loud that her head throbbed, but the canned K-pop couldn't quite muffle Alex's crying or Nadine's screams. Nadine had made sounds like that once before, when she'd thought Bonnie had lost her at the mall. It was her gut-song of abandonment. It brought back the chemical stink of polyester and Bonnie's footsteps light with adrenaline's panic. Bonnie tried to float on flirty lyrics, on love songs promising kisses and squeezes. On cheap lavender body wash. On hot water like an envelope, enfolding her securely. The house trembled. Water floated in the air beside her. She squeezed the damp towel with a rictus fist. The children screamed. She only had to be a bad mother for a few minutes. Just a few more minutes and everything would work out pretty much okay.

THE SCREAM

ANDREW CULL

The end began with a single scream.

We watched the man stumble between a group of Japanese tourists. The woman recording reeled back with a yelp when she saw him. She swung her cell up to his face, catching the horrified expressions of her friends behind him as she did.

Someone yelled, "Daijōbu desu ka?"

The sun flared on the screen of Alex's iPhone. I leaned closer, blocking out the glare with my shadow. A message from Sandy popped up on the screen: "Where r u?"

The man in the video moaned. His hands were clamped over his face, white fingers gripping at the flesh as if he was trying to hold his skull together. He dropped onto his knees. The cell camera followed him down.

His groaning began to change. The muscles in his neck were spasming, taut cords twitching and straining. Something snapped, a loud pop that sent the woman recording scuttling back. In her panic she recorded the floor, the feet of other commuters gathered to see what was happening. The groaning became an awful wail.

"Dear God."

"Sandy sent it to me." Alex didn't look up. "It's Edison Central. The police have closed it off, she said."

When the woman's camera found the man again, his hands had slipped from his face. His mouth had stretched so far open that it looked like the twitching muscles in his throat might dislocate his jaw. His head jerked back, pulling his gaping mouth even wider. It jerked again, and I had to look away. The man's agonized scream seemed endless.

"*Christ*. Turn it off." I couldn't watch anymore.

"They're saying it might be a terror attack. Gas or something released inside the station."

"Gas doesn't target just one person." Bob's voice made me start. I hadn't realized he'd been standing behind me.

"What, then?" Alex scrolled the video back with his finger.

"Turn it off. I don't want the kids seeing that." I looked across the park to Sarah and Georgia, sat on a picnic table deep in conversation. Georgia perched on the tabletop swinging her legs over the side, while Sarah knelt on the bench beneath her.

Since Sarah turned eight, she'd grown less interested in parks for any of their rides, and more interested in finding a quiet spot, generally as far away from me as possible, to talk with Georgia and sip the latest Starbuck's frappe variation. They swapped tall drinks, sipped each other's, laughed and then swapped back. I was grateful that they hadn't heard the video.

"Now?" Behind me, Alex sighed into his cell. "Yes, okay. I understand. Sandy, we're five miles from Edison Central. Even if it was a gas attack…"

Bob joined me watching the girls. "You okay?"

I nodded. I wasn't.

"I miss the days when we only heard about terrible things, didn't have to see every single one of them."

"I miss those days too, Dad."

Alex paced as he talked. "Yes, yes, I remember the July London attacks. I know there was more than one bomb, but Sandy, they haven't even..."

After 9/11, we'd all tried to get back to normal, but what we'd known as normal before that September day was gone for good. Normal now was waiting. Waiting for the next bomb, the next mass shooting, the next virus. 9/11 had long, skeletal fingers that could easily reach through twenty years to wrap themselves around your heart. In 2015, Tom and I had Sarah. That same year, he was diagnosed with cancer. It was inoperable. We waited for the chemo to work. It didn't. We waited for a space on a clinical trial. It never came. We waited until he died in January of the next year. Normal now was waiting.

"No, no, I don't think you're being unreasonable. We'll see you soon. Sandy, it's okay." Alex hung up his cell. I was already heading across the park to collect Sarah.

* * *

ON THE RIDE HOME, Sarah pouted and prodded about our reasons for leaving early. I deflected as best I could, my mind replaying that video over and over: the man's ever-widening jaw, that awful wailing. As we'd climbed into the car to leave, I could have sworn I heard a scream in the distance.

* * *

"MOM, WHAT THE HELL?"

A car had swerved across the road ahead of us. Its front end had collided with the median barrier. I stopped a way back. There wasn't any smoke, any shattered glass, no skid marks on the road. The driver hadn't been going very fast when they crashed.

"I'll go and make sure everyone's okay." I opened my door and made to step out. Sarah called me back.

"What if it's a carjacking, Mom?"

"I don't think they're gonna want to swap that car for ours, kiddo," Bob said.

I looked back to the car. I wasn't sure what brand it was—a Lexus, a Tesla, maybe—but I knew it was expensive. Still, between Sarah's caution and the knot I had in my gut from Alex's video, I dragged my heels as I approached the crash.

"Hello? Is everyone okay?" I called.

No answer. Damn it.

I arrived at the driver's side window. A woman sat facing away from the glass.

"Hello? Are you hurt?" Still nothing.

I assumed she was talking to the car's passenger; I could hear muffled sounds coming from inside the car. I leaned closer, reaching out to tap on the pane.

"Hello?"

As I did, I caught sight of the car's passenger: A man, I guessed in his sixties, his cheeks glazed with tears, an expression of utter horror contorting his face. He'd pressed himself back as far as the cabin would allow. He was frantically running his hand over the door behind him, trying to find the handle but unable to tear his gaze away from what he was seeing.

"He...he...hel..."

He found the catch and he ripped it back, throwing the door open. He fell out of the car, dropping momentarily out of sight. Now I could hear his muffled voice clearly.

"...P! HELP! OH, GOD, HELP!"

I heard one of the doors of our car open. Afraid it was Sarah, I turned to look back. At the same moment, the woman in the car in front of me threw her head back. She spasmed backwards with such force that her head slammed into the glass, leaving a splatter of blood and hair on the pane. She began to wail. She gripped her head with her hands, fingers tangled in her gray hair.

Her head jerked back again, this time crushing her fingers against the window. More blood smeared on the glass. I stumbled backwards, almost losing my balance as I turned to run. It was Bob who'd climbed out to see what was happening. His confused expression quickly turned to alarm as he saw me.

"Get back in the car! Get in the car!"

As I ran, the woman's awful wailing grew louder behind me. It felt so close that I expected to turn and see her racing after me.

I was back in the car before Bob.

"What's going on? What happened?" His questions were lost in my panic. Behind us, another driver honked. Cars had started to back up on the road.

I started our car and peeled forward, mounting the sidewalk to get around the Lexus. Even then we scored along its trunk as we passed.

"Shit! Mom!"

"Please don't look, Sarah."

All the time, the woman slammed her head back against her window, only now her gray hair was black, slick with dark blood.

* * *

I DON'T KNOW how many times Bob asked me what happened before I found the words to answer him. He was scared, obviously, and not doing a great job of hiding it in front of Sarah. She just sat silently watching me from the back seat. I was sure she'd seen the woman we'd fled from. As we drove away, the passenger (*her husband?*) ran around their car. He'd waved his arms madly, trying to flag down some help. The car that followed us had almost hit him in their panic to get past.

"It was the same as the video."

"Christ." Suddenly our car felt very small, too tight for all the awful thoughts squirming through my mind. I wound down my window.

Bob turned back. "You think they were at Edison Central too?"

I drove. Maybe the woman in the car was having some kind of seizure. Maybe it wasn't related to the video at all. Maybe she needed my help and all I'd done was run away. I stopped about a mile down the road, got out and called 911. I instinctively walked far enough away from the car that I thought Sarah wouldn't be able to hear. When I got through to someone, I told them about the accident, gave them the address. I hung up when they asked for my name.

* * *

THIRTY EXCRUCIATING MINUTES LATER, we pulled into our street. Along the way, I'd noticed several cars pulled haphazardly off on the side of the road. I tried to convince myself they were simply breakdowns, the usual abandoned cars you see at the side of the freeway, coincidences I was interpreting as something else, but I was sure I'd seen at least one figure crouched beside one of those cars.

The woman was kneeling in the middle of the road.

I slowed to a crawl as we approached. Her body was arched so far backwards that she shouldn't have been able to support herself; still, somehow, she knelt screaming silently into the sky. Her mouth was stretched open, even further than the man in the video. Her eyes were unblinking, staring behind her, watching us as we approached.

"Turn around, Kate." Bob's voice was barely a whisper.

"Our house is on the other side of her." I had no plan other than getting us home. I wasn't going to fail Sarah in that.

The car jolted as we rode up onto the curb. Sarah let out a yelp. Aside from that, we were all silent. I was holding my breath.

I'd chosen to pass the woman with her on my side; that way, she'd be as far away from Sarah as I could manage. She passed alongside the car's hood, and slowly she gained on my window. That's when I heard it.

Faint at first. The sound of strained rasping, air wheezing from her impossibly gaping mouth. The woman was still breathing. No, she was still screaming. Only her body had contorted so unnaturally, her muscles pulled so taut, that she could only manage to snatch the thinnest of breaths to cry out with.

I wound up my window against the terrible sound.

As we passed the woman, I couldn't help but look into her tortured eyes. They didn't move or acknowledge us. Could she even see me anymore? I was having trouble breathing. I gripped the wheel, trying to keep myself together. It was so terrible, so unthinkable. In one of the buildings close by, someone wailed.

I panicked. All the fear that'd built as we passed the twisted woman poured out. I sped forward, almost slamming us head-on into a telephone pole on the sidewalk. I took Bob's wing mirror off as I swerved to avoid the post.

I stood on the brake and the car skidded sideways back out into the road. We jerked to a stop that made my seatbelt lock.

"Fuck. Fuck. Are you okay? Sarah? Dad?"

I put my hand on Bob's arm.

"I'm...okay," he said, although I wasn't convinced.

"I'm so sorry, Dad."

Behind me Sarah's seat belt unbuckled. I spun to see what was happening. She was up on her knees looking out the back window.

The wailing was out on the street behind us now.

"Sarah, get back in your seat."

"Mom! Mom!" She waved frantically out the back windshield. "That's Jenny Derby."

"Sarah, honey, please sit back down. We have to go."

Jenny was Sarah's age. She'd lived on the same street as us since Sarah was a few months old. Framed in the back window, Jenny stumbled towards the car. This couldn't be happening.

"What? Mom, we can't just leave her."

"We have to go. *Now,*" Bob urged.

Jenny didn't make it to our car. She buckled to her knees in the road. Her hands were clamped around her bottom jaw, her fingers hooked into her mouth. I guessed she was trying to force her mouth to close.

Maybe her fingers were locked, contracting like the cords in her neck, but when her head jerked backward she didn't—maybe she couldn't—let go. Her mouth gaped, wider, wider, her head pulling so violently against her locked hands that her lower jaw dislocated. It came out of its socket with an awful crack.

Jenny's wailing was unbearable. Her bottom jaw hung useless, gripped in her hands.

I took off before we could witness what happened next.

* * *

WE DROVE WITHOUT SPEAKING. Sarah sobbed against the back seat. Bob stared out of the window at the passing countryside. After what happened to Jenny, I'd torn out of our street, driven in a blind panic, too fast, without direction, unable to pull a single thought out of the red haze that descended over my mind. I had no plan, no idea what we could do next. When I saw the sign for Mount Callaghan, I took the exit.

Before Sarah was born, Tom and I spent a lot of weekends hiking the trails at Mount Callaghan. We'd camped there, too. Sarah didn't know, but she'd been conceived there. We hadn't planned to stay on the mountain that night, but our car broke down. We were carefree enough back then that we'd embraced the whole thing as an adventure, had a dinner of trail bars and bananas, and slept across the back seat of our car. Nine months later, Sarah was born. I desperately wanted to comfort her now, but that would mean stopping, and until I knew what to do next, I couldn't stop.

"It's going to be okay, honey," I said, even though I knew they were just empty words. I had no idea what was happening, what awful thing would happen next, if I could even protect us from any of it. The incline was growing steeper, narrower, the canopy of the trees lining the sides of the road met overhead. Sunlight strobed over the car's hood. I drove the ascent to Mount Callaghan.

One of my fondest memories of our camping trips was of the silence of the place. It was so peaceful. Tom and I would often hike a whole day without seeing another person. It was that memory of a vast emptiness that guided my hand to take the road we were driving.

Whatever was happening, I hoped that being away from other people would help me keep Sarah and Bob safe a while longer.

Bob turned from the window.

"That poor, poor child." His voice was a hoarse whisper. He thumbed tears from his eyes.

"I know." I put my hand on his arm. I called Bob *Dad*, but he wasn't my father. He was Tom's. We'd been close since we first met, not long after Tom and I began dating. My father died when I was a teenager, and Bob had easily fit into a space that'd long been empty in my life.

About eighteen months after Tom's death, I got a call at three o'clock in the morning. It was Bob. He'd taken a pretty nasty fall down the stairs at his place. He managed to drag himself along the hallway to the phone and called me. I asked him if he'd called an ambulance. He repeated that he'd called *me*.

Later that night, as we sat in the ambulance that *I* called, I asked him what he was doing up at three in the morning anyway. The painkillers must have kicked in because I don't think he'd have told me otherwise. He said he fell at eleven on his way to bed, but it'd taken that long for him to accept that he wasn't going to be able to pull himself up the stairs to his bedroom and that he needed help. That was when he'd hauled himself along the corridor and called me.

I wheeled him out of the hospital two days later. All the way home, he argued that he was perfectly capable of looking after himself. That he could roll the *damn wheelchair* on his own. Not that he needed it, of course. I told him that was fine. If he was so healthy, he could look after Sarah and me until the plaster came off his broken leg. I drove him to our house and he ended up staying with us for almost a year.

I had no problem with that at all, and Sarah loved having him live with us. She hadn't had a chance to get to know her father, and Bob was always ready with a tall tale about Tom's adventures growing up. He always finished with "and that's how I got this gray hair," pointing to a different one each time. I'd known and loved Tom for more than ten years, but Bob always seemed to have a new story about him that I hadn't heard before. I missed Tom terribly, and sitting listening to Bob talk, well, it felt like it brought him closer somehow.

The road was getting steep. Bob leaned across and switched on the radio. He scanned the channels until he found a news report. The newsreader didn't seem to know much more than we did. They speculated that a number of terrorist attacks had occurred across the city. That a nerve gas might have been released. They cut to a reporter at Edison Central. At that point, the line seemed to go dead. The host cited technical difficulties, called the reporter's name a few times— only the line wasn't dead, it wasn't completely silent. There was a faint whistling of air, the same wheezing I'd heard as we passed the twisted woman in our street. At the other end of the line, someone was trying to scream.

"Dad, please turn it off."

Bob didn't move.

"Dad, please."

I turned to see Bob, staring straight ahead, his arms locked across his chest, hands gripping at his sides.

"Are you okay?"

The road doglegged ahead of us. I swung around the curve and almost into a truck that was parked side-on, blocking the way forward. Two figures, dressed in head-to-toe protective gear, appeared from the woodland at the side of the road.

"Road's closed. You can't go this way," one of the figures called.

"They've got guns, Mom," Sarah whispered from the back seat.

The figure talking to us had a handgun, held down at his side.

"Turn around," called the second man.

"Government quarantine," the guy with the handgun added.

I noticed movement in my rear-view mirror, another figure stepping out from the woodland behind us. This figure was dressed differently: their protective gear consisted of the kind of N-95 mask we'd all worn during the pandemic, and they wore hunting camo, with a rifle slung over their shoulder.

I cracked my window open. As I did, I noticed one of the men in front step back away from us. "We live up here. We're just heading home," I lied.

"Close your window, ma'am."

"Road's closed," a voice barked from beside the car. The masked hunter had drawn up alongside us. More alarmingly, they'd drawn the rifle from their shoulder.

"Mom..."

"I said, we live up here. We're just heading home. Let us through, please."

"Close your window and back the fuck up," growled the hunter.

I kept the window open; it seemed to be keeping the men at a distance for now.

"Head to my house." Bob struggled to get the words out through clenched teeth.

"Dad, are you okay?"

"Grandpa?" Sarah leaned between our seats.

"Sit back, honey... please."

In front of the car, *Handgun* was pacing. He gestured to the hunter next to us. I didn't like the way he was waving his gun around.

Bob opened his door.

"Dad, no." I grabbed at his arm. The muscles spasmed beneath his shirt. I only held on harder. "Oh no, Dad, no."

"Just get to my house. Keep Sarah safe..." Dad wrestled his arm from my grip. He staggered out onto the road.

"GET BACK IN THE FUCKING CAR!" The hunter had his rifle up, pointed at Dad.

"NO! PLEASE!" I begged.

Dad began to wail. Ahead of us, Handgun opened fire.

I slammed my foot on the accelerator and raced forward. I only meant to put the car between Dad and the gunfire, but I rammed into Handgun head on. We slammed into the truck barricade, crushing him between the two vehicles. His screams were awful.

Handgun's accomplice didn't stop to help him. He turned and raced away into the woods.

I fumbled the shifter into reverse. I had to get back to Dad! A gunshot rang out behind us.

"NO!"

In the rearview mirror, I saw the hunter stumble backwards. Even though the shot had done a terrible amount of damage to Dad's head, he still wailed into the sky. The hunter raised his rifle again.

I stood on the accelerator.

My tires squealed over the asphalt. The hunter's second shot exploded as we collided with him. He crumpled under the trunk. The car jerked upward and then dropped as we rolled over him.

I didn't stop.

We kept speeding backwards.

My foot was jammed to the floor. My heart was going to explode. I screamed in anger, screamed with the unbearable grief of it all, screamed because there was nothing else I could do.

The back end of the car swung across the road,

I couldn't stop.

I wasn't in control anymore.

We ran up the verge, into the woodland, and slammed into a tree.

* * *

THE BACK WINDSHIELD HAD SHATTERED. A branch stuck through it like an arm reaching in to take hold. Sarah had fallen into the footwell behind mine and Dad's seats. She wasn't moving. I tried to reach for her, but a bolt of pain shooting across my chest made me snatch my hand back.

"Sarah?"

I unclasped my belt and threw open my door. I tried to step out but my legs gave way underneath me and I collapsed onto the dirt.

I crawled to the back passenger door and hauled myself up. When I saw the bullet hole in the window, something inside me snapped. As I'd reversed at the hunter, I'd heard his gun discharge, a huge noise close by the car. No! No! I was just trying to protect Dad. I hadn't stopped to think what might happen if we put ourselves between the hunter and his target.

I ripped the door open.

Sarah groaned.

"Mom?"

"Sarah? Oh, honey, I'm here." I climbed onto the back seat and, even though the pain knifing across my chest was excruciating, I pulled Sarah up next to me and clung on to her.

"Are you okay? Are you hurt?"

"I just fell. Is Grandpa okay?"

"No, sweetheart, no, he isn't"

"Why is this happening, Mom?" Sarah started to sob. She buried her head against my side. I held her with all the strength I had left in me. We cried together until the sun no longer flickered in the canopy above us, and the woods around us had swallowed the last of the day.

Exhausted by her grief, Sarah finally fell asleep against me. I gently laid her across the seat and ventured outside.

The evening was quiet, the woods around us that'd concealed Handgun and the others were eerily still.

The hunter lay where we'd hit him. As I approached his body I wished for a sound to distract me, for any other sound than the one I heard coming from Dad. The hunter's first bullet had removed most of Dad's head. Even in the near dark, I could make out the glistening wreck of his skull. Jagged edges and bone where his face should have been. He should have been dead, surely he *was* dead, but still he knelt, the remains of his head arched up into the sky, air whistling out of his lungs. Even in death he screamed.

I picked up the hunter's rifle. I wanted to cover Dad, but I didn't have it in me to get any closer to him. I fumbled through the pockets of the hunter's vest and found some extra rounds. When I'd finished, my fingers were streaked with his blood.

I buckled Sarah into the back seat, laid the rifle where Dad had sat, and started our car. I managed to rock us back and forth until the car dislodged from the tree and rolled back onto the road. Between crashing head-on into the barricade truck and reversing into a tree, the car was in bad shape. I had no idea how far it would carry us. I hoped it would get us to Dad's place. His house was another ten miles past Mount Callaghan. The land it sat on had once been used to rear cattle. It was a large house without any neighbors for miles around. It seemed like a good place to stop, to take stock, to hide if need be.

As I drove past Dad's corpse, I prayed that his screams would fall silent soon. He'd saved us. I prayed that I might live long enough to save Sarah, too.

THE DOOR IN THE BASEMENT

RUTH ANNA EVANS

It was good—*really* good. Took Jazz's mind off of everything happening outside their bedroom. Legs up, chest flushed; she was close—*so* close.

"Please," she said, gripping Joel's wrists so her fingernails sank into his skin. Joel cocked back, prepared for a deep, satisfying conclusion.

An alarm sounded. Not *an* alarm. *The* alarm. The one the officials never even tested for fear of mass panic. It was only to be sounded for the *real thing*, when it was certain, no other possibility. The End Alarm. The screech blazed through every digital device they had, a rounded ringing, grating, almost-alien sound that couldn't be confused with anything else.

"Don't stop," she whispered to Joel. "Keep going."

For years, everyone had been asking each other what they would do if they had five minutes, and her answer had been a great cup of wine and a really good scary movie. But really, she wanted to do this, with this man.

But he pulled away, eyes wide.

"Shit, fuck, shit!" he swore, stumbling out of bed, stepping into his pants and pulling them on in one motion.

"Where are you going?" She felt emptied out, shocked by the sudden rending away.

He stopped for a millisecond and looked at her, his eyes completely different than before.

Then he took a deep breath and looked away, shoving his shoes on his feet.

"You can come if you want to," he mumbled. "And sorry in advance."

"What the hell are you talking about?"

But Joel was already out the bedroom door. Jazz gathered the blanket around her and followed him toward the basement.

Everyone knew a basement was no protection. There *was* no protection. It was The End.

They had only minutes, and he was being an idiot. Jazz wanted to cry. She'd imagined snuggling in bed together in a warm afterglow when time and space ripped apart around them. Not everyone had that opportunity, and she did. She'd felt so lucky, had thought he wanted that too. But here she was, standing naked under a blanket, shouting down the rickety stairwell into the cold, dank basement.

"Where are you going?!"

"Come on if you're going to!" Joel shouted back up at her.

Jazz descended the disgusting stairwell. She couldn't remember the last time she was down here. Joel went down regularly to do some guy-shit or other, but she stayed away from the spider eggs and damp.

At the bottom of the stairs, Joel moved a stack of crates away from a wall.

"How is this going to help anything, babe?" Jazz asked. "Let's go back to bed, we only have..."

She shut her mouth.

Behind the crates was a door she'd never seen before. It was black steel, dented in places but with a deep sheen. It was a door that meant business.

Joel didn't look back, but the panic on his face was obvious even at this angle. No one knew how long they had after the alarm, but it was between moments and minutes. He reached for the doorknob and yanked it open.

Jazz's mouth fell open. On the other side of the door, where she expected a tiny hideaway stocked with water and canned corn, a couple of cots, maybe, was a finely decorated room, a couch, and a woman who looked remarkably like herself. Bigger boobs. Better skin.

"You and I don't know each other," Joel said to Jazz, quiet but clear.

"Joel!" the woman said, standing from the leather couch. "What were you doing in there again?" She didn't notice Jazz. "And what's that noise?"

Joel stepped forward and pulled the door almost closed behind him, just enough so the latch wouldn't fall into place.

Jazz felt heavy, stunned. Like her heart had stopped beating. Her husband somehow had another woman in a room in their basement? Or—what? Another dimension was connected to theirs through this unexpected black steel door? She didn't know what to be more upset about: that the world was ending, that the man she loved had left her behind, or that the other woman was prettier than her with a better couch.

She pushed the door open. Joel had gotten his other woman out, so the room was empty. It was a basement—the same basement that she was leaving, she realized now. Only, money had been spent on this one. There was tasteful wallpaper. Carpeting, thick. The room smelled good, like a vanilla candle, her favorite. She pulled the door closed and the incessant screeching of the End Alarm fell silent.

Then she saw something that shot a pang through her heart. A tiny white rocking horse with a long mane, braided childishly. Its face was scribbled pink with marker. Draped around its neck was a macaroni necklace. It had the feeling of being well-loved by a well-loved child. In this house—in this world—Joel had a *child*. A daughter, perhaps.

The thing she'd never been able to give him.

Side piece. The name stuck in her head like a slur. *Other woman. Barren mistress.*

And then words for him: *Cheater. Asshole.* But what really hurt was how much she still wanted him. Wanted this life with him. Wanted the house. Wanted the child. The future. But she was standing naked in a sex-smeared blanket in another woman's basement, and behind her was a world moments from breaking completely.

A little voice reached around the corner. "Daddy!"

Jazz and Joel always pretended it was okay. That with The End so near, a child would have been a selfishness. But she knew he wanted a baby, and she knew she wanted one, too. It was because of her they couldn't have one. It was a silent truth between them. It was why she didn't comment about the amount of time he spent in the basement.

"Where were you, Daddy?" The child sounded about six.

"Coming home to you." His voice was warm. Fatherly.

"Can we play?" The voice was getting closer.

"Not in there, sweetie, let's play in your room." His voice was raised a little. She heard the message in it. *Leave now. Get out.*

"No, I want to play with my horse." They were right around the corner.

Jazz jumped back and swung through the door behind her, pulling it shut firmly. *No.* She couldn't see her husband with his child by another woman. She couldn't let the child see her, naked, looking like her mother, only not. In a way, the girl was her child, almost, and she wanted to spare her such terrible confusion.

It took her a minute to realize the alarm wasn't going off.

And then, "Babe!" A voice behind her, deep.

Strong arms wrapped around her.

"I thought you went out. I didn't expect you down here waiting for me like this." An erection pressed into her back. The man nuzzled her neck with a bearded chin. She always asked Joel to grow a beard, but he never did.

Jazz turned to see who was there and found a warm mouth on hers, familiar but not. After the cleaving she'd just experienced, the abrupt interruption, the abandonment and rejection, her body reacted instinctively. She relaxed and opened herself up to the stranger who was not a stranger.

He picked her up, and, blanket and all, carried her up the stairs. They were simple, wooden, and clean. There were no cobwebs. She got a look at the man's face. He looked like Joel, only stronger. Smarter.

He was bigger too, and fit her just right.

She was almost there, back arched, knees trembling.

The Alarm went off.

"Goddammit!" she gasped.

New-Joel froze, then pulled away quickly.

"Finish," she said, reaching for him and gripping his shoulders. "Please."

"I have to go," he said, separating from her and rushing into his clothes. He darted a furtive glance at her. "You can come if you want to."

"No," she said, flopping back on the pillows. "Apparently I can't."

"Seriously?" He asked. Then, "Nevermind. I have to get ho—"

"You have to get home?"

"We don't really have time for this conversation right now. Are you coming?"

And then there was a flash, so bright the word bright meant dim, and in a second Jazz saw all the Joels, all the Jazzes, and all the little girls and all of the lacks of little girls.

Then the doors all swung open, the times and spaces mixing and mingling until there was no time left, no space, no Joel, no Jazz, no little girl or lack of little girl. Only doors in basements, hanging open in the emptiness.

SILVER ALERT

WENDY N. WAGNER

The new dent stood out on the side of my mother's Subaru, the metal dimpled and scraped, a pale line of damage tearing through a Sierra Club sticker and two decals for her favorite drive-thru coffee place. I scrubbed at the streak with my finger. Telltale paint flakes came off. Good: not another car. She must have sideswiped something else—probably the street light at Java Brothers again. It was a good thing she tipped so well, or the staff would have surely turned her in to the cops by now.

As if linked to my thoughts, a siren screamed on the street behind me. I glanced back, but the police car had already streaked past. A man in a black suit stood staring after them, and something about his stooped posture made me give him a second look. I forced myself to turn away and head toward the house.

Balancing the bag of cat food on my hip, I unlocked Mom's front door. The scrape on her car returned to the forefront of my attention. "Mom, didn't the doctor say you shouldn't be driving?"

The smell of chocolate and coffee filled the living room, their sweetness overpowering the faint bitter skunk of her other major vice. One of the black cats—Puka, I thought—jumped down from the ottoman to twine around my ankles. Mom looked up from her copy of *The Atlantic*, reading glasses free-soloing at the tip of her nose, travel coffee mug in hand. "Doctors. What do they know?"

I pushed past her, headed for the kitchen. *Count to ten*, my girlfriend Linda always reminded me. *Don't let her get to you.* I concentrated on the simple act of putting away the groceries. Mom had never trusted politicians, rich people, or doctors. I couldn't be angry with her for sticking with her worldview now that she was pushing eighty.

Mom's hand closed on my shoulder. "Chandra." She rubbed her thumb along the muscle and loosened it, just as she always had. It was amazing that her hands still had that kind of strength when so much of her was falling apart.

I grabbed her hand and squeezed it tight. "I just worry about you so much, Mom. You know that."

She sighed and went to the kitchen sink. The line of orange pill bottles looked daunting beside the jelly jar she used for a water glass. "I know." I couldn't see her face, only her bowed shoulders. She looked so little and frail, nothing like the woman who raised me by herself, who'd hiked the PCT before Cheryl Strayed made it cool, who'd lived in trees to save them from the men with chainsaws.

My breath hitched in my throat, and I turned back to the grocery bag. Couldn't let the Tofutti Cuties get melty.

From my pocket, my phone sent up a chirp. I took it out and frowned. It was the second Amber Alert of the day. Local, too. Maybe it had something to do with the police car I'd seen outside.

Mom's voice pulled me back to the kitchen. "I had to get out of the house," she explained. "Every time I look outside, I see more people out there."

I closed the freezer. "Like neighbors?"

Mom shrugged. "Sometimes. But most of them don't look familiar. Maybe they're homeless? I don't know. They just keep looking in the windows."

"They're called 'houseless' these days, Mom. And maybe you should call the cops." I went back in the living room to check that the windows were all locked. Mom wouldn't let me put in a Ring door-bell, let alone a full-on security system.

The black cat jumped onto the back of the wing-backed chair, staring outside intently. I stooped to see through the ficus and the philodendron. The man in black now stood on the sidewalk beside Mom's mailbox. He wasn't looking at the house, but his appearance so shortly after my mother's declaration sent gooseflesh up my arms.

"Is this one of the people you saw?" I called.

The cat hissed and slashed at the window.

"Chandra?" Her voice wobbled up in pitch. "Can you come here?"

I didn't want to take my eyes off the man. He didn't look houseless, not in that suit jacket and what appeared to be dress shoes. Even the part in his gray hair looked crisp. He reminded me of our family doctor, but of course, Dr. Henkel had been dead for decades.

"Chandra!"

The fear in her voice yanked me away from the window. It took me a second to find her, because she'd stepped out onto the screened back porch, where she stood clutching the fluffiest of the cats to her chest.

"What's wrong?"

"Maeve is scared," Mom whispered.

I could actually hear the cat growling, a low engine-like rumble. Maeve, the cat who every letter carrier knew by name. The cat who once caught a mouse just to give it a bath and offer a cat treat.

We peered into the backyard and the lot beyond. Mom's backyard stretched out longer than most city lots; the house behind her had burned down years ago, and the lot stood abandoned. Friends joked the property had to be a tax write-off for a foreign corporation or maybe a drug lord. Since the fire, the place had become a wilderness of weeds and small trees.

The fog had definitely thickened since I had arrived. It filled the neighboring yards, obscuring the houses. I could only make out the shabby chain link fence dividing Mom's property from the empty lot; the trees beyond were merely a suggestion in the mist. And yet I thought something moved between them, a shape human-sized or bigger. My tongue went dry in my mouth.

"What do you think is out there?" I rubbed my arms. The fog radiated a damp chill.

"I don't know," Mom whispered back. "I thought I saw the lady from Java Brothers, but that can't be right, can it?"

"The barista?" I couldn't help the incredulity in my voice.

"No, the lady who jaywalked in front of me. The reason why I hit that street light."

I tugged her arm. "We should go back inside."

"I've seen her here before," Mom complained. "The lady in the white dress. I think she's following me."

I closed the back door and locked it. "A lady in a white dress."

Mom nodded, eyes wide. Her glasses had slid all the way down now, just dangling from her beaded glasses chain. "Sometimes I think she's my neighbor. The one who died in the fire."

Sadness squeezed my throat. The doctor warned me this could happen. The combination of everything—macular degeneration, the stroke, diabetes, the cancer medications—was taking a toll on her brain. *It's a perfect storm*, Dr. Edwards said. *If she'd come to us years ago...* But Mom hated doctors, and so she'd skipped out on decades of preventative maintenance.

I steered her toward the kitchen table. "It's okay, Mom. Let me make you a cup of tea."

She glared up at me. "*It's okay?* Are you serious? Feel Maeve's side. She's shaking."

I laid my hand on the cat's side to humor her. The cat's ribs vibrated. I glanced at the back door, but the view through its panes revealed nothing. Maybe my mother's fear was infecting the poor animal.

"We should keep her inside," I said, filling the kettle and putting it on the stove. "There's probably a coyote or something in the back, and it's scaring her." I opened the cupboard, but Mom's favorite blue-and-white mug was missing. I checked the dish drainer. Nothing. "Mom? Where's your Earth First mug?"

She didn't answer. I glanced back at her and saw her head bent over the cat, her voice too low to be heard. Was she losing her hearing now? I'd have to add that to my list of questions for next week's appointment.

"Mom?"

She still didn't answer. My stomach gave a squeeze. What if it was something worse than her hearing? She'd obviously been seeing things if she'd dodged her dead neighbor while driving to get coffee. No one in my family had ever suffered from dementia, but you could still get it even if you didn't have the genes. Linda's grandpa died from it, and everyone else in her family had stayed sharp as a tack into their nineties.

"It's okay, kitty," Mom cooed softly. She looked up at me. "I left the mug upstairs by my bed. Silly of me to forget it up there."

I forced a smile. "I'll go get it."

The stairs looked twice as steep as usual—the weirdness of the morning draining my energy. The worry was the worst.

My phone chirped and buzzed, but I ignored it, dragging up the willpower to go upstairs.

I stopped at the top of the stairs and rested my forehead next to a photo of my mom in her college graduation gown, kid me in a yellow sundress. She'd always been so much stronger than me. Larger than life. She wasn't just my mother: she was an icon. A keystone figure in so many communities. It had been impossible to imagine her old or sick. When she had her stroke, and I'd sat outside in that hospital parking lot waiting for a nurse to tell me whether Mom would live or die, it was like watching my world slide off its axis.

The third cat, Snorri, brushed past my legs and streaked down the stairs. The youngest of the three, he sometimes still acted like a kitten. Mom adopted him when she got out of the hospital, and caring for him had been part of her recovery plan.

I went to her bedroom, where the Earth First mug still sat half-full of Sleepytime tea. Its smell brought a smile to my face. Mom never let her supply of Sleepytime run out. I bent to tip the cold tea into the nearest plant and froze. The man from the sidewalk now stood in the front yard.

"What the hell?"

He didn't move. Didn't look my way, either, but simply stared out into the side yard. My fingers tightened on the mug's handle, the ceramic biting into my joints. A circle of frost had formed on the grass around his feet.

I spun and raced down the stairs like Snorri. "Mom! Mom!"

At the base of the stairs Mom crashed into me, and I barely caught her before she fell backward. The Earth First mug hit the ground and splattered tea across the floor, its forty-year-old handle snapping off and spinning toward the front door.

"Are you okay?" I stared into her face, gripping her arms almost as tightly as I'd gripped the mug.

"You're hurting me, Chandra!" She wriggled loose. "And you broke my mug." She sank into the couch and began to cry.

"Oh, Mom, I'm sorry." I sat down beside her, put my arm around her shoulders. "I'm so sorry. I saw—I got scared, and I ..."

I ran out of words. What could I tell her that wouldn't frighten her more than she already was? I forced a deep breath and made a plan. After all, if there was someone in our yard, there were people who could help us with that.

"I'm going to clean up this mess, Mom. And maybe I can fix your mug." I took my phone from my pocket and dialed 911 as I went back to the kitchen, opening the cupboard under the sink to find a rag to mop up the tea.

A robotic woman's voice answered. "All circuits are busy. Please hang up and try your call at a later time."

My hand froze on the stack of old tee shirts my mom kept around for rags. I'd heard that message a thousand times in a thousand movies, but never in real life. I hit the "end" button and picked up a tee shirt advertising the Portland Rock Gym. The ancient cotton fabric smelled like my childhood, organic detergent and patchouli incense.

At the back door, a cat wailed.

"It's her," Mom gasped beside me. Her eyes looked glassy with fear, but she took a step toward the cat and the door. Her socks squelched, sodden with spilled tea.

"Mom, stop! You'll slip!" I sprang up to stop her, but my head slammed into the bottom of the sink, and I dropped to my butt, my eyes full of sparkles.

She opened the door. "She's waving to me, Chandra."

My phone chirped an alert, but I dropped the thing on the counter as I rushed after my mother. "Don't go out there, please."

Mom evaded my grasp and stepped outside. "She says … it's my time."

The air on the porch bit with winter-cold teeth, my breath condensing in front of me like it was January and not May. And I could hear something outside, a voice, a woman's voice, softly murmuring something I couldn't understand. I grabbed the doorframe to keep my jellied legs from collapsing. "Don't."

Mom rotated slowly, and when her eyes fixed on me, a gray film covered them over so they were the same color as the fog bank that now filled the yard. "Humanity's time is up, don't you see? That's what the ghosts are trying to tell us."

I grabbed her arm. "Mom!"

With a hiss and a snarl, Snorri shot past us, clawing his way up the side fence and vanishing into the mist. Mom kept walking, pulling me along with the strength of her youth.

"I'm coming!" she called. "I'm coming now."

Every step across the porch felt colder. The air around her arms steamed, the moisture condensing like damp air in a freezer. My fingers stiffened, went numb. I lost hold of her arm and stared at my hands, the pink gone from my fingers, the skin shifting to a yellow so flat and dead it was nearly gray. "What the hell?"

When I looked up, I saw the woman in white. The mist made gray swirls around her yellow hair and slim figure, but her dress hung limp, untouched by any breeze. The air choked out of my lungs.

"I'm coming," my mother said, moving faster. "I'm coming."

"Mom!"

But she was already stepping off the porch into the backyard, her step quickening as her arm rose, stretching toward that eerie figure in white. I rushed after her, but it was like running into a storm. Hail battered my cheeks and sliced at my eyes. Frozen grass crunched under my feet. "Mom, come back!"

I could barely make out her shape through my slitted eyes, her outline blurring as if her skin had turned to mist. I lunged toward her, but my fingers felt only the cold and wet.

"Mom!" I screamed. The chain link fence slammed into my hips and I slid to the ground. The grass beneath my knees turned to soft, ordinary plant matter as the mist withdrew. I clung to the fence and called for her over and over again, but nothing moved.

The phone chirped in my pocket. I wiped my eyes on my sleeve and pulled it out.

Silver alert: 82 year-old man vanished from his yard, the phone blinked. I swiped the notification away angrily. The only old person I cared about right now had just been sucked out of her yard, as impossible as that sounded.

The phone lit up with another alert: *Silver alert: 90 year-old woman taken from care center.*

Amber alert: 8 year-old reported missing.

Silver alert: 76 year-old man missing from his office.

Notification after notification flashed up on my screen, more missing people than I'd ever seen. I opened Chrome to check the news, but CNN's website had crashed. I turned my phone to "do not disturb" to block the waves of notifications while I dialed 911 over and over again.

Somehow my feet made it back to the house while I tried to get someone, anyone to answer. My hand shook as I slid the deadbolt on the back door. I wiped my breath from the glass to check on the fog, still thick along the fence line. It pulsed ever so slightly, like a stomach churning after Thanksgiving dinner. There was a sound, too, a murmur so soft I almost couldn't make it out. My breathing slowed, grew rhythmic. Matched *its* rhythm. My hand closed on the lock and turned the knob.

My phone buzzed, and I screamed and jumped so hard the damn thing flew from my grip and spun out on the kitchen floor.

The silly xylophone tune of Linda's ringtone repeated as I dropped to my knees to pick up the phone. I'd forgotten that her number (and Mom's, of course Mom's) overrode the do not disturb setting.

"Lin?" My voice quavered. "Are you all right?"

"I don't know, Chandra." Her voice echoed a little, like she was talking through a tin can and not a brand-new cell. "There's this weird fog that's come up from the river, and I can't see any of the other buildings. Not even Big Pink. And now Brian and Kelsey are missing."

I squeezed shut my eyes so I could picture her office building, fairly central to Portland's other office towers, even that pink monstrosity on Broadway Boulevard. She worked on the twenty-sixth floor with the other IT specialists, so she had a great view of the city. "They're probably just helping one of the partners or something."

"They had to help set up laptops for a presentation at that hotel," Linda said, her voice shaking harder. "I was supposed to go with them, but when we got down to the street, they just *took off*. It was so weird, Chandra! I should have tried to look for them, but it was so silent and scary. There aren't even any cars on the streets."

I took a deep breath. "Linda, where are you?"

A little pause. "I'm in the lobby. I went back up to get my jacket. It's really cold out all of a sudden."

I took a step forward as if I could get close enough to stop her. "You're not going outside, are you? Do *not* go outside, Linda. Don't do it!"

"I think I can see them now," Linda said, her voice no longer frightened, almost dreamy. "They're waving at me from out in the fog. And they're saying something."

"Linda!" I heard that rush of air that meant a door had opened, and ice filled my innards. "Linda!"

"It's my time, Chandra," she said, and the phone made a hollow, thwacking sound, the sound of hard plastic falling to the ground. Her heels clicked, clicked, *clicked* on the sidewalk, and then—

The silence was thick as the fog, an anti-sound that pressed against my eardrums and summoned up the oceanic rush of my pulse. I ended the call, but the sound continued all around me.

My feet tingled, and I realized I was still kneeling on the kitchen floor. I forced myself to my feet. The back door radiated a chill into the center of my spine.

When I looked back outside, the fog had come all the way up to my mother's raised beds. The man stood in between the herb bed and the flower bed, looking at me with empty gray eyes. But what drove the knife of sadness into my belly were the whispers coming out of the fog. The voices, barely louder than the blood rushing in my veins, of my mother and my girlfriend.

Maeve threw herself against my legs, screeching with fear. I slapped the deadbolt back into place and scooped the cat into my arms. We were both shivering.

The fog murmured and pulsed. I hugged the cat tighter. It wasn't my time yet, but it would be soon.

A SWEET SOIREE ON THE LAST NIGHT OF THE WORLD

GWENDOLYN KISTE

I t's ten o'clock in the morning on Thursday when we learn the world is ending. By noon, Vera has sent us all invitations to a party.

You are cordially invited to celebrate the impending apocalypse. Please wear your very best attire and be ready to party until dawn. Or until death do us part.

My husband glares down at the embossed lettering, his gruff hand trembling. "It's like she knew this was coming."

I can't help but let out a small laugh. Vera's always been ahead of the rest of us.

The location makes me laugh, too—her favorite graveyard across town. The one with all the shiny obelisks and the marbled mausoleum and the headstones with the names and dates wiped away unceremoniously by the cruel hand of time. She and I used to hang out there when we were only girls, our whole lives stretched in front of us like a promise the world wouldn't keep.

"We'll get out of this town one day," she'd whisper to me, and back then, I honestly believed she was right. We'd curl up together in the grass, reclined in the shadows of the dead, drinking whatever concoction of sweet liqueurs and herbs and secrets she had tucked away in her bag.

I never asked what was in it. She would pass me the bronze flask, and I'd take a sip.

If it was good enough for Vera, it was plenty for me.

My husband tosses the invitation on the table and proceeds to call every important contact in his phone. Councilmen and state representatives and even the head of our town's emergency planning committee. As if anybody ever planned for this. Meanwhile, I watch the grainy reports on television and refresh the news online. It's happening everywhere, one city after another. And we can't run, even if we want to. All the airports are closed down. The same with the interstates and the byways and even the little county highways. The world expects us to wait right here and take our turn at death.

"Are you sure?" my husband asks, his fingers gripped knuckle-white around his phone, his voice splitting in two. It's the same story, no matter who he calls. A simple story really.

People are expiring all over, but they're not doing it with any sort of pomp and circumstance. It's happening quietly, their bodies slumped over at kitchen tables and in boardroom meetings and at office desks where they always suspected they might die one day. There's no theatrics to their end, and there isn't any pain either. They're here one minute, and the lights snuffed out the next.

Not such a terrible way to go, if you ask me.

It's past three in the afternoon and my husband's still hollering in the den. I slip into my walk-in closet and rummage through the narrow rack of clothes I'll never wear again. Pressed suits for business and cotton frocks for pleasure and jeans with the knees ripped out from times long gone by. Times I used to spend with Vera. There's grass stains on the cuffs, a parting souvenir from our graveyard retreats.

She and I don't talk much these days. I'm surprised she even bothered to send us an invite. She must have hand-delivered it, but we never saw her on the front porch, never heard her steps as light as a ghost's. It's sometimes as if Vera doesn't exist at all.

A siren blares in the distance, and I reach into the back of the closet and find what I've been looking for. A red satin gown, crystal-jeweled and cut on the bias.

The last dress I'll ever wear.

My husband is still on the phone when I come back downstairs, already rouged and ready for the evening, even though it's only four o'clock.

"Is it nerve gas?" he asks over and over again. "Is it a natural airborne toxin? Is it something we can stop?"

"Maybe it's just fate," one of his old college professors tells him on speaker, hopelessness soaking through every word, and my husband grits his teeth and hangs up.

He doesn't bother to call anyone else after that. Instead, he takes a long, hot shower, fogging up the entire second floor, and gets dressed for the party, donning his black suit and crisp white shirt and his leather dress shoes he had polished for a client luncheon next week. A day that won't ever come now.

"I don't see why we have to do this," he says on the drive to the graveyard. It's almost sunset now, the final hours of our lives trickling away from us like sand in an antique hourglass.

"We owe it to her." My hands are clasped tight in my lap. "We owe it to Vera."

"We don't owe her anything," my husband says with a scoff, his eyes shifting toward me. "*You* don't owe her anything."

We park on the street outside the graveyard, our engine cutting out with a heavy thud. Up and down the block, people peer out the front windows of their homes, eyes limned red from sobbing. Far off, there's a siren again and then another and a scream somewhere nearby, but my husband only shakes his head and starts toward the front gate of the cemetery. He hates to be late. Even if there's barely a world left, that's no reason to have bad manners.

Everyone we know is already here, a sea of tuxedos the color of midnight and tight pearl necklaces strung around reed-like throats. One by one, we all exchange our dubious greetings, each woman extending a dainty hand, her diamond ring polished so bright that you can almost see your own reflection staring blankly back at you. These are all couples from the country club and the homeowner association and the Rotary, all respectable, decent people.

That's what we tell ourselves anyhow.

We find our way to the center of the cemetery where there are strings of twinkling lights strung up in the bare branches of dead trees, and tables draped in silk cloths, bedecked with pale votive candles and the plumpest roses you've ever seen.

A divine night of finery and finality. Exactly the way Vera wants it.

She isn't here yet. I search through the faces, an anonymous crowd of friends, but I don't spot her anywhere.

Across the city, dozens of rooftops are on fire, the night sky blazing a glorious pumpkin orange. We pay no attention to the local carnage. The global apocalypse, of course, is all anyone can talk about.

"They're claiming it's not so bad," says a man whose name is Duke or Dutch or Daniel. "When it comes for you, it's quick and quiet."

"Like falling asleep in front of the television or something," his wife insists.

"I hope that's true," says another couple, their smiles stiff and courteous as corpses.

"It's definitely true." Duke or Dutch gives us an emphatic nod. "Those are the reports all around the world."

"Maybe it won't reach us at all," my husband says, and something shifts behind him, the whole party going silent and still.

She emerges as if from nowhere, as if she and the gray shadows are kin.

Vera, arrayed in mourning black, her gown slit up one side, a velvet cape tied in a tight bow at her neck, everything about her looking like a most glorious afterlife.

"Enough with this morbid talk." She beams at us, brighter than every constellation in the sky. "Let's enjoy one last evening together, shall we?"

And with that, we begin the festivities. There are canapés with prosciutto roses and chunks of aged cheese as fragrant as the dead. Someone plays Mussorgsky on their phone to drown out the cantankerous melody of the firetrucks that never stop passing by.

Nothing can touch us in here. That's what we pretend. Our own private merrymaking like we're gathered to ward off the Red Death. In a way, it's not so different from any other evening. We've never cared enough about anyone. We've never even really cared about ourselves.

But then Vera always cared more than enough for all of us. Those eyes the color of creeping ivy, watching over everything.

She ladles blood-red punch into miniature cocktail glasses, and everyone can't get enough.

"To the end of civilization," someone says, holding up their drink, and the others chortle in refrain.

I stand alone and empty-handed, my heart in my shoes.

"Does it have to be this way?" I used to ask Vera back when we were young and foolish and full of faith. "Do people have to be so terrible?

"Maybe not," she'd tell me. "Maybe things will change one day."

Then with that sly grin on her face, she would climb the nearest obelisk and stand atop it like a conqueror. Like a queen. At least until the caretaker came and chased us away.

"We'll see you next week, Gus," she'd yell over her shoulder at him as we ran, the two of us hand in hand, the bitter wind in our long, flowing hair.

Gus is long dead now, felled by cigarette tar and remorse, and there's nobody left to care for this place, the grass gone wild around all the tombstones, the rusted fence toppled over, the ancient wreaths faded as gray as bone.

Across the lawn, two couples stand at what's left of the front gate, their nervous eyes set on the flaring skyline, vague screams rising up like the mournful lilt of a violin.

"Can't we help them?" they whisper, a distant siren ringing in our ears. "Can't we do anything?"

They aren't like the others. These couples are newcomers to town. That's why they don't fit in with the rest of us. The only reason they're here is to have somewhere to go. Somewhere safe to spend the last night on earth.

What they don't understand is that being with us means you're never really safe. Vera learned that the hard way.

Of course, we've all learned lessons the hard way. Nearby, my husband is telling a joke only he'll laugh at, his arm looped around the waist of another man's wife. A sight as familiar as the phase of the moon.

My husband. He would never raise his hand to hurt me. But he'd never raise his hand to help me, either. We exist in the same space, passing each other like dim acquaintances.

But Vera's always been more than an acquaintance to me. Even when we were girls who'd just met on the first day of high school, we already knew everything about each other, our secrets laid bare with a glance.

"Don't worry," she whispered. "I won't tell anyone if you don't."

Each chance we got, we'd sneak away. On our lunch break and after school and sometimes even past midnight when our parents were dozing in their dark, dreamless beds. Together, she and I would fall back in the grass of the graveyard, gazing up at the universe glinting above us.

"The stars burn all the time," she told me. "Their flames never rest, never take a holiday."

"It's like they're burning for us," I'd whisper, and Vera always laughed.

"For you and me," she said, and we'd drink deep from her flask.

"A toast to the meek," I'd say. "May they inherit the earth."

"Not the meek." She would grin at me, her hand entwined with mine. "To the resourceful. They're the ones you have to look out for."

Even now, she's still grinning, her cape flowing behind her, not a hint of fear in her eyes, not even with the specter of doomsday veiled over us. A radio crackles next to a tombstone, and the party hovers closer.

"They're claiming there are pockets of survivors," someone says.

"How?" my husband asks.

"They're not sure yet. All they know is there are some people left behind."

"That doesn't sound very fun," Vera says, and she's looking at me. "Who wants to be the one who's forgotten?"

My cheeks flush at once. A shiver trembling through my bones, I try to turn away, but Vera keeps watching me, keeps remembering. Because that's exactly what I did to her—we grew up, and I left her behind. I left her because it was easier that way. But only easier for me, not for her. Nothing's ever been easy for Vera.

We were already out of college when things fell apart. Vera and I still met in the graveyard, though not as often as before. I had my gaze set on the next horizon, on a life that was more than a flask and a tombstone and a stolen midnight.

"You care too much about what this town thinks," she told me, and I didn't argue.

She was waiting on me that night, the one that split our lives in two all those years ago. We tried to keep our meetings secret, but everyone knew she would be there. Dutch knew. He hopped the half-broken fence and found her alone, his hands eager for something she wasn't willing to give.

She fought, she ran, she escaped. That should have been enough— she should have been safe. But there were things she didn't count on, the secrets small towns are determined to keep. Vera told us the truth about what happened. We all knew it then, and we all know it now. But it turns out the truth doesn't matter as much as you'd think. After all, the truth isn't worried about being respectable. It doesn't care about your manners or your country clubs. The truth exists whether you want it to or not.

And Vera was nothing if not unvarnished truth.

"We can't have a troubled girl like her around here," they all said, and I never argued. I told myself it wouldn't have mattered, but I wonder now if that's really true.

Soon, her life was like a row of precarious dominoes, falling one after another. A lost job. An eviction notice. The stares and the glares and the gossip. Her eyes searching every crowd, desperate for a friend, desperate for me. But I would only look away when I saw her, shame churning in me like poison.

She disappeared for a year. A moment and an eternity, all wrapped into one. Everybody was sure she was gone for good, and they grinned about it, as though they'd just pulled off a marvelous caper.

"She never did fit in with us," they'd say, and I tried to smile along with them. I tried to ignore the dull ache inside me, the guilt that stole the breath from my chest.

I met and married my husband while she was away. Under the circumstances, it seemed like the most respectable thing to do.

"Another round of drinks," Vera declares, and she turns toward the silk-draped table, already reaching for the punchbowl.

But I catch her hand first, her skin warm, the scent of her lavender perfume nearly overwhelming me. For an instant, everything else fades away, and it's just the two of us, the way it used to be. The way it always should have been.

"I should have been better to you," I whisper.

It's the first time we've ever spoken of this.

Vera stares back at me, a glint in her eye, strange and distant. "Yes," she says, and passes me a martini glass, bright red and filled to the brim, "you should have been better."

"I'm sorry," I say, even though it's not enough. The world is falling apart at our feet, and a word like sorry doesn't seem to mean much now.

Not that an apology is ever worth as much as we pretend. It's just a subtle demand, a polite way to tell someone to move on. To let it go.

This town certainly thinks she's moved on. When Vera returned at last, it was as though nothing had changed, that same smile on her face, that same devious fun in her heart. From then on, she threw the best parties in town in the most unusual locales. Abandoned warehouses and former supermarkets and the balconies of old movie theaters.

Everyone would attend—for the novelty, for the gossip—and Vera would always play the role of the perfect hostess, draped in satins and silks and taffetas, her delicate hand always passing out one of her famously fearsome drinks. By the end of each evening, however, the masquerade would slip a little, not enough for anyone else to notice. Just enough for me to see, that sharp flash of something in her eyes, a mortal wound we'd inflicted, one that would take a lifetime to finish her.

One that might finish us too.

There are more fires at the skyline now and more mournful cries from mouths we can't see. But it's a party in here, and Vera ensures everyone's thirst is quenched, handing out her specialty cocktail from two punchbowls. It takes me too long to realize there's a difference between them.

The couples from the country club suddenly aren't swanning around the graveyard anymore. Their knees gone soft as jelly, they stagger a step in one direction before wobbling back the other way. The men shed their tuxedo jackets like cicadas sloughing off their skin, and the pretty little pin curls in all the wives' hair have gone limp and useless as yesterday's promises.

"What have you done?" Dutch asks Vera, collapsing to his knees. She gives him that sweetheart grin of hers, and I squeeze my eyes shut, because I already know the answer.

"They kept talking about how the deaths were so quick, so quiet." Even with my eyes closed, I can tell she's still smiling. "After everything, that just didn't seem fair."

The blood comes faster than I expect. By the time I look again, it's already everywhere, leaking out of noses and coughed up in thick clots the size of silver dollars. There's screaming for a little while, mingling with the soundtrack from across town, but that doesn't last very long. Once the shrieks have faded away, all you can hear are the gurgles of regret lodged in the backs of their throats, as they gag up what's left of their mangled insides.

Only not everyone is down for the count. The two couples who'd been loitering near the front gate, the ones who are new in town, are still standing, their jaws slack, their eyes wide.

"Don't worry," Vera says to them. "You'll be fine."

They gape at their empty cocktail glasses, smeared with fingerprints and red lipstick. Their drinks were identical to the others. Except apparently for one particular ingredient.

Vera was always so clever, always a dozen steps ahead of the rest of us. It's as if she's been waiting for an apocalypse. Waiting for a night just like this one. She must have been planning a final fete ever since she returned.

With the shadows engulfing me, I stumble back a step. I haven't taken a sip yet, the liquor still swirling in my martini glass. There were two punchbowls. My breath twisted inside me, I try to divine in the dark which one she proffered me.

The others are writhing and oozing all around us, their bodies contorted in strange inhuman shapes, their faces as pallid as the moon.

The two couples that Vera spared are sobbing now, their cheeks streaked with salt tears. "We'll call someone," they're stammering, as they edge toward the rusted front gate. "We'll call the police."

Vera waves goodbye. "Good luck with that," she says, as they vanish into the night.

I want to vanish too, but Vera glances back once, her eyes suddenly on me, and I freeze under the weight of her stare.

She sees me here, the cocktail still waiting in my hands.

Vera doesn't say a word. She only gives me another smile, as bright and impossible as starlight, before she drifts toward the mausoleum we once called our own.

I edge backward, but I'm not alone. My husband is clawing at my feet, a spray of bright red blood on his starched white shirt. "Please," he wheezes, but as I stare down at him, it's like looking at a stranger.

The radio is still crackling in the grass, the announcer's voice thin as piano wire. "There are more reports of survivors in every city," she says.

This might not be over. I could still run. Vera wouldn't chase me. There might be enough time to escape all of this.

Except I won't do that. Not now, not after everything. My heart tight in my chest, I smile a little to myself. Then I take a long, deep drink of my cocktail.

I never ask what's in it. If it's good enough for Vera, it's plenty for me.

With the moon sinking low on the horizon, I make my way across the noiseless graveyard and settle down on the earth next to Vera. And I wait.

She glances over at the radio, a few staticky updates still clambering through. "It sounds like some of us will get through this after all."

"Maybe," I say and set my empty martini glass next to a forgotten gravestone. "Maybe not."

We fall back in the overgrown grass, the sky glimmering bright above us.

"For you and me," Vera says, her hand entwined with mine, and together, we watch the universe burn on forever.

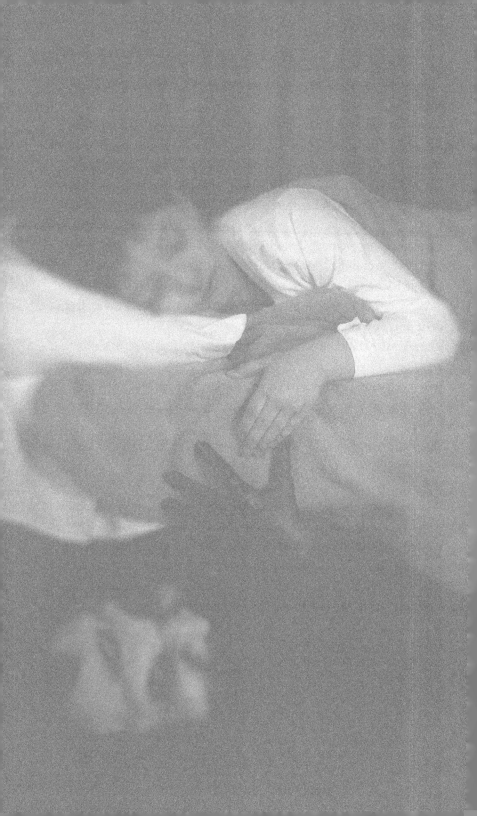

THE BOY WHO PRAYED FOR THE WORLD TO END

OLEN CROWE

Mason Quaid sat on the edge of his bed and looked out his window. The world was ending—had ended—will be ending. And he smiled. The sky was the same color as his burnt sienna crayon in his craft box on his desk. The clouds, the ones still in the sky, were asparagus. The sun was the color of outer space (that was his favorite crayon in the Crayola box).

Everything looked just like his picture, and for that he was happy. The god, his god, under his bed had listened. Mason was scared the first time he prayed to him. He didn't know exactly how to pray, but he got down on his knees next to his bed and clasped his hands together. Bowing his head, his prayer began with *Dear god...* Mason knew it was a good start because his bed warmed, and he felt all cozy while he prayed.

Mason had only one request. He didn't realize what he was saying at the time; the words simply rolled out of his mouth. When he finished, he drew the picture. Mason thought his god would appreciate that.

He only wished he'd remembered to draw his parents into the picture. A single tear tracked down his cheek, and Mason wiped it away. They had never believed in his god anyway. They spoke of

Christ the messiah, Yahweh, Elohim, Adonai, and the Holy Spirit. Mason never cared much for polytheism, and the plethora of names gave him a headache. Still, he loved his parents, and he hoped their gods had saved them.

But, there was only one god. His name consisted of three consonants Mason was not allowed to write or speak, and he lived under his bed.

For now.

Mason shifted on the mattress and kept his eyes trained on the world outside. No more school, no more visits to restaurants, no more playing with friends on the playground.

If Mason could reverse time, he would have gone outside one last time to play basketball with his dad. Then he would have eaten some ice cream, chocolate and vanilla swirl with too many maraschino cherries dumped on top. Then he would have called his friends to say goodbye.

On second thought, he wouldn't have said goodbye. That would have made them scared. He would have called them to talk about video games and how best to build the fort in the woods they had been working on all summer.

The world was truly a lonely place when it was ending.

How could his god not have warned him about this? The tiniest amount of anger built in his chest. Like Lego blocks, the anger built up and grew larger and more concrete until it was sturdy and strong. Anger turned into hate, and Mason hated—With a cry he leaped out of bed. Tears tore at the corners of his eyes. Mason turned to see what had burned him, but there was nothing on the bed.

"I'm sorry," he muttered. He walked to the window and stared outside some more. His neighbors' houses were no longer there. Nor did he see his street or road signs or trees or... anything.

The Quaid house (now belonging only to Mason) stood by itself in a dandelion desert (the disgusting yellow Crayola color he had chosen for his picture, not the flower; that would have been too beautiful for an apocalypse). The scene turned his stomach, and

Mason wanted to vomit. He quickly unfastened the locks on his window and stuck his head outside and—nothing. The sensation in his stomach had ceased, and an overwhelming silence invaded his ears.

During their conversations his god had never told Mason what his plan was for after the end of the world. Mason wished he could have said goodbye to his parents, but then he didn't realize they weren't going to be part of the plan. He'd told his tied-for-second best friend, Bianca Ashbury. She lived across the street. Well, she didn't live there any longer, and Mason wondered what happened to all of the people.

He hoped they hadn't died. Maybe they just went somewhere else. Somewhere beautiful and happy. That was what Mason hoped the end of the world would have been. He hadn't wanted this.

Looking outside made him sad so Mason returned to his bed. He threw himself on top of it, and then jumped up forgetting that it was on fire, but, luckily, he wasn't burned a second time. His god was no longer angry with him, and that made him happy. He closed his eyes and counted to at least five thousand. He was a good counter and could regularly count past a thousand, but this was the highest he had ever counted. Mason was mad when he lost count, but he made it a point to not let his anger turn into hatred again. He loved math, and he loved counting, he told himself.

He also loved burnt sienna skies and ~~green~~ asparagus clouds.

Apocalypses were boring. Mason sighed loudly and stared at the ceiling.

He wished he'd drawn a water slide, a pet cat, and a skateboard. His parents wouldn't ever let him have any of those things. He also wished he had remembered to draw Bianca's house across the street and her standing in her room waving at him through the window.

All of a sudden, Mason jumped out of bed. He *did* forget to draw something! He had to draw something right now. He ran to his desk and pulled a piece of construction paper from the top desk drawer. He wanted white, but he used all of them last week drawing pictures for his friends at school. The next best was a light pink so he used that.

Mason sat at his desk and furiously drew a beautiful picture that would make the end of the world so much better.

After several minutes Mason held the new drawing up—

and frowned.

He wanted to cry.

What he meant to draw was everything he had just thought about and more. He wanted to correct his mistakes and create an apocalypse to remember. One that wasn't filled with loneliness and regret.

What he was looking at was something he did not remember drawing. He recognized his desk and his bed, but his bed had been flipped over. A mass of gray swirls (the color was really called outer space, the same as the sun) snaked out from under the bed. The tentacles stretched all the way out the window and scraped at the sky.

Mason knew he didn't draw this picture.

Don't let anger turn into hate.

"I like this picture," Mason said. "It's a pretty picture." Despite it being a beautiful and perfect picture, Mason needed to lie down again. But when he turned around, he realized what he really wanted to do was throw up. Not like the first time. He meant it this time, and his stomach felt funny.

Mason's entire room had turned a light shade of pink: walls, floor, everything. Even the air had a pinkish hue like he was looking through costume store glasses. Well, not everything was pink. His bed wasn't pink and neither was his desk. Nor were the tentacles that grew from the box underneath his bed where his god lived. They stretched outside, and if Mason wanted to, he could have walked to his window and saw that they were scraping the burnt sienna sky. He didn't want to look, though.

In that moment, Mason wished for the loneliness to return. He much preferred it to the primal, infinite terror that burned in his gut and screamed in his ears.

He stumbled backward, mumbling something both hideous and incoherent. He yelled what he believed was his mother's name, but the sound that came out was jarring and dissonant. Stumbling, stumbling backward, Mason fell—

and landed in the chair next to his desk.

One more picture.

Had he thought that, or did something else think for him? He pulled another piece of construction paper from the drawer and went to work. His hand worked furious lines across the paper. He yelled out more sounds that were meant to be pleas to his mother and father, but every time he spoke, the sounds that came out scared him. Eventually, Mason stopped talking.

It didn't take long for him to finish this drawing. Sweating and tired, he closed his eyes and held the thing up in the air. He didn't want to look at this one. He hated—

No he didn't. He opened his eyes.

Mason stared at a blank, black piece of construction paper.

He vomited all over his desk. His vision blurred and darkened, and a vile, creeping sickness bled into his rosy pink room.

Loneliness, Mason quickly found out, had been the most beautiful part about the end of the world.

TUESDAY

BRITTANY JOHNSTON

"—New York City, Philadelphia, and Washington DC are devastated. An estimated 7,500,000 people are assumed dead, with numbers rising by the hour. Moscow and Cairo are still assessing casualties. The full death toll is incalculable. We've just received a warning of incoming impacts in Los Angeles and Houston, both cities ordering immediate evacuation. The Vice President urges Americans to avoid all metropolitan areas; the National Guard has been deployed—"

Laura was fifteen during 9/11.

She remembers sitting in her English class, everyone watching in silence as smoke and fire spilled across the New York skyline—courtesy of gritty televisions meant for VHS copies of a recurring cycle of three Disney movies and one overwrought Shakespeare reenactment. Kimmy Johnson, the bombshell blonde who cheated off her in chemistry, gripped Laura's hand in a vice, ugly tears reddening her perfect face.

She thought that would be the defining horror of her lifetime.

Then there were the shootings—so *many* shootings. Bombers, massacres, police executions in the streets. One tragedy after another until they blended into a red noise in the background of every newscast. The photo-ready devastation and the thoughts and prayers with neatly marked expiration dates. Every headline grew less and less notable as the scrolling lists of victims became so never-ending she stopped trying to keep track of the latest nightmare.

Two decades later, she thought there would be no defining horror of her lifetime.

This time, it's a 70-inch flatscreen. Laura's boss insisted on it, even though it's only ever turned on for corporate videos (*time theft is a severe problem, one that can have a detrimental impact on the entire staff...*) and the occasional football game.

Stupid waste of company money, but that is Jason's specialty.

This time, the smoke billowing from what was once Manhattan is the height of quality. In crystal-clear, glittering definition, they see the sweep of a now empty horizon, a city's charred husk. A woman is dragged out on a gurney from the outskirts of the impact zone. She's almost unrecognizable as a person, her skin blackened and flaking, yellow-but-singed chunks of fat melted into the vivid red and pink muscle that ruins the medical sheets. Surround sound carries the screams to every corner of the office, and all the way down Laura's spine.

This time she's next to Kathy, 68, a stickler for the copier protocols. The woman curls into the fetal position, hyperventilating into a two-day-old In-N-Out bag.

We're next.

It's what everyone's thinking, what every horrified face around her reads. They're in downtown LA in the middle of the afternoon, and there's no time.

They can't escape.

They're going to die.

But Charlie is five blocks away.

Laura sheds her blazer and kicks away her heels, grabbing Adam's sneakers from his office couch while he gapes at the screen, his phone pressed against his ear, his wife's shrill cries audible to everyone in the room.

No one notices her run to the stairwell.

Five blocks. Five blocks. Laura can make five blocks.

There are others on the stairs. More will come. Dozens run down in panic, pushing, shoving, paying no heed to the **CAUTION** signs. Mallory, manager of the PR company two floors up, stumbles and crashes into the stairs. No one stops to help; no one *stops*.

Instead, the crowd tramples over the body, gurgling screams and pleas ignored as blood rapidly soaks through Mallory's salmon Armani suit. At least two more people go down, slipping into her mess. Their cries are just as ignored, and they join her in a flesh-colored mosaic on off-white sheeting, seeping into the concrete below.

When Laura gets to the flight they're spread out on, she elbows her way to the railing and grips on with both hands. The cool metal attempts to slip through her sweaty grasp. She steps through, resolutely ignoring the wet warmth dripping into her shoes, soaking the fabric.

And the *crunching* under her heels.

A few floors up, someone teeters over the railing and plummets past with a cut-short scream. No one notices the crash.

Somehow, she makes it to the bottom. A mass of panicking bodies pulses around the door. They block out the sun's light as they try to push their way out, some people getting crushed into the metal lining of the entryway, skulls cracking against the still-lit EXIT sign. Grasping hands are all over the threshold, some trying to pull themselves through and others trying in vain not to be pushed down.

Lazy post-impressionism, a bored Mr. Carter (Laura fucking *hated* Art History, damn him) chirps in her ear.

Blood and bone are striking mediums.

Instead of throwing her body in for canvas fodder, she breaks left, darting down the service hallway to the back exit, a handful of others following her.

Too many plow right into the pit.

This exit is farther from the parking lot, but she's not stupid enough to go for her car. The roads will be worse than the stairs, and she doesn't intend to die in a pile-up fifteen feet from the office—if she makes it that far.

Laura slams into the heavy door, hardly registering the impact of others pushing her through, all of them falling onto the sidewalk. She scrambles to her feet even as her knees protest, aching and throbbing where they hit the stone. Most people turn to the parking lot, where they'll die. It's a waste of precious minutes.

Horns and the awful screech of bending metal are audible from here, the slightest wisp of smoke rising from that direction. Instead, she heads for the break in the fence, the one maintenance has been neglecting for three months. When she was twelve, Laura and her cousins in Missouri snuck into all the places they shouldn't. They dodged through countless fences and unlocked windows, and for the briefest moment, she's there again. The long grass tickles her feet—there's a chill in the air. The sun creeps into the sky.

But the wires digging into the meat of her arms, drawing blood, pull Laura back.

By now, alarms sound all over the city, sirens joining them, though few, too few, and it's not surprising. What's the fucking point? Laura can't help one last look at the office, swallowing hard when she sees the bodies falling from the windows; their forms abruptly halt when they *plop, plop, plop* into the ground below. Smoke and flame pour from the upper level, and Laura wonders, inanely, which idiot managed to start a fire.

Maybe it was the new guy with the three packs of cigarettes on his desk.

Get moving, Laura; you don't have time to rubberneck.

Her grandfather wasn't a warm man. Her grandfather wasn't a good man. It's always his voice when things are at their worst.

Thomas was a Vietnam veteran who didn't mind the killing as much as he should, a drunk, and a fucking asshole. Laura's grandma, his second wife, died right after he came home from the war. Thomas never remarried. Instead, he spent the next forty years of his life alone in a hunting cabin his father left him; he sequestered himself there until the place was rotting on top of him.

Then he drank some more and rotted with it.

"Fear is the great equalizer, kid. Doesn't matter if you've read all the books in the world or if you're the toughest son of bitch you know. A human being that's truly afraid is nothing more than an animal. We're all just beasts, running around, pretending to be something we're not."

When he said it, the gleam in his eye conjured images of squealing soldiers and protruding bone, of gunfire and bombshells, of Thomas, raining bullets and playing god, hiding amongst scared men and relishing the sound of death rattles.

Laura's thrilled he's dead.

Maybe she'll tell him that soon.

Four blocks.

She curses her aversion to the gym as she runs. People knock out shop windows, carry away televisions, stumble out with liquor bottles (that one, at least, makes fucking sense). When she passes an alley, a man pushes a woman to the ground. The woman's hand reaches out as soon as she catches sight of Laura. A hand over her mouth stops her plea, and only the desperation in her gaze calls for aid.

Laura swallows the bile and keeps running.

Three more blocks.

Laura's forced to slow her pace when she comes to a major inter-section. The *smell* stalls her steps before the sight itself, a semi turned on its side, some sort of chemical leaking out to cover the street. At least five cars are smashed into the side of it, some already on fire, some looking like they're going to blow in minutes. People drag themselves out of the wreckage through puddles of whatever rancid liquid the truck carried, screaming as it eats at their boiling skin. Some die only a few feet away, limbs sprawled, bleeding and bent, faces pressed into the asphalt.

The traffic light has crashed into the street, loose wires and flying sparks igniting some areas of the chemical spill, the flames an off-color. It puts out an intense heat as Laura tries to wind her way through.

Someone grabs at her leg, and she doesn't look down as she kicks them away, once, twice, *harder* until they fall with a gasp. A foot, all alone, almost trips her up as she darts around the forward section of the truck, and its owner (she assumes) lies a few feet to the left, hands grasped around a body almost wholly flattened, brain matter splattered several feet around it.

The nearest car goes up in flames.

Laura jumps away, feeling the heat lick at her arm, and her heart drops at the sound of a shrill, terrified cry. Her body refuses to move. When she looks closer at the vehicle, Laura sees the "Baby On Board" sticker, surrounded by four stick figures, just as it melts away.

Two blocks. Don't stop.

Laura crosses and jumps over the smaller puddles, praying the shit doesn't eat through her shoes.

She makes it to the next street just in time because as the truck finally explodes, it sends raining body parts all the way to her, little bits of flesh coating her skin, bone shards serving as effective shrapnel. Then, there's the *actual* shrapnel, and Laura keeps running, the world around her a cacophony of agony.

People are impaled or ignited by still-flaming bits of debris. A car door lands on top of a fleeing old man. It takes his head *almost* off.

"Daddy!" A woman screams.

Several more minor things hit Laura's shoulders and back, twisting and burning, and her shirt is soaked. Her progress slows as her limbs grow heavier, even with the adrenaline pumping through them. Her right arm starts a persistent pain that flares with every stride.

Then, the goddamn gunshots start.

Laura jumps nearly a foot when they start echoing from behind her, and she makes the mistake of turning around to a young man gleefully mowing down the surrounding people, glass shattering everywhere.

Oh, what the fuck?

Maybe this shit happens because we deserve it, and she can't remember if that was Thomas.

Last block. Almost there.

The building rises behind a line of palm trees, swaying gently in the breeze like any other day.

Of course, it's beautiful outside. Shining sun and not a cloud in the sky. What else would she expect?

Charlie, Charlie, Charlie.

The second thing she notices is that someone, for some reason, took the time to lower the flag to half-mast.

Who would do that?

The question is answered a moment later when Laura turns down the walkway. An old woman, a stern-looking creature with greying hair pinned tightly back, lays in front of the flagpole, blood flowing from a pair of scissors dug deep into her abdomen. She has a small medal, gleaming against red, clutched tightly in her hand, lifeless eyes staring helplessly up at the sky, watching the flag wave against blue like nothing is wrong in the world.

Laura steps around the corpse and flies through the double doors. She's glad they aren't locked. She doesn't want to waste time looking for a window to break.

But inside is worse, so much worse than out there.

Everywhere, *everywhere*, it's crying. Laura didn't come through the main door, but from the level of destruction, it's clear she wasn't the first one here. Books, backpacks, and papers are strewn about. Kids wander the halls, some curled up in corners and some pushing past her through the doors, alone. Wails echo off walls, and kids of varying ages look up at her with frightened eyes that beg for answers.

Are you here to help us? Can we go home?

She can't care about them. No one gets to go home.

Construction paper art is stomped onto the floor. A few voices try to calm the kids while some classrooms have obviously been abandoned, leaving the little ones to stew in fear and panic. Laura turns down the third hall and hopes Miss Adams isn't one of those people. She passes the principal's office and sees blood spatter on the wall —*you could have done something for the kids,* she thinks. But Laura lets the malice go as quickly as it came.

It's not like she will, either.

When she finally gets to the second to last door, she's both thankful and terrified to see it closed. She notices the lights are off, and panic tears at her (where is he, where is he, where is he) but then notices the music.

Baby Beluga?

With dread in her stomach, she slowly pushes open the door.

Inside the colorful room, numbers and letters are decked with glitter all along the walls. Over a dozen little mats are laid along the floor, small sleeping forms tucked in blissfully as their minds wander fictional seas.

In the corner, Laura sees Miss Adams.

She's young. Laura thinks it's her first year teaching (her last, too). Her arms are wrapped around her knees, and she looks up in terror until she recognizes Laura. Then she sobs, muffling the noise with a hand. Miss Adams quickly steps around the kids and pulls her into a hug, even if they've only spoken a handful of times.

"Charlie is asleep, over by the calendar. They're all asleep. I just couldn't...I can't stand to wake them. What's the point? They'll just be afraid. It's better this way."

Laura nods, forcing herself to keep her voice down, and is glad the other woman doesn't react to her appearance. "Thank you—" she whispers, the tears finally coming, heavy and ugly in her words. "*Thank you.* For staying."

Miss Adams (What was her name? Her first name? Did Laura ever learn it?) nods and squeezes her hand. "I couldn't go. Couldn't let them be alone."

Laura returns the grip and ignores the blood she leaves on the other woman's hand. She pads as quietly as manageable to the corner, keeping an eye on the calendar.

It's Tuesday, she notes. She always hated Tuesdays.

Then Laura sees him and falls apart.

Her Charlie-Bear: all chocolate curls and dimples, even in his sleep, his stuffed Paw Patrol puppy in its dumb little fire hat tucked as tightly as possible under his skinny arm.

She smiles, and it hurts. Laura hates everything, *everything* so very much.

"Oh baby," she whispers, not loud enough for him to hear. She wants to hold him more than anything, to pull him into her arms, but she can't be that selfish. Can't risk waking him, not like this, when he looks so peaceful. When he can *stay* that way, drool leaking from his mouth onto the pillowcase, like they're at home, like there's nothing wrong, like he can run into her room at four in the morning and demand pizza.

"Baby, I'm sorry."

Her beautiful, lovely, silly little boy.

"I love you so, so much. All the bad things? None of it matters. Everything was worth it for you. You made every day worth it."

She lays beside him, not bothering to look at her phone, Miss Adams, or the other kids. Sure, her mom is probably calling, there might be a few friends who had the presence of mind to text, and there might even be news popping up on her screen, telling her how long she has left.

But it doesn't matter. Laura doesn't want to spend one single second doing anything other than staring at his pudgy face and listening to his little snores. And because she *is* selfish for the most part, and he sleeps deeply, she lays her hand on his, relishing in the *bump, bump, bump* of his pulse under her thumb.

The song changes to the Five Little Monkeys, who never stop jumping on the bed, and Laura listens, holding on as tightly as she can without disturbing him.

The fourth monkey falls, and everything goes bright beyond belief.

I love you.

Until the end.

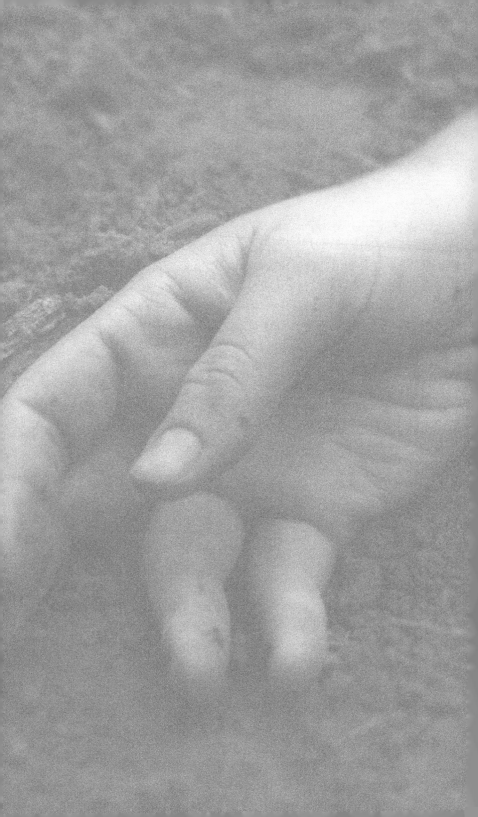

DIRT AND BLOOD AND SILENCE

ELOU CARROLL

All is silence and dirt and blood, and Giulia presses her hand on Lenore's cheek and her cheek is cold. She slaps that cheek once, twice, three times, but Lenore does not stir and all is silence and she is—gone.

Lenore cannot be gone. Lenore is only sleeping.

Giulia sobs but the sound of it is far away, quiet, barely there at all. She heaves in breath after breath, but all she can hear is the thrumming of her own heart like the revving of an engine unwilling to start. Giulia is unwilling, too, to start this new life—this *after*. The beating of her heart screams, *Not her, not here, not now.*

The pulsing heat replies, *Then when, then where, then who?*

Giulia rests her forehead, so hot, on that cheek, so cold, and cries until her throat burns.

Her hands are red.

There is someone across the road, their body waving in the heat. They shout, fanning their arms, but Giulia cannot hear them. She presses her fingers to her ears, begging them with gentle touches, coaxing, pleading.

Her hands come away redder.

Giulia thinks of paint. Sangria Sunset, the shade they'd picked for a feature wall in their living room two weeks ago. They'd laughed and joked and flirted until Lenore kicked the can and spilt three quarters of it across their brand new carpet. Lenore broke her foot but Giulia was so angry she sent her to Accident and Emergency alone. They never did finish painting.

When she looks up, the living room is gone. Beneath the rubble, she can just see the stained carpet. If she could, she would go back there—go back and laugh because it's *just* a carpet. Go back and press her hands into the wet paint, scoop it up and smear it on the walls and say, "There. All better. Now, let's get that foot checked out, hon."

Go back and tell Lenore she loved her, instead of telling her exactly how much the paint cost, and exactly how long it took to fit that carpet.

The cast is still on Lenore's foot. Giulia's black-marker *I'm sorry* facing the heavens as if it might change things, as if they can be changed now.

She could be sleeping; Giulia tells herself that Lenore is sleeping. She was—is—she *is* a heavy sleeper. The world could end and she wouldn't even stir—didn't even stir. But it's morning now or noon or after, and it's time to wake up.

"Honey, wake up." Giulia cannot hear herself speak. "Baby. Lenore. Come on, Lenny. It's time. It's time. Len. Lenore. *Lenore.*"

Giulia shakes her now. Her fingers, still red, sink into Lenore's pyjamas and pull so hard the material rips. But Giulia doesn't stop and before she knows it she's screaming. She can hear that. It's not her, though. It cannot be her. It is an animal and the animal is in pain.

They put them down, animals that sound like that.

Hands cup her underarms, drag her away from Lenore and pull her across the rubble that was once their house. It is only in her unwilling retreat that Giulia sees Lenore's eyes, open and glassy.

"No, no, no, no, no." Giulia is a record—stuck and stuttering—a thing fundamentally broken. Her own eyes are wide too and her mouth hangs low with its *no, no, no*ing. Her feet scrabble against the broken brickwork, catching and smashing a vase she'd always hated. Any other day, it would be cathartic, but today, its breakage rips at her chest and she howls all the harder.

"We have to go." The words are low and muffled behind her. Listening to them hurts, but not as much as looking at Lenore, so Giulia listens harder. "It's not safe here. We have to go."

She thinks she asks, "Who are you?"

And whoever they are, they reply or they tell her, "I just moved in across the street. Didn't have time to introduce myself before…"

"Before," says Giulia and her body goes slack. Numb. "Just leave me here."

They don't. Instead, they continue to pull.

"You're going to hurt yourself," they say but they don't let up and Giulia's legs snag and snarl on broken masonry. She might be bleeding. She might be missing chunks of skin or muscle or worse, but she doesn't notice—doesn't care.

Giulia thrashes in their arms and screams, "Leave me. Let me go. Go away!"

They don't.

For a moment, it is summer and Giulia is on the Backslider at the Broken Broadside Theme Park and Amusements. Lenore is strapped in beside her and the floor falls out from under them. Giulia is weightless.

A laugh threatens to choke her before she realises she's being hauled over their shoulder.

"Let me go."

"Not going to happen, neighbour." There is a smile in his voice—it is a man who has her, she can see that now, can hear it. He is smiling, despite everything.

Giulia stills. "Wait," she says. "Wait. Stop."

He does not stop and Giulia does not remember there having been a house up for sale, or a room up for rent. This street, Sycamore Crescent, has cupped the same seventeen families for the last six years. Giulia knows her neighbours. Lenore insists—insisted—on having them over in turn for dinners, and together for barbecues and garden parties and Christmas Eve carolling. She called it community building, planting real roots—and this man has ripped them up, is tearing her garden down.

"Who are you?" Giulia rakes her nails across him. "Who the fuck are you?"

He doesn't answer. He never told her his name before. She wasn't paying attention. She hasn't been paying attention since the world—her world—ended. Giulia barely has looked past their plot as if the wreckage of their house had been the entire world, and it was, once. Now, its shell seems as hostile as the hands that hold her. Lenore's mouth, hanging open, in the shape of the word *run*.

Giulia cannot run. She can only kick and claw and scream.

But even that is useless, her captor is too strong.

All is pain and wreckage and wrong. Sycamore Crescent is gone. Every house shattered. Beyond that, Elder Road, Oak Tree Lane, Birch Place, Alder Street, all of them rubble and ruin. Some people stumble between the downed buildings, others rove—searching, seeking, finding.

He is one of them, and he has searched, sought, found Giulia.

And he is smiling.

"Where are you taking me?" she asks so quietly that she can't be sure she actually said anything at all. She doesn't ask, *What are you going to do when we get there?* or *Why?*

Her heart hammers out an angry, *Why him, why here, why now?*

His heavy bootsteps reply, *Why not me, why not here, why not now?*

Of course he's here now. There are always people like him in the movies, aren't there? Picking through the remains of the world for anything they can take, anything they can consume, and smiling while they do it. Giulia has met men like him, women too. Before, she might have walked on by. Pretended she hadn't noticed. But it is after, and she is here.

And so is he.

For a moment she's glad Lenore isn't here to see this. Just a second, that's all it takes.

Giulia might as well have killed Lenore herself.

She thinks she swears under her breath. It has been a few minutes since she last fought him. Maybe he thinks she's given up. Giulia wonders if he thinks it still as her teeth sink into his back.

"Fuck," he roars and when he drops her, his skin comes away between her teeth. He looks at her like an animal—hadn't she sounded like one just now? "What the fuck is wrong with you?"

She imagines how she must look to him, covered in dirt and blood. Dried blood down the sides of her face from her ears, his own blood dripping from her mouth. Her mess of black hair, like a storm cloud atop her head. Novelty cupcake pyjamas torn and stained and barely covering her in any way that matters. Giulia locks eyes with him, seconds pass in silence and he looks away first.

Giulia laughs then. More than she has laughed in days, weeks, if she's being honest. That fight with Lenore—about the paint and the carpet and Lenore's foot—their last, the last fight they would ever have—lingered. Then the laughter turns to sobbing. Howling. Changing. This is the part of the movie where the wolf tears off its skin.

When had she seen her smiling last? *Had* Lenore smiled since the argument?

"She'll never smile again." Giulia watches her teardrops steam and dry on the pavement, spiralling from her face like a ribbon. She smiles herself, but the smile is hollow.

"What?"

Giulia doesn't answer and her would-be captor doesn't wait.

"Fuck this," he says and he leaves her there, surrounded on all sides by the remnants of *before*. By neighbours that didn't make it, their faces just as still as Lenore's.

The rovers retreat, taking with them pilfered pieces of lives that are no longer. Giulia wants to run after them, to tear them to bits with her teeth, to rip the tins and clothes and valuables from their hands and put them back where they belong. But where they belong is gone.

Instead, she returns to Lenore. She holds her cold hand, her own so hot. She sits down next to Lenore in the blood and the dirt and the silence, her heart drumming an *I'm sorry, you. I'm sorry here. I'm sorry now.*

To this, the heat and the air and the dirt and the blood and the silence have no answer, and Giulia is alone.

TEN TOTALLY FREE PLACES TO WATCH THE END OF THE WORLD

NICK BOUCHARD

Ten Totally Free Places to Watch The End of the World
By: All remaining NTM staff writers (Kate, Pablo, Rakesh, Joe)

Monday, June 19th 2023, 9:03AM PDT
(T-Minus 23 hours until impact)
Glendale, CA

Unless you've been living under a rock or a totalitarian regime for the last four years, you know that The End of the World is almost here. Use this simple guide to avoid selling your soul or your ass – or both – to get a front row seat to The End of the World.

(Image Description: Graphic of Earth, cracked like an egg with a mushroom cloud falling out instead of yolk)

It's known as C/2019 Q2 – Garrett. The comet was named for an amateur astronomer and prolific publisher on all things lunar. His monthly e-zine, Luna Bin, remains the most widely read publication of its kind.

One: Aunt Franny. We've all got one. That funny old aunt with

the rundown three-story Victorian or neo-industrial home. You haven't spoken in years and she'll be more than glad to hear from you. Bring a chainsaw, fell some of the taller trees and cobble together a little rooftop platform. Don't worry if it collapses, you're going to die anyway. And odds are you'll be sipping a very nice chamomile tea as the Rainbow Wall of Flame sucks the oxygen out of your lungs and instantly dehydrates you in its pyroclastic surge.

When interviewed by the good folks at *Wake Up Sarasota*, Henry Garrett cried. Having a comet named for him was *the* crowning achievement of his life. He went on to say he wished he'd never been born – as if that might negate the existence of the comet.

Two: This one is for our west-coasters. At last check, the Golden Gate Bridge wasn't overrun by a biker gang trading blow jobs for rooftops like they are in downtown LA. This promises to be a real party though. Expect the bridge to be jam-packed with revelers. There are at least ten Facebook groups dedicated to getting so many people to jump up and down on the bridge that it collapses. Could be fun. Won't cost a dime.

Three: The northeastern US, the expected impact zone. There is almost no ViewFeeing in the northeast. For every thirty people trying to get out of New Hampshire, one is going in. The prediction is that it will be bright and then you'll be dead. Fast. You won't see the Rainbow Wall, but you could see Boston without traffic.

In a recent survey, we found that just ten percent of the 'ViewFees' were actually monetary. After The End of the World money will be useless, so these folks are just hedging their bets. The other ninety percent are divisible into three major categories:

1. Sex Acts – there are several places, like the top floor of pretty much every skyscraper, where getting in requires giving it up.
2. Food – this has several subsets, but there is a preponderance of locations charging an admission, which

amounts to providing a meal of exceptional quality. Some places just want a week's worth of pizza. Don't worry, we can't understand why either.

3. Salvation – not surprising that many religious groups are requiring a conversion commitment to get through the gates.

Four: Lake Erie. Any of the Great Lakes will do, but we picked Erie because its name seems appropriate. Toronto's CN Tower has one of the dearest ViewFees because it is expected that impact will be visible followed by up to five hours of Rainbow Wall viewing. On the Great Lakes, you won't see impact but you will get the Wall and probably get to watch the lake vaporize as you suffocate.

All of us still here in the News That Moves offices wanted one last clickbait story before we go take in that perfect view. This is the story. We nearly ran a piece called The Best Way to Survive an Extinction Level Event. The article was two words: You don't.

Five: Consider Black Rock Desert. If you've never been to Burning Man, this is your last chance (and you get to *be* one). The official website says this special, absolutely final festival – Burning (hu)Man – now in its second week of dehydrating debauchery, will culminate soon. They have erected a special five hundred foot tall installation of two people holding hands. It will be lit by the Rainbow Wall and consumed along with the revelers. Free admission, just bring enough bottled water, or you'll die before you're killed.

The impact is expected to be quite a show. Some say Jesus will emerge from the flames with an army of angels to carry the saved to their eternal reward. Some say Satan will be going door-to-door skinning children alive. Most scientists expect a wall of rainbow-colored flame – its colors fueled by the incineration of literally everything it touches – to burn outward from the impact, boiling the seas and burning the innocent and the damned alike, though they're expected to have suffocated before incineration.

Six: Equatorial Pacific. We now leave Mainland, USA. As with the Great Lakes, many places on the ocean should be perfect viewing right up until you're boiled while suffocating. We've selected the Equatorial Pacific for its relatively warmer waters, which will make for a much more comfortable last few hours. The Rainbow Wall reflecting off the ocean from horizon to horizon is "not to be missed" according to this morning's Twitter trends. However, the northern Atlantic will be too rough – a tsunami of unimaginable size is expected to follow impact.

Seven: Europe's West coast. Any spot you can find on the coasts of Ireland, England, France, Spain, Portugal, or even Morocco. Seismologists, oceanographers and other experts – who at this point wish they'd partied more in college – speculate that the Rainbow Wall will catch and overtake the mile-high tsunami within view of these coastal areas. The ocean is expected to recede several miles. Boiling waves will force a blistering cloud of steam ashore. Death by scalding is particularly unappealing, so it shouldn't be too crowded at the beach.

Eight: The Alps/Himalayas. Where better to spend The End of the World than atop an iconic mountain in an iconic range? It's not free if you pay a Sherpa, but for the most part, if you can get to these mountains you're more than welcome to start climbing them. Let's face it, most of us have at one time or another dreamed of conquering Everest. And if you fall and break your ankle or get lost, no need to worry, you're going to die.

Nine: Hawaii/Pacific Islands. There is a better than fifty percent chance the pacific islands become volcanically active as a result of C/2019 Q2 – Garrett's impact. Everybody loves Hawaii and who knows? Maybe in a thousand years, your preserved corpse will be studied like the bodies at Pompeii who suffered death by pyroclastic surge before it was cool. If it's any consolation, it should be quick.

North Korea denies the existence of the comet. Any discussion of it is now a capital offense. Ignorance is bliss, am I right?

(Image Description: Cartoon dog smiling, drinking coffee while house burns around them. Caption: This is Fine)

Ten: Last but not least, Siberia. Siberia is a harsh, oil-soaked tundra. With three quarters of Russia's land and just a quarter of its people, not many folks seem to want to live there, but dying there might be just fine. You'll get to see some apocalyptic-level eruptions as the underground pockets of oil explode in celebration as the Rainbow Wall approaches.

I'm guessing some of you have money or something else you've traded for that one in a million chance to survive. We've got tons of people who will attempt to orbit the Earth for anywhere from a day to six weeks. NASA is sending up two dozen genetically diverse survivors. Tough, intelligent people who likely won't succeed in reinvigorating a charred Earth. Some smaller vessels* still have seats available in exchange for cuddling, servitude, anal sex, and more.

*Commercial airliners are not expected to reach an altitude safe from the pyroclastic surge.

The most expensive seats, however, are at the southern coast of Australia. There is already widespread lawlessness as armed power-brokers have taken over. The hope is that being the landmass closest to opposite the impact zone, and the Rainbow Wall having to travel across Antarctica, that maybe the flames will die off. Just to be clear this is a more than distant possibility, but people are paying quite a lot for this shred of hope. The experts all agree that the only thing dying off will be life on Earth.

PS: If you find yourself in sunny Glendale, feel free to join us on the roof here at News That Moves. We don't have a view, but we've been hoarding burgers and booze and we plan to get toasted and toast to being toast.

Correction: An earlier version of this article said the Space Needle was in Toronto. Forgive us, we get the CN Tower and the Space Needle confused – especially when we know we know that death is upon us.

(Image Description: CN Tower and Space Needle separated by NOT EQUAL symbol)

ANYMORE

L. MARIE WOOD

H is hands were on her and then they weren't.

He was pawing, prying, panting in anticipation, pressing down so she couldn't get up, couldn't move, couldn't breathe...

... but then he wasn't.

He wasn't because he *wasn't* anymore.

He wasn't hot anymore, not game anymore, not *him* anymore.

He wasn't... anything, not anymore.

He said nobody would notice.

He said even if they did, nobody would stop him because they'd be too busy saving their own asses to care what he was doing right out in the open.

Because it was all over.

He laughed at her.

Called her stupid.

Because she didn't see it, didn't believe it would happen, didn't think the world would be wiped away.

As he lay on top of her, tears springing from his eyes like fire hydrant flow interrupted by a big stick, drenching his face as he pulled at himself, tugged at it, flaccid thing that it was, terrified into permanent inaction, but still he pulled and pulled and pulled. With the other hand he squeezed her breast, twisted it like the crank of a Jack-in-the-Box, fingers bruising, digging into her flesh. He heard her squealing, but no, he didn't care because it was over, it was over, it was *fucking* over, goddamn it, couldn't she see that? Who gave a shit anymore?

When his head split in half, a diagonal slice that looked like it was made with a sword, she didn't cry for him. The squealing that issued forth from her mouth minutes before died in her throat. The sky behind him first went black, then blossomed with the most brilliant of reds like Heaven was on fire. She choked on her screams as people dropped around her, falling to the ground dead, dead, so very dead. She could see inside some of them, holes bored through their foreheads to show their brains, through their chests, all the way out of their backs.

Carol from the diner. She must have left food in the window to run out of the place before the lasers came to kill them all, cold and impersonal like sunlight through a magnifying glass over an ant colony. The beam cut into her body, opening her with the precision of a surgeon. Carol fell right behind where she and Buster, the bastard who died with his limp dick in his hands, lay in the street. Carol fell on her back, her stomach open where she'd been sliced, intestines spilling out like they were too big for the cavity they had been crammed into.

Walker and his wife. Was her name Maggie? Margaret? Misty? Marla? She didn't remember, and it didn't matter, not anymore. They fell next to where she lay under that bastard, Buster, close enough that Walker's arm flung onto her shoulder when he landed, their eyes burned out, burned clear through their heads.

She could hear the hiss of the beams coming from some unseen thing in the sky. Must be a UFO, she thought, but even then, she wasn't so sure. It was just something she would have said twenty minutes before, when all she had to worry about was what she was going to have for dinner.

Aliens.

That's what people thought of when terror came from the sky, right? That's what they said in the movies, like aliens didn't have anything else to do but to mess with the good people of Earth and take over the planet like squatters.

Buster smelled of cheap cologne and his own piss and shit.

She looked left, saw the kid whose only job was to gather up the carts from the parking lot and bring them inside. He couldn't have been more than sixteen, probably went to the high school down the street from where they both lay. The carts were on top of him – the little ones meant for just a few items; the big ones for Thanksgiving dinner-type shopping. There was even a cart designed for kids to pretend they were driving sitting on top of him, the handle attached to a racecar cockpit with a steering wheel and everything. This one had landed on his head after the wind that came behind the lasers swept through, wind strong enough to push carts full of food abandoned by their owners across the lot...well, at least partially: some carts still had limbs attached to them, fingers gripping tight in death even as the arms they belonged to were severed at the elbows. The wind was strong enough to uproot street signs and carry them over the highway and up the hill to where she was pinned beneath Buster. Decatur Street. That was at least a mile away, she thought. She wondered what was happening on Decatur Street then, whether or not someone was surveying the aftermath like she was from a similar perch, stuck beneath the rubble and rot.

She looked right and saw more of the same. Downed bodies covered in blood, organs on the ground covered in the dirt that had been pulled loose in the windstorm, innards dredged in viscous fluid and coated in soil like a snack ready to be pan fried and served up to who? The aliens? The gods?

Something stringy and wet flapped toward her propelled by the wind but tethered to something on one side. She recoiled beneath Buster, disgusted because she knew the pink, fleshy thing was sinew even though she had never seen a picture of sinew to know for sure.

She wriggled, desperate to get away from it, single-minded in that effort now that she'd convinced herself what it was. It kept flapping toward her, reaching for her. She was sure that if it touched her, it would consume her, eat away at her like acid, skin ulcering like a canker sore on the sensitive pink of one's lip, falling off in big clumps... flesh eating disease in the end because why not? She laughed, the prospect enough to break her resolve, to tip her over the edge and send her into hysterics.

And nobody cared.

A thought came to mind as her laughter trailed off, an elaborate picture show forming in her head, displaying everything in graphic detail.

Maybe the stuff she thought was sinew was really a spore like in that old alien invasion movie. Maybe if it touched her, she'd see it turn *into* her, first morphing from the stringy crap into a blob, then forming a face that looked like hers, a body that was tall and slender, gangly when pressed into action, like her own. Maybe it would open its eyes and stare at her, shoot a fleshy appendage out to touch her face, feel the contours so the replica would be better... more authentic. Then she laughed again, the sound harsh in the deafening quiet. She laughed in part because of the beast made of sinew, the monster after her essence, but mostly because she realized she was going to die beneath that bastard, Buster, after all. She was going die after surviving the fucking apocalypse, managing to dodge hot globs of flying flesh and lasers intent on cutting everyone in half. She was going to die because she couldn't breathe underneath him anymore, his dead weight like a ton of bricks on top of her thin body. She was going to die because she was afraid to get out from under him, afraid to stand exposed in the crowded parking lot where she'd be utterly alone. The laser would find her if she did.

When the librarian fell, she'd lost her shoe.

The old guy who picked up trash off the street lost his teeth when his head hit the ground unprotected, unshielded, smacking against the asphalt hard enough to break the thin skin over his skull and spew blood. She had to crane her neck to see him, could have avoided that particular sight, but she couldn't stop herself from moving, from stretching, from trying to see. His mouth was open, jaw permanently set in a surprised 'O'.

It was quiet. Quiet, but not silent.

Fuzzy.

The way static might sound.

She listened to it. Closed her eyes and tried to fall asleep to it. Maybe when she woke up she'd be ready to move, ready to make a run for it, just in case the laser was waiting for her.

Maybe when she woke up, she'd be dead.

She squeezed her eyes shut.

Buster's blood dripped onto her face, into her mouth.

The sinew monster took another swipe at her, getting closer this time.

She shrieked at the thought of it making contact, attaching itself to her skin, sucking at her with toothy mouths that dotted its flesh. She found strength she didn't know she had, pushed Buster's mutilated body over to the side, and stood on shaky legs.

She was out.

She was out.

She turned around in a circle, surveying the lot.

She was alone.

Bodies strewn, torsos here, limbs there. Scalps, fingers, livers, hearts – she thought of Humpty Dumpty when he fell off the wall, a grizzly puzzle with the pieces lying on a table, some right side up, some upside down. She grabbed at her arms, reached for her legs, looked at her shoes, still on her feet, and wriggled her toes, checking even though she could feel herself, knew everything was still where it should be, but because nobody else around her was intact, she looked anyway, to be sure. Then she looked back at Buster. That asshole, Buster, who always looked at her with kind eyes when he said hello; Buster, who always seemed to be coming when she was going, always happened to be wherever she was; Buster, who she thought was harmless right up until he threw her to the ground to have his way because the world was ending.

Buster, who had saved her life by getting on top of her.

She saw the bodies around them and realized something that made her angry.

He'd been right.

Nobody cared.

Carol, the librarian, the garbage picker, Walker and whatever his wife's name was, all the people who had met the laser close by her and Buster, so close they could have touched them, screamed at him, pushed him off of her – none of them cared what Buster was doing. They were too busy trying to save their own asses to worry about anything else.

But the laser saw.

The laser knew all.

The kid with the carts was looking at her with a smile on his face as a bubble of bloody spit grew large on the corner of his mouth, like gum.

And that didn't matter either.

Because he wasn't anything anymore.

THE END IS VERY FUCKING NIGH

W. DALE JORDAN

"Lord God, even as your vengeance is spewed forth upon the earth, we pray for your salvation and forgiveness for this, your errant child, fallen from grace, a slave to the sin of homosexuality. Forgive him, Father God. Cast out this darkness. Save him, Father!"

I couldn't help rolling my eyes, even as I strained against the ropes my parents and their *fucking* pastor used to tie me to an old wooden armchair in the church. All around us, "the faithful" fell to their knees, weeping and praying and praying and weeping. Some gave up and just fell over, lying face down on the floor in some weird combination of prayer and duck-and-cover drill.

I was pissed, but I also pitied the assholes.

When the end came, and make no mistake, it was here, they weren't caught up to Heaven the way they'd been taught. Instead, like everyone else on this rock hurtling through space, they had a front-row seat when the oceans surged up over the coasts, wiping out everything in their path. It didn't take long for stories of tentacled creatures in the whitecaps, feasting on drowned bodies, to spread.

Actual fucking sea monsters were coming for us, and nothing in their Bible prepared them for that.

Poor bastards.

At first, they were in denial because, in Genesis 9:15, God promised never to destroy the Earth by floods again. Then that megachurch run by the guy with the good hair down in Houston was flattened. One of the last broadcasts to come out of the area on the news showed him screaming his head off as purple tentacles wrapped around him, and his head burst under the pressure.

The truth hit fast for them after that.

The end was very, *very* nigh, and there wasn't a damned thing they, or their God, could do about it.

We were at the top of the Texas panhandle, and it was coming at us from all sides. Even now, the air was damp. Of course, that could just be me sweating. It doesn't take long for the temperature to rise when you're the sole focus of a church full of Pentecostals determined to save your soul at the last minute.

A part of me, somewhere deep down, understood what was happening.

They were helpless. They'd lost all control. So, they latched onto the one thing they thought they could accomplish in what time they had left.

They were going to save someone's soul, and I was the lucky bastard they picked.

I don't know if they planned it, or if it was just convenient because I drove up to check on my parents when I realized what was happening.

"Jacob, baby, please," my mother pleaded. "Turn to the light. Accept Jesus into your heart. We're running out of time."

"Mama…"

"Yes, baby?"

"Mama?"

She leaned in close.

"The sin of homosexuality is in the act itself, right?"

"Yes, baby, it is."

"So, it's not so much a state of being as it is the act of having sex with another man, right?"

"Yes—"

Her brow furrowed.

"So, exactly how much fucking do you think I intended to get done between the time you kidnapped me and when the Gulf of Mexico shows up in the parking lot?"

She slapped me.

Hard.

Intentionally.

Her face clouded, and her eyes flashed pure hatred for a good three seconds before she regained control.

I wasn't shocked by the "Amens" and "Hallelujahs" that followed the slap. I wasn't even mad. But if they were going to make the end of the world all about them, I would get my sucker punches in when and where I could.

"Pray harder, children. The devil is strong, but God is stronger!"

Ugh, the platitudes. I couldn't believe this was how I was spending my few remaining hours.

I turned from mom and strained to peer out the window. Storm clouds gathered in the distance, and unless my imagination was working overtime, something massive and shadowy moved through them when the lightning flashed. My heart thumped loud against my chest once, twice, three times.

Fuck it. I was not going out like this. This chair had to be thirty years old. That's two years older than me. I was getting out of it one way or another.

I pushed myself to my feet, still bent at the waist with my ass in the chair, and threw myself sideways to the floor as hard as I could.

The chair arm and at least one or two of my ribs snapped with a crack that put an end to all the weeping and wailing in the room. No one moved as I stood. I grunted at the flare of pain in my side and looked around the room at them. Shock, anger, and disbelief stared back at me. I looked at my wrists. The chair was broken, but the ropes hadn't loosened, even a little.

"Son," my dad whispered. It was the first time he'd spoken to me since he threw a burlap sack over my head that morning. I wheeled around and spat at his feet. His fists clenched, but he didn't move toward me. He took a deep breath; his voice was surprisingly calm when he spoke. "Son, we're all gonna die here. There ain't nothing you can do about it. Nobody's survived the water or the...things...in it. But, son, Hell is forever. Don't you see? Your mom—we—just can't stand the thought of being separated from you for all eternity. Knowing you're burning in Hell because of this sin."

I took my own deep breath before I responded.

"Dad, I'm not going to argue. I don't want to spend what little time I have left...I spent the first fifteen years of my life terrified of dying. Y'all never gave me one good reason to want to go to Heaven. You spent all your time talking about Hell. Lakes of fire. Eternal torment. Satan and all his demons just waiting to torture any human being who didn't live like a saint, and what has it gotten you? You're gonna be wiped out within an hour or two, just like everyone else on this fucked up planet.

"When I realized I was gay, I prayed and prayed for God to change me. I did everything possible to 'live right' and be the person you wanted me to be.

"And you know what? God never answered. He never changed me. I've spent a lot of time thinking about that over the years until I finally reached my own conclusion. If the God you taught me about existed, then he either couldn't or wouldn't change me. This is who he wanted me to be. I don't know if that means being gay ain't the sin you think it is or if he's trying to make sure Hell has a nice fat population, so Satan doesn't get bored. Either way, it's out of my hands, especially now.

"I'm going. I'm leaving. If you make it to Heaven and I'm not there, you just go on and have a big time without me, okay? I give you permission to have the best damned time you ever had. Y'all say your prayers. Do what you need to do. But I'm not staying here. Okay? I'm out."

No one said anything. I waited for one of them to speak up. I figured the pastor, at least, would do his best to get them riled up again, but even he was silent when I turned away, dragging the old chair behind me.

I was almost at the door of the sanctuary when I heard a sound that stopped me dead in my tracks. It was a belt clearing beltloops in one quick, smooth motion. I knew before I turned around what was happening.

I just couldn't fucking believe it.

My dad's eyes were grey steel as he looped the belt over his fist. Mom stood to his right with the pastor on his left.

"Honor thy father and thy mother," the old man intoned as thunder cracked over our heads and the first drops of rain spattered the church windows. In the distance, I could hear the sound of waves and a metallic screeching.

The end was here, and my dad had decided to dole out some corporal punishment like he hadn't in a decade and a half.

"This really the way you want to spend your last few minutes, old man?"

Even I was surprised by how steady my voice sounded.

"Spare the rod, spoil the child," mom whispered so quietly I could barely hear her, and dad took a tentative step forward, then another.

The thunder was louder now. Lightning flashed so bright it was nearly blinding. The roar that followed wasn't human, but it wasn't any animal I'd ever heard before, either. Something in the sound sent my dad running. The fist holding the belt pulled back over his head, ready to bring it down on me with the full force and weight of his body behind it.

He was within three feet of me when the windows broke, and water flooded into the church like a tidal wave.

"HAROLD!!"

Dad stopped in his tracks when my mother shouted his name. He turned in time to see her swept off her feet and crushed against the opposite wall. The sound of her neck snapping rivaled the water and thunder.

"Marjorie!"

Dad forgot all about me, running into the rushing water as if there was something he could do. I almost called after him but lost my voice when no less than two dozen long purple-black tentacles appeared from beneath the rushing rapids. One of them speared him through the chest with less resistance than a hot knife through butter. Another wrapped around the pastor's head and pulled him beneath the rising tide.

I turned away as screams erupted from the congregation. The chaos outside had infiltrated their holy of holies, and if the water didn't kill them, the creatures in it certainly would.

I pushed open the door and half-stumbled through it into the devastation of the parking lot. I nearly lost my footing in the waves but managed to grab onto the flagpole just outside the church. With all my might, I bashed the chair against the metal structure until it gave way, disappearing into the dark beyond. I clung to the flagpole, turning my face toward the storm.

Rain lashed my skin, and I pushed myself higher up the flagpole as the water rose far too fast, pushing cars across the lot like toys.

Metal scraped against metal.

Beneath me, one of those strange limbs shot from the water, wrapping itself around the pole as that inhuman roar split the sky.

I looked up and, for the briefest moment, caught a glimpse of some Eldritch creature with a body comprised of tentacles that even now drew its prey to a sharp, beaklike maw.

A moment later, the pole bent toward the water's surface, and the dark of the night took my last breath.

WHEN THE HORIZON BURNS

ELFORD ALLEY

I've been digging for an hour when the world ends. My spring project: a koi pond for the front yard. A perfect outdoor task for an unseasonably warm February morning. An ice storm waits, but for now the low gray clouds lift and the sun breaks through. I've shed my jacket. The dull ache in my lower back is reason enough for a break. I drop the shovel, peel off my gloves, and drop them in the hole. I make a slow fist and undo it to stretch my fingers. Kicking off my boots, I swing open the storm door and go inside.

Every window is open. The breeze rushes through the house, pushing with it the dust of a long winter. The baby is napping. Even at two, he still sleeps twice a day and we're thankful for that. Phoebe sits with her legs crossed at the kitchen table, still in her pajamas. A comfortable day. She takes a sip of coffee and scrolls on her phone.

Makes me think of a quote. Who was it? Vonnegut? He said to take time to say to yourself, "Well, if this isn't nice, what is?"

Phoebe stands, clutching the phone in both hands.

"What's up?" I ask.

Her eyes scan the phone screen, back and forth and back and forth. Her mouth falls open, lips quivering.

I laugh, not because anything is funny. I ask again and she runs to the TV. She's shaking. I follow her and ask again what's happening, voice raised. She pushes her phone into my chest while turning to the news.

"Nuclear Detonations on the East Coast" reads a scrolling headline.

What a well-mannered way to put it.

The image is an overhead map of the eastern states, angry red dots popping up over various cities, spreading like mites. The TV echoes the same. All communication is lost with several states. More bombs falling. US responding in kind. No answers, only silence from each leveled city.

I drop the phone and pull Phoebe to me. I tell her it's okay. We're in Oklahoma for Christ's sake, who would bother? But I feel like we need to run. Where to? What's the minimum safe distance for the apocalypse? Phoebe sobs, digs her fingers into my chest and I squeeze her tighter. Eric wakes in the next room, his wails joining hers.

What do we do? I run, pace the kitchen, gather up water bottles and canned foods. They pile on the counter. Do we have a can opener that isn't electric? Load up the car! We'll load up the car, and we head west. Maybe north? Far from anywhere, far from the radiation. Does it spread with the wind? It does, but maybe we'll still be out of reach. That's where the rich build their bunkers, right?

One minute into the world's end, and I'm wondering what I truly know about nuclear weapons outside of movies and TV. Phoebe's stopped sobbing, but she stands perfectly still, watching the news and blinking away tears. She sniffs and wipes her nose.

"Phoebe?"

She looks toward me, but her gaze is far beyond.

"Phoebe, we're going to be okay."

She motions to the screen. Every major city on the map bathed in red. The coffee maker bubbles. The scent of cinnamon rolls on the counter. A comfortable day. I embrace her again and put myself between her and the TV. I promise we'll be fine.

"The world is ending."

No, I tell her. No. Just get Eric and anything he needs. Pack some clothes, for all kinds of weather, coast and all. I tell her I'll load the car with food and supplies. Flashlights? Do we need batteries and soap?

She walks down the hall to Eric, while I load every non-perishable item our kitchen contains. Canned pumpkin pie mix? It's nonperishable, right? Outside, I hear birds. They're singing because tomorrow will be here, and they need to mate.

Through the window, screaming, doors slamming, tires screeching as cars pull away. Panic buries the birdsong and I stuff whatever I can into old shopping bags. Forks? Spoons? I should fill up the empty water bottles.

"Phoebe? How's it going in there?" I call out as I run down the hall to her. I peek into Eric's room. His bed empty, toys strewn, but the dresser drawers are closed. No suitcases being filled. I call out again down the hall.

Quiet.

I jog to the bedroom, our bed unmade but otherwise the same as we left it. I call her again. Wait. The water in the bathroom is running. Maybe she's filling bottles too? I push open the door.

Phoebe kneels on the rug in front of the tub. Water pours from the faucets, whirls around the Eric's partially submerged body, naked and—

Floating, face down.

"He didn't hurt. He can't hurt now."

Her voice is calm, level, steady.

The waves from the pouring water jostle him, enough that my heart skips and I wonder if he's alive. I fall to the tub, turn him over, but his lips are blue, eyes wide and vacant, unblinking. His head lolls, nearly severed, as I lift him.

Someone's screaming, I can feel it in my skull, my chest, and suddenly I know it's me. I drop the body into the water. It splashes like a massive stone. I scream and scream and there's a hand on my back, gently rubbing. Something wet, something warm spreading across my back.

I look at Phoebe. She's no longer crying. She raises one hand to touch my face, and red gushes from the wounds carved down her arm.

"Come here. It won't hurt."

Her face, the same gaze as before but now there's serenity. She sniffs and nods, asking me if I get it yet. If I understand.

"We-we need to stem the bleeding." I swallow. "A towel, we need a towel."

I grab one from the counter. There are still doctors right? There still will be?

"No!" She cries.

She lunges, stabbing at me with the knife in her other hand. The pocketknife from the hiking backpack. I crawl away, desperate to avoid the blade. On my feet again, I stumble out of the room, avoiding her weak swings toward me, the knife cutting air.

"We can be together!"

At that moment, with the horizon soon to burn away everything, I don't want to die.

She nods and brings the blade to her throat. I slam the door shut. It clicks. She gasps, gurgles. Then, only the sounds of pouring water.

I stumble down the hall, bracing myself with one arm before I collapse. I scream and slam my hand against the wall until I'm sure I've broken bones. Then, for good measure, I hit it again and cry out in pain, cradling my hand against my chest. I stand and staggerto the living room. The news continues. More bombs, more cities beyond communication.

The broadcast reveals smartphone videos of mushroom clouds blooming and flattening cities in their path, the video shaking and breaking away as the blast forces hit the witnesses.

"Phoebe, we gotta go."

I remember. But I keep talking.

"Did you pack Eric's bag? We gotta remember the rattle cats. He goes nuts without them. Want to grab some of your books?"

Outside, a pit sits for a future koi pond.

"I have to bury, don't I?"

I turn off the bathtub faucet and fish my son from the water. I wrap him in a baby blanket, then another as the blood soaks through. Him first. Phoebe lies on the bathroom rug, blood soaking and congealing into the bright yellow fibers. When it's her turn, I pull the rug, and bring her slowly into the living room. I grab her legs because her arms are too slick with blood.

After rolling her into the pit, I place Eric in her arms.

I throw in her jewelry next, Eric's favorite toys, including both plush cat rattles. I put the baby books in plastic gallon Ziplock bags. In a thousand years, you'll never know we were here. In ten thousand years this will be a prairie again, and bison will trample it in herds unfathomable. Even if the bombs never come this way the houses will be gone, grass will cover and consume the concrete. I shove the dirt into the hole and start stacking the rocks and stones I bought for the walkway and pond border. I stack them like a pyramid, I look for others.

Next door, a neighbor stands on his lawn, pistol in hand. Just moved in. I'm not sure I know his name. Paul? He watches the people throw things into their cars and scream away.

"Hey Dan."

He waves without glancing my way.

"I'm gonna borrow some rocks, okay?" I lift one from the border of the yard. He puts the pistol to his head and fires.

"Goodbye, Dan."

Just an hour into the apocalypse. Here we are. I build. A tall pyramid of stone, a monument, a burial mound with the most precious of treasures entombed within. The ground rumbles as I stack more. Maybe Oklahoma isn't far enough. I'm leaving a monument for them. In a thousand years they'll find this, right? Someone will. They'll find a grave like no other and they'll see these baby books and think, what a wonderful family. What an amazing mother. Look at this kid. They'll see only bone and have no idea what happened. I'll be gone.

We all will.

But they'll be here, even after the horizon burns.

If this isn't nice, what is?

ALICE

CHRIS MASON

No one had come to check on her. Alice considered this as she looked out at the empty street. Not fourteen-year-old Becky, who'd taken selfies in the driveway of the house opposite while her mother threw bottled water and blankets into the back seat of a white Mercedes. Not Gary Mather from next door, who'd exited his house minus the wife and carrying enough military grade weaponry to start a war. Not even Ben and Antony from number eight, who returned to their SUV four times to pile in crates of their beloved vinyl record collection. Only Natalie Hosking, dressed in cargo pants and hiking boots, had thought to pause as she passed on foot with a backpack slung over her shoulder. An apologetic smile aimed towards Alice all she'd managed before hurrying on.

The sky changed from dull pink to magenta. A forest of thick black lines grew on the horizon. Alice turned away from the window and closed the curtains.

"What do you think, Tinks? Time for a cuppa?" The grey ball of fluff at Alice's feet rolled onto its side, cocked a leg and licked its arse. "I'll take that as a yes."

She shuffled into the kitchen, her hip letting her know it was time to sit. Her sciatica was bad today. The bulb overhead pulsed and dimmed. It was okay. If the power cut out, she still had LPG and a box of matches. Enough to boil water for a pot of tea.

The panic and confusion hadn't surprised Alice. *Where did they think they were going? The next town? The coast? Then what?* Amid the slamming doors and screeching tyres there had been yelling and gunshots.

Then the long silence.

Perhaps, if she'd been younger, she might have left too. Found herself squabbling with strangers over food and refuge. Pretending survival was an option. Alice was no expert, but she was pretty sure this was the end. *The* end. Not that anyone said as much. No one was talking, and therein lay the problem. It was like governments around the world had given up. Decided whatever it was—a black hole, mother nature at her finest, or the second coming, who knew? —it was way too big for the US, EU, Russia, China, or all combined, to deal with. There'd been no launch of military intervention. It was everyone for themselves. Which begged the question... how exactly was one supposed to behave in an apocalypse? Alice thought a little kindness wouldn't have gone astray. She sipped on her Orange Pekoe. Seemed like kindness was in short supply today.

Alice took down a copy of *On the Beach* from the bookshelf. When she'd read the book in her early twenties, the cold war a lived thing, she'd lost a fair amount of sleep over it. She didn't live in Melbourne, but south of Adelaide was close. What she couldn't stop thinking about was the way the characters kept going about their daily routines, putting one foot in front of the other, while the clock ticked down on their small town lives. (To tell the truth, she'd much preferred the movie because at least it offered Gregory Peck as a distraction to the end of the world). Now, with decades of hindsight under her belt, she understood. Keep breathing until you don't. It's all you can do. Death was coming for everyone at some point, it was only a matter of how and when.

"Looks like it's just you and me, Tinks." The cat jumped onto the table and skidded across the lace cloth, knocking over the sugar bowl.

Alice sighed. There was no way the cat wasn't going straight to hell. She hoped she wouldn't be sharing the same elevator.

* * *

THE SOUND of a dog howling woke Alice. She glanced at the wall clock. She'd been asleep over an hour. How could she have dozed off? She'd always wanted to know how the world ended, and now she had the chance to see it up close and personal, she'd risked sleeping through the whole damn thing. She straightened in the chair, her left leg cramping. Getting old was a pain in the arse, but it was better than the alternative. She'd seen more sunrises than most.

The dog continued to howl. Alice squinted and listened. If she wasn't mistaken, the sound of distress was coming from next door.

Alice stepped out onto the porch. The air was warm. Black ants covered the terrazzo.

"Not long now," said Alice. Tinks, who'd followed her to the door and would go no further, flicked his tail in agreement.

In the half-light from a sky now shot with red and the ever-encroaching lines of black—*they look like ant trails*, thought Alice—she crossed her front lawn and into the property next door. A high fence and locked gate prevented her from accessing the backyard. The garage and front door, however, had been left wide open. Out of politeness, she announced herself as she entered the hallway of the Mather residence. Alice didn't expect a reply and got none.

A German Shepherd paced the patio on two metres of chain secured to the back wall of the house. Both food and water bowls were empty. Alice knew Gary was a shithead, but this took the cake. Couldn't he at least have let the dog go free? Let it enjoy a few final hours rolling in grass or pissing on trees.

Alice shushed the animal. It growled at her, more fear than aggression.

"You want to bite me?" said Alice. "Because that's not going to help."

The dog seemed to understand she was there to assist. It sniffed her outstretched hand then woofed, tail wagging. She reached for the collar and unclipped the chain. The dog bolted into the kitchen.

Alice wasn't surprised to find the pantry full of boxed cereal and beef jerky. Gary didn't look like the type of guy who dieted on tofu and greens. Neither did his wife. She didn't look like she ate much at all. Alice opened the fridge. There was beer and steak.

"Looks like it's your lucky day, dog." She threw the meat onto the terracotta tiles. "Enjoy." She went out back and retrieved the water bowl and filled it. While the dog ate, Alice took the opportunity to explore the house. It was crammed with big boy toys. A 100-inch TV screen took up one wall of the living room. On the other was a mock English bar and a pinball machine. The low coffee table had a stack of hunting magazines, a full ashtray, and a bong. In the corner was a southern cross flag and a framed photo of Gary astride a large fresh-water crocodile, the jaws secured with wire.

Upstairs the master bedroom was neat and clean. In the bathroom was an empty vodka bottle, and Gary's wife, Trish. She'd slit her arms from elbow to wrist and floated in a bath full to the brim with water the colour of cheap red wine. Long hair fanned her face. She looked anything but peaceful.

"Well, I guess that's one way to do it," said Alice. She wondered who else hadn't made it out of their homes.

* * *

AFTER LEAVING the dog to do its business on Gary's front lawn, Alice decided to check for abandoned pets in the other houses nearby. She didn't bother with number four or ten. One was vacant and up for sale, the other empty due to the occupants being on holiday in Bali. They'd left a week ago so might have got a suntan and some beach walks in before doom, descended. Alice studied the street and felt number eleven beckon her. *No harm going for a lookyloo.* The house had intrigued her since its completion six months ago. The architecture was modernist with an abundance of glass and angles designed to deceive the eye. It wasn't large compared with some of the other houses in the street, but it stood out, unashamedly defying the norm. Alice didn't mind it. She'd had only brief glimpses of her new neighbour as he'd driven past—a blurred figure behind the windscreen of a fancy sports car, used mostly on weekends.

The garage doors were closed. Alice tried to recall if she'd seen the car leave. The burnt orange metallic paint job would have been hard to miss, but then again there had been an awful lot happening on the street. She checked the front door. It was locked. Alice squeezed down the side path between hedges of manicured azaleas. There was a light on in the kitchen. She peered in through the window. On the workbench was a mug of steaming black coffee and a plate with two slices of toast on it. There was also a trail of ants circling the sink.

"I was wondering who shut that dog up," said a voice from her left.

Alice turned. A man appeared from the back of the house. He wore aviator sunglasses and a black kimono. Golden dragons danced down the sleeves. Her cheeks flushed pink. "Sorry, I'm not snooping." Then as an afterthought, "Or looting."

"Of course not." He removed the glasses, and offering his hand, smiled. His teeth flashed white in a handsome face. "Reg Woden, I don't believe we've met."

"I'm Alice." She shook his hand, surprised by how cold it felt. She couldn't guess his age. He looked old and young at the same time. "I live in the cottage at the end of the street. I keep pretty much to myself."

"I've noticed." He glanced at the sky, now brewing purple with flecks of green and silver. "We've got a bit of time. How about we sit out by the pool? Get to know one another."

"I—,"

He grinned. "It's a one-time offer."

Alice brushed back her hair. She wished she'd put a comb through it.

The pool was not a rectangle of chlorinated water but a water feature with koi and waterlilies—a reflection pool. It was set in a garden of carefully raked gravel, moss rocks, stone lanterns and bamboo. There were two wicker chairs and a table on raised cedar decking beneath a large Japanese maple. It was a picture of tranquillity.

"I like what you've done to the place," said Alice.

"I'm happy with it," said Reg. He offered her a glass of lemon water from a pitcher on the table. "So, you decided to stay?"

"I'm eighty-three. What am I going to do, run around and pretend I'm Charlton Heston?"

He laughed. "Good movie, the *Omega Man*." He pointed at the vivid swirling sky. "Tell me, is this how you thought it was going to end?"

"I had my money on mutually assured destruction. We do love our bombs."

"Disappointed?"

"No. It means humans aren't completely stupid." She paused and thought. "Asteroid would have been nice though. Spectacular *and* quick."

He looked offended. "This is not spectacular?"

"The colours have been amazing," Alice admitted. "Not exactly the bleak nuclear winter many had in mind. Although the dark is coming."

"True."

"It's all a bit weird, really. What do you think?"

"Oh, you know, seen one apocalypse, seen them all."

It was Alice's turn to laugh. "Well, the Gods certainly got creative on this one."

"You believe in God, Alice?"

"Ask me again when I'm on my last breath."

"Is that a no?"

"It means I'm flexible."

Reg grinned. "I knew I was going to like you. And for the record, I'm glad it wasn't an asteroid, because we would have had no time to talk."

Alice relaxed. She was out of practice in the art of conversing. The last time she'd talked to someone was when her sister Linda had called. Linda lived in Queensland and Alice was used to one-sided phone conversations. Linda could prattle on for hours about nothing much at all. When Alice did manage to get a word in, Linda finished her sentences for her. By contrast, Reg was easy to chat to. It was nice to have pauses that allowed for exchange for once.

"Do you have family? A significant other?" asked Alice.

"I've loved… and lost over the years. I tend to travel alone much of the time."

"Children?"

His green eyes twinkled. "I'm the father of many."

Alice wanted to ask *how many* but had a feeling Reg might be hazy on the figure. Instead, she said, "You didn't want to be with one of them? I mean, knowing the end is nigh and all."

Reg shrugged. "To be honest, I'd rather be here with you."

If he was trying to charm her, it was working. Her reply was coy. "But you don't know anything about me."

He gave her a look that said maybe he did. "Go on then. Give me the highlights."

Alice took a deep breath and searched for the sun. She figured it still must be up there because a scrap of light was coming from somewhere. Armies of ants marched around the still pool of water. She wondered why the tiny creatures were so intent on gathering their masses. Were they smarter than they looked? Would the humble ant and not the cockroach claim its place as sole survivor of a dead planet?

"Two husbands. The first, killed in a car accident. Cancer took the other one. I've been on my own for over thirty years."

"Children?"

"Also, two. And sadly, both gone as well. Rory got hit by a car riding his bike to school. He was in a coma for a week, before… well… a tough decision had to be made. He was twelve. I had Stephen longer.

He got to be a man. Blocks gave way while he was working under a car."

"Ah, I'm sorry. Are you alright?"

"Yeah. I've got no more tears left in me. And it wouldn't matter if I did. Not going to change anything. But it hasn't been easy."

"You've had some bad luck."

"Just a bit." Alice sighed. She'd not talked about her losses in a long time. It felt strange and somehow right to reveal it now. "Reg, what are we doing?"

"I believe it's called 'shooting the breeze'."

Typical, thought Alice. After all these years, she'd found someone prepared to listen, and now she had at the best an hour to cram it all in before the bell rang.

They changed the subject and talked about all manner of things until Reg checked the sky and said, "You haven't figured it out yet?"

Alice frowned, confused.

"C'mon Alice."

She gasped. "I knew it. You're not real."

"Interesting, but incorrect."

He leaned back and the kimono gaped to show a bare chest tattooed in ancient script. "I'll help you out. Perhaps this isn't the end of the world. Perhaps it's only the end of *your* world."

"You're saying this is all about me? Hah! That'd be a first. Next, you'll be telling me this is all a construct. Like some *Matrix* plot?"

He chuckled. "Not quite, but I do admire the fact you've kept up with—"

"Give me a break. I might be old but I'm not entirely boring. I do know who Keanu Reeves is!"

"Oh, Alice. You are a delightful creature."

Alice wasn't sure if he was being condescending or not. His tone didn't reflect it.

"Here, I'll show you what I mean. Comfortable?"

Alice nodded. *Sure, why not?* She'd come this far. And isn't this what she'd been doing her entire life? Accepting the unpredictable, the unthinkable, the downright horrible. Rolling with whatever the universe threw at her. *Lay it on me.* Reg snapped his fingers.

Her eyes fluttered shut. Her breathing slowed. Her mind flooded with memories; vignettes whirling so fast it was like flipping the pages of a photo album, images providing snippets of her life in rapid succession. She was not afraid, but grief featured heavily, and her body convulsed with each grim reminder. Slowly, she rose from the chair like a marionette, a great master pulling the strings. Her head rolled back and her feet dangled inches from the ground. Alice drifted towards the reflection pool like a leaf on the breeze.

Alice.

If this was death, she had no qualms with it. The pain in her knees and hip were gone.

Alice.

So was the ache in her heart.

Alice.

Her eyes opened and for a moment she could see nothing but ants crawling over her field of vision. No, not ants. Black dots. Black dots elongating into thin lines. Weaving across the last of a bloodshot sky.

ALICE. Look at me.

She blinked.

Reg floated above the reflection pool with her. He held out his hand and she took it. A tingling sensation spread from her chest to the tips of her fingers and toes. Then a kaleidoscope of colour enveloped her. Alice sucked sweet air into her old lungs and breathed long and deep.

"Come, let's ride the stars together tonight," said the voices of many.

There was but one question on Alice's mind, for she knew now what this was. "Why me?"

"Why not?" Reg squeezed her fingers. "You've seen what happens in the end. Now I'll show you how worlds begin."

SMASH HIT

MATTHEW M. BARTLETT

Carrie killed us all today. It's Tuesday. Of *course* it's Tuesday. Kearns always said nothing good can come from a Tuesday. Poor dead Kearns. Poor dead Carrie and Conway. Poor dead me, and soon. Nothing more terrible, as the poet said.

Nothing more true.

* * *

WE WERE ALL AT HOME, none of us working. Kearns was unemployed; he is—was—in his second month of collecting government benefits, unrelated to current events. Carrie's employer had shut down all operations and furloughed everyone. Only Conway was actively employed. One of the factory's products was earplugs, and even though those were pretty much useless, his company got special dispensation. He'd scheduled the time off in advance, planning to fly home to see his folks, which, obviously, wasn't gonna happen.

Mine was a glorified data entry job, a work-from-home gig, but it wasn't considered safe to be online anymore, so the firm had me in a holding pattern while the board tried to figure out what to do.

They had no idea.

None of us did.

The stories in the newspaper—supposedly the only safe way now to consume news, according to, who else, the newspapers themselves —were contradictory or just plain false; one day there'd be an article, the next the inevitable retraction or correction, the day after that, the correction correcting the previous correction. Then a new article, and the process would start all over again.

Hard to believe it had only been two weeks.

* * *

THIS AFTERNOON, around 2 p.m.: Kearns, sitting on the couch in his shorts, one leg crossed over the other, said it was a rap song, it had to be rap.

"How come, because you're a racist?" said Conway from the easy chair.

"Fine, if it's not rap, then I bet it's country."

"Classist."

"Classist is better than racist, right? Wait, did you say *classist* or *classicist*?"

"It's called Country & Western," I said, which broke everyone up.

Carrie piped up. "I heard it's whatever you want it to be."

Conway said, "That doesn't make any sense."

Carrie: "What about this does?"

* * *

"GOOD QUESTION," I said. "I have questions too. What if you hear it and survive long enough to sing it to someone else? Would, like, your own rendition be enough to make it do its damage?"

"Also," said Carrie, "how much do you have to hear for it to be fatal? What if you hear, like, just two notes? Three?"

"I can name that tune in four notes, Alex, and it'll fucking kill you."

"Alex hosted Jeopardy," Kearns said. "Who hosted Name That Tune?"

Carrie and I ignored him, and she pressed on: "Also, shouldn't this be easier to avoid? Don't listen to the radio. Don't put on the television. Don't go online. And yet..."

And yet the body count is astronomical.

"I guess the problem is people," I said. Isn't it always?

Conway stirred from his pile of blankets and started recounting the article from a few weeks ago, and I tuned him out. It was old news, happened only a few days in, before everyone had a handle on exactly what was happening, when people still thought it was safe to be outside. A couple of degenerate teenagers drove by a playground blasting the radio, which was tuned to a hijacked station broadcasting the song on repeat, like a musical marathon of murder. The three in the car had noise-canceling headphones on, but they hadn't counted on having them knocked right off their heads. So there's eight or so children and their parents twitching on the ground, ears clicking and clacking, heads coming apart, the driver's shocked at what he sees, the car skids out of control, careening up someone's lawn, crashing right into their living room, the driver dead from the impact, the passengers and the couple in the house, well, we all know what got them.

The police cordoned off the area, because even with all the damage, the goddamned car radio still worked. The media even made a point of saying the radio was a Blaupunkt. I doubt that boosted their sales, given everything. The military shot the car to pieces from a helicopter just to shut the radio up.

The cops shut down the broadcasters. There were few details. You can fill in the blanks.

And that was just one example of people being people. There are a lot more. You think you get used to it, but it eats at you, like maggots, crowding into a thick ball in your stomach, and, especially after dark falls, chewing on the part of your brain that regulates hopelessness and despair.

* * *

HAVE I mentioned we're a band? Yeah. Obnoxious, I know. I didn't even want to bring it up. We're not one of those bands like on shows or in movies where everyone's hot and young and hip, looks like a model, plays generic rock wearing miniskirts, half shirts, bandanas around our wrists, stuff like that. We wouldn't even be allowed to *open* for that band. We don't even have a name. We play mostly covers, but I have a few originals I was holding onto, thinking I'd introduce them to the band...someday.

We're in our late thirties, early forties. The only one of us who isn't flat out ugly is Kearns, and he's got a gut like a basketball. He plays drums, though technically he doesn't know how—he can keep a beat, that's all. Carrie, bucktoothed, with a receding chin, is the bassist, Conway with the unibrow and the jug ears plays rhythm guitar, I'm lead guitar and vocalist, and my features all seem to have come from other faces, don't mix well.

Regarding our skill level, the joke, and this is from Kearns, is that as bad as we are, even *we* couldn't write a song that kills the listener.

Anyway, we were pretty giddy at the thought that my soundproof music room could save us. I guess I'm the serious one in the group— the only one who studied music, the only one who saw it as something more than folly, as a possible escape hatch from a life of office drudgery. I'd had soundproofing and sound absorption professionals put the room together, paid them with money from the settlement I got after the accident a few years ago, and even had a little left over with which to buy a decent amplifier. Not long after, I'd invited my friends to stop paying exorbitant rents to evil corporations and come live with me in the raised ranch I'd inherited from my parents when they passed.

So with the perceived protection of the band room, though we were obviously duly sad about the massive loss of life, we maintained a cautious optimism—maybe we had a shot to survive. I probably wasn't the only one who imagined we could somehow come up with a solution, stop the song, go down in history as heroes.

Stupid.

We moved the couch and some chairs and blankets and the refrigerator to that soundproofed basement room, and there we lived, in extremely close quarters, with no windows and very little in the way of distractions, driving each other crazy. Every day, one of us, earplugs in our ears and noise-canceling headphones duct-taped over them, scurried upstairs through the dust-covered living room to grab food delivered by drones, and the paper, which, after a two-day interruption when everything started, landed on our doorstep every day, no sports, no entertainment, just mass deaths in China, the UK, Africa, Russia, the Netherlands—everywhere.

I worried about the delivery drone being hacked, the earphones and earplugs not being effective. Add it to the list of shit to worry about, I guess. One thing was clear, despite all the contradictions and retractions and corrections. This thing had a 100% mortality rate. You hear the song, you're a goner.

* * *

"I MISS GOING ONLINE," Carrie said, and the deep, profound sadness in her voice would have been funny if not for the fact that she meant a lot more than just *going online*. In those four words she referred to the presumed (but come on) death of her parents. She'd had an enviable relationship with them, texting every day, playing word games, talking all the time. She had to help them with technology a lot, and technology probably played a role in killing them. The last thing she did before we bricked our phones and burned the chargers was to text them a carefully thought-out list of strategies for survival. She never saw whether they responded.

She was also mourning the loss of streaming music and movies, which now functioned mainly as presumed Trojan Horses...but, yeah, mainly her parents.

"The trolls on the net," Kearns said quickly, before she started to upset herself talking about her folks. "And we thought Rickrolling was bad. Click to open an email, you're dead. Click on your go-to Pornhub video, the one for when you want to get done quickly so you can get on with your day? Dead. Click on a news story? The song starts playing your funeral dirge. I mean, that's what it is, isn't it? Country, pop-country, hip-hop, classic rock, new wave—whatever the genre, it's all the same death song, and they can't play it at your funeral, and even if they could, there are no funerals anymore, because they're an exposure risk."

"You could put your computer on mute," Carrie offered, obviously grateful for the direction in which Kearns had taken the conversation.

"Good try, except hackers can unmute your computer easy. And remember the guy who hadn't even plugged in his speakers?"

"Yeah," I said, "We all remember that story, and that it was debunked a few days later."

"And then there were all the people debunking the debunker, and now no one knows what to think."

Kearns was right, of course. And so out of an abundance of caution, they blocked the Internet, claiming "public safety."

I miss going online too.

I miss cat videos.

I miss memes.

I miss YouTube commenters telling us our songs suck.

I miss Wordle.

I miss my online friends.

I miss the version of myself that existed there.

He knew everything.

His opinions were dead on.

He wasn't afraid.

* * *

FOR A WHILE, we figured deaf people were safe. A few enterprising souls even performed impromptu self-surgery.

It didn't work. Go figure. I guessed it was vibrations. Or black magic.

I don't know. The paper says the government has brought in "experts."

* * *

LAST NIGHT I dreamed I listened to the song. I was driving down the road to an ex-girlfriend's house. To the east swayed vast wheat fields separated into ruffled regiments by the wind, and cliffs rose up from the western horizon like a rocky tidal wave. It was summer. My hair was whipping around my sunglasses, and the radio was blasting A One Story Town—until it wasn't.

A deejay with an echoing, fifties baritone introduced the next song as a really killer-diller, a shriller-thriller, a rocker and a shocker and a real tick-tocker. I then dreamed the song in its entirety—the chorus, the intro, the verses, the pre-chorus, the bridge. Heavy drums; big, blocky, doomy guitar chords over a slinky, sultry lead and a thudding bass. The vocals, tobacco-torn but passionate. The song had an irresistible hook, the kind that makes you drum the steering wheel, press down hard on the gas pedal, sing along in a cracked voice, not hitting the high notes, but not giving a shit.

A buzzing in my head rose until it drowned out the song. The mountains and cliffs tilted downward as though bowing, then stretched to impossible heights, blotting out the sun, filling the sky. The wheel grew icy cold to the touch, and in my ears I felt and heard a wet, frenetic slithering. The knobs popped off the radio like they were shot from a gun, and the antenna glowed red hot, turning the air to a shimmering haze that blurred a horizontal swath of countryside.

Then I saw it: a car approaching head on, as though it had materialized from some other dimension, in my lane, spilling a black tornado of smoke from its pipes. As it rapidly closed the distance, I realized it was my own car, driven by a blackened, ashy cadaver in a cape and cowl of raging fire. Its mouth hung open in a demonic grin. Red light danced in the black caverns of its eyes. Though its features and clothing were burned away, I knew it was me. The song was gone now, the buzzing too, the only sound now a rising and falling siren, a howl of terror, the raging roar of flames. I thought I would wake when the cars hit each other, but instead I flew in slow motion through a windshield gone to water, my cinder-fleshed doppelganger mirroring me, flying right at me through the summer air. It was only upon the second impact—my head crashing into his—that I woke up, stifling a scream.

* * *

YOU GET BORED. Especially when the end of the world is so quiet. There aren't marauders. No scrappy heroes roaming the countryside in search of some bastion of institutionalized silence. No walled cities with armed guards. No speeches about what it means to be human, about what we've lost, about coming together and fighting. The daring and wicked are dead. So are the resourceful and brave.

You get bored.

You nap.

I'm not even the napping kind, but I napped. Peer pressure? Nah, just regular pressure. We'd had dinner delivered, half-decent Chinese. It had been Carrie's turn to go up and get it from the porch. After the chicken fingers and the fried rice and the shrimp in lobster sauce, we fell into a funk, talked a little more about how we'd first heard what was going on. Kearns and Conway, ever stoic, ever turned-inward, contributed little. They looked drawn, overloaded with all they kept inside.

After a while, it was just Carrie and me talking. It got a little intimate. We both cried. I think we knew our little group wouldn't last. I said some hopeful things I maybe even half-believed. I thought something might happen between us, if she just came over and got under my blanket with me. I guess I could've used that. Not long after I had that thought, I heard her snoring softly.

I woke up in pitch black to the sound of a G-sharp diminished chord—the first chord from the song in my dream. Then the sound of a hand slapping out a rhythm on wood. Conway's light came on, sending our shadows all stark and angry to the ceiling. Carrie sat cross-legged in front of the drum kit, a strange smirk on her face. Her headphones, the pair she'd worn to grab the food, were on over her ears. A fault line like a lightning bolt shot down the lefthand casing, ruptured foam in the split. When Kearns and Conway tackled her, she was singing. I'd never heard her sing. She sang like an angel. Something she'd hidden from us.

I'm sitting here now with my dead band. Conway held Carrie down while Kearns broke her neck and collarbone with the neck of the guitar. She sang and laughed until they crushed her voice box. They fell back, cursing. Finally, snuffling and sniffing, they looked at each other, then at me. Their eyes said terrible things, apocalyptic things. I shrugged. I said, "I think that's it."

They both went over and sat on the couch, looking anywhere but at Carrie. I looked at her. My friend, her throat flattened, her mouth open in an eternal sneer, her eyes, which looked flat and fake, somehow. Conway bawled like a baby. Kearns put his hands over his eyes and pointed his elbows at the ceiling. I heard the popping in their ears, like snare drums. Watched the veins push at their foreheads from the inside. The popping got louder. Something shot out of Conway's ear and hit the wall hard enough to crack the plaster. Kearns slumped, leaking sludge from both ears. Something moved inside my own head.

* * *

I THINK THAT, when people die, their voices should vanish from audio recordings.

Some things are better remembered.

Maybe if that was how it worked, this wouldn't be happening.

See, I believe that whatever this song is, it's from a dead person. If someone performed it, they heard it, right? And it killed them. It only stands to reason. Or maybe it's like the opinion piece in Sunday's paper said—a dark magician mimicking the stylings of some dead artist, irresistible to people who absolutely must hear one last song from their favorite performer, even after all the previously withheld tracks are exhausted on extended reissues and box sets.

But what if it's not a person? What if it just *happened,* a strange phenomenon of sound, a sonic alien invasion, the ultimate earworm, that killer-diller, shriller-thriller, bursting out from all the speakers on the beach, from all the car radios and sound systems in the shops, that inescapable, irresistible smash hit of the summer.

I AM THE VANITY MIRROR SHAPED LIKE A SKULL

MADISON MCSWEENEY

They enter my mind with a sound like branches snapping, a frozen forest coming apart as they force their way through to me. The shambling infected, and the last of the kind ones. The ones who cannot speak but still say things like *I'm sorry you're in here* and *You deserve more dignity than this.*

Selfish creature that I am, the words aren't enough for me. I want their help. *Where are you?* I ask. *Near me, or on the island?*

The clang of my cell door opening breaks our connection. Two guards wait for me over the threshold, looking like lizards in their goggles and face shields. Standard biohazard procedure, I'm sure. They're not trying to look intimidating. Yeah, sure. One is lightly gripping what looks like a stick that culminates in a leather collar. The other brandishes a prod that I know can dispense an electrical current, if he so chooses. They call my name and I stand. I'm afraid if I hesitate, they'll put the leash on me.

Two stupid thoughts cross my mind as they prod me through the double doors—I wish they hadn't sewn my jaw shut, and I hope my family isn't in the courtroom. Both pure vanity. It's not like my mouth will do me any good—I haven't been able to speak coherently for three weeks. But the thick black stitches that crisscross my lips—they look so *monstrous*. No better than being wheeled in wearing a Hannibal Lector muzzle.

It sounds petty, I know. But I never really had anything going for me except my looks. I was never a natural mechanic like my father and wasn't much for academics (dyslexia; undiagnosed until adulthood and doesn't matter now). But I had striking blue-green eyes and sharp cheekbones, and my mother was convinced if she dragged me to enough child modelling auditions, I'd be discovered. She was right. I made a decent living displaying myself before the outbreak claimed me.

I don't love how sickly I look, but I can cope with it. But what they've done to me... fuck it. I was going to say, *What they've done to me, I can't abide*, but I have been, haven't I? I bark up a hysterical laugh, which chokes in my throat and comes out like a chirp.

The guard jabs me with his prod. I wince as my skin bursts at contact, viscous blood dripping down my back. "Get to it, supermodel," he snarls. "It's not in your interest to drag this out."

I blink and try to make sense of that. It's certainly not in my interest to speed *up* the process. The absurdity of the comment almost takes the sting out of the "supermodel" crack.

He could have called you worse, someone tells me. *They deemed me a ghoul, when they took me.*

Are you here? I ask her. I feel something like fingertips stroking my spine, tentative like a funeral smile, and she replies, *I'm in the woman's holding. I'll be up after you, I think.*

I'm sorry.

Me, too.

The courtroom is built to intimidate: Greco-Roman ornamentation and stained cherry wood rendered grim and cheerless. Grey sunlight that streams through the rectangular windows. The carpet is covered in stains, something I notice as I lurch down the aisle to the plain wood table where awaits my court-appointed attorney. She's slumped in a plastic chair, exhausted at noon, sawing away at her nails with a silver file. I've heard they do dozens of these hearings a day, sometimes up to a hundred; the lawyer is just here to check a box.

There aren't many observers. No one wants to be in the vicinity of people like me if they can avoid it; even the judge appears to be wincing, looming high above us like a king. I recognize my parents near the back, my father in a plaid button-up, my mother in the blouse she reserves for Easter and funerals.

My brain fills up again, the alien thoughts crackling like firewood. The roaring grows louder as the individual sounds grow more distinct, different voices emerging through the din.

Keep your head up.

Nothing to be embarrassed about.

They're afraid of you. *Remember that.*

What does this remind me of? The denouement of that David Bowie song. Something off *Ziggy Stardust*, the one where the rock star has a breakdown and all the space aliens he's been communing with beam in to offer solidarity. What was the title of that one? Oh yeah— "Rock and Roll Suicide." And didn't Bowie say the aliens, at the climax of the song, were actually ripping poor Ziggy's soul apart?

Great.

As the judge lifts the gavel, a final voice leaves me with some pragmatic wisdom: *If it makes you feel any better, none of them actually hate you. They just don't understand you're still human.*

"Xavier Dorian," the judge intones.

My name.

I try to open my mouth to respond, the words tripped up by my numb tongue and blocked off by the stitches. Mortifying.

"Nod if you can understand the proceedings that are about to take place."

Is there some other procedure for patients who can't understand the proceedings? I wonder. Would that be better for me?

Not really, one of my new friends replies, startling me. I hadn't intended to send out that question. The psychic connection must be involuntary.

I nod.

"You've been brought here today under the *Infection Control and Prevention Act* for Failing to Register as a Carrier. Do you dispute the charge?"

An argument erupts inside my head, fellow sicklies bickering over whether there's any point denying it. *It's a kangaroo court,* says one. Someone else asks if I could claim that I *did* register and the government lost my records. *And what?* another voice scoffs. *He registered and thought the government just decided not to follow up? The law says you have to self-surrender if you get sick. Him standing there, clearly infected, is all the evidence they need.*

This is awful. Maybe with time (time I don't have) I'd get used to the hive mind, but right now I just feel like I'm losing mine. I shut my eyes as if cutting off my vision will silence the voices. *Please shut up,* I beg. *I'm sorry, I just can't use any of this advice.*

The judge repeats the question and I shake my head. I'm sure everybody shakes their head. I would have registered but I couldn't believe I actually had it. I was afraid. Thought if I just waited it out, I'd get better. Etc. Etc. None of these justifications mean anything, legally speaking. Not that we can speak them at all.

The irony of our disease is this: soon after we lose our verbal communications skills, we gain a sort of mental communion with the other infected. Telepathy. We can't talk to the non-infected anymore, but we can understand each other fine, have rational, affectionate conversations. But so far, none of us has been able to articulate that to the non-infected. We're all too far gone, speech-wise, before we fully understand our condition. So as far as the rest of the world is concerned, we're zombies.

The judge scowls, asks me outright: "Did you, in fact, register?"

I look at my shoes. Not actual shoes, but a set of vinyl boot coverings tossed into my jail cell, to protect the floor from my bare feet. Underneath the crumpled fabric, my feet are swollen, purple, leaking black pus. I still cringe whenever I have to take a step.

The judge clears his throat into the hot mic, and for a second I think he's about to hock phlegm into a spittoon. "I'm assuming that's a *no*." When I don't answer, he cocks his head at my lawyer. "Do you need to confer with your client, Sandra?"

She sits up, blinks rapidly, like a sleeping student called out by her professor. The nail file halts its back-and-forth but remains poised over her thumb. "Do you need an interpreter?" she asks, a sort of Hail Mary to make it sound like she's been following.

I shake my head, and the judge impatiently repeats his question. *No*, I silently indicate. *I did not register.*

"Well, in that case, the law is clear."

When the judge says "guilty," I initially think, *this is it*. The trial is just a legal formality; he'll want to pass sentence quickly so they can bring in the next moaning shamble. Instead, he lectures me.

"All residents displaying symptoms of ARC-17-V are required to submit to testing, quarantine, and registration. Failure to do so puts not only the health and safety of the community at risk, but the security and survival of our entire society."

No one in power wants to say "zombie apocalypse" but they come pretty close.

"As I said," he continues, "the law is clear. Being afraid is not a defence. Being in denial about your condition is not a defence. By foregoing registration, you have chosen your own comfort over the lives of your fellow Canadians." He clears his throat again, looks at some papers in front of him. "I see from your file that you're a male model. I assume you've become used to a certain degree of luxury and comfort. Perhaps the quarantine village isn't quite your style."

That gets a smirk out of me, earning another death-glower from the judge.

The quarantine village is an island off the coast of Nunavut. Anyone who tests positive gets flown up there in a cargo plane. The government tries to spin it as something between a sanitarium and a colony, claims to provide the residents with enough rations and supplies to function as an autonomous community. But I've heard the stories, on the news as well as from the voices in my head.

There's no food, not enough space, and the patients cannibalize each other.

And that's the cruelty of the place—we wouldn't do that if we weren't there. Contrary to the images you see in the media, we aren't mindless flesh-eating automatons. The convulsions, the lurching gait, the uselessness of our tongues—these are issues of muscular control, not mental capacity. And we only bite in self-defence, like if some yahoo takes it upon themselves to exterminate us. Or if we go crazy, like we all do on that island. No one with any sense of self-preservation would allow themselves to be sent there. That's why there's hundreds if not thousands of us in hiding, locked away in our apartments, cowering in our loved ones' basements, living off the land in hastily purchased mobile homes.

But no, this is a *me* problem. As far as the judge is concerned, the issue is I'm a pampered model (*male* model, there's a difference, Xavier) who just can't stand the thought of roughing it.

I wonder what he'll use to condemn the next guy. I wonder how quickly *he'll* surrender himself, when he inevitably gets sick.

"Do you have anything you'd like to convey to those assembled, before I pass your sentence?"

Another sick joke. I break the judge's gaze and turn back toward my parents.

My father's expression is one of pure revulsion, my mother's a mix of shame and horror. No grief, though. Because I'm not their son anymore. I'm their future. A reminder of what fate awaits us all. More than that, I'm the bringer of that fate. Like the judge said, I'm the grim reaper in designer jeans, dooming society to collapse because of my selfishness. I'm that painting of the woman sitting by the vanity mirror that looks like a skull.

I try to smile at them, despite the butchery that's been done to my mouth. Because the approval-seeking kid inside me can't bear to deny them their final goodbye. A goodbye they clearly don't plan to say.

They've grieved you already, someone tells me.

They don't realize you're still you, another voice adds. *If they did, they'd say something.*

My eyes well with tears and my heart feels like it might explode. *Are we all so gentle with each other?* I ask. *Does the sickness make us better?* I wish I could have more time, that I could explore the bounds of this telepathy, get to know these people. More than anything, I wish I could be part of this chorus, consoling strangers in their final hours.

"Mr. Xavier Dorian, I sentence you to death. The sentence will be carried out immediately after these proceedings. If you wish to have a witness accompany you to the execution, you..."

My lawyer files her nails.

I feel like someone's opened my chest and scooped everything out. Rib cage, lungs and all. The sentence is no surprise—it's literally the mandatory minimum—but there's only so much you can do to steel yourself against an old dude in judge's robes casually announcing they're going to kill you. I search the courtroom for sympathy. My mother has her head in her hands, like she's trying to hide. Dad's scrolling on his phone.

I want to scream.

I always loved attention. Now at the most dramatic moment in my life, no one will even look at me.

The bailiff's prod jams into my back again, in case I have any creative ideas. At its opposite end, I can feel the man's grip stiffen, like he's pressing his finger to the button that says "electrify."

The judge, housekeeping: "Mr. Dorian, do you require a witness?"

I grunt and point at my lawyer. There's nothing she can do to help me anymore, but I suspect she's never watched an execution before. She should have to look upon this process she's lending legitimacy to.

Her eyebrows rise in alarm. She opens her mouth as if to argue, then remembers herself and stands up. To my surprise, my parents rise, as well. That quiets my pounding heart a bit. Maybe I will get my goodbye.

The procession begins. My feet make gross squelching sounds as we exit the courthouse.

The Ottawa River is cold and cruel. To the east, I can see Parliament Hill and the Peace Tower, our red and white flag hanging limp atop a sickly green copper spire. On the other side of the water, Gatineau smokestacks turn the sky into a sea of fog. At the edge of the precinct, just a metre away from where the parking lot becomes a cliff, is a new building: a hastily constructed concrete shack. A single storey, about the size of a one-car garage. Its only ornament is the Government of Canada seal branded into the heavy bronze doors.

This is where they'll put a bullet in my skull.

I guess technically it'll be a *bolt*. They use something called a "penetrating captive bolt gun," which is what slaughterhouses use for meat cows.

When we reach the death-house, I realize I haven't heard a voice in a while. That withers me. Have they really left me to die alone? Is this my fault, for telling them to go away during the hearing? I send a plea into the ether. I don't know if anyone hears.

The chamber is even more grim than I'd imagined. Single room, grey stone walls. Propped against the eastern wall is a burly man in a black plastic folding chair, reclined as if asleep, bolt gun in his lap.

I'd been hoping for a window. Let me look out on the water one last time before I close my eyes.

I whirl around in a panic, start babbling at anyone who might listen – my parents, my lawyer, the fucking executioner – begging them to see reason. But it's marble-mouth gibberish. My parents and lawyer recoil from me. The executioner just looks bored. The guards are the only ones who spring to action, Cattle Prod Guy jumping between me and the witnesses, leash guy brandishing his stick, trying to force me toward the wall. As if it could restrain me.

Then again, an electric shock definitely could.

"Stay back," orders Cattle Prod Guy, adding, as if everyone doesn't already know, "Any skin-to-skin contact puts you at risk of infection."

As if I could touch anyone if I tried.

They let me wear my own clothes for the trial—thank God. Earlier extermination hearings paraded out the unlawful infected in grey coveralls, until the proceedings became so numerous that makers of institutional clothing were bringing in a small fortune in taxpayer dollars. Over the last few months, the process has been "streamlined" to reduce the time between arrest and sentencing; now everything moves so quick, a costume change would just be red tape.

As a result, I'm in the outfit I was wearing when they detained me, dark jeans and a black sweater. My favourite sweater, as it happens, which is a small source of comfort. Not so much my court-issued accessories, the pair of oven mitts secured under the silver grip of handcuffs.

So if you're counting: my mouth is wired shut, I'm in long-sleeves and pants, my hands are neutralized, and even if I could wriggle out of this pseudo-footwear, my feet have limited mobility due to the shackles. So what are they afraid of, a forehead nuzzle of death?

For the good of all that is holy, why is *everyone* so afraid of me right now?

The scary stick, the kinky-looking leather collar still hanging uselessly from it, has only driven me back a few feet. But now it's Cattle Prod's time to shine. The end of the rod lights up with blue sparks. The guard's black mask hides his face and eyes, but I imagine they're lighting up just as much. To his credit, he restrains himself from shocking me on the spot. "Don't make this harder on yourself than it has to be," he says, savouring every word like morsels of the tenderest steak. He gestures towards the X made in tape on the floor. "Stand there and get on your knees."

I've never been electrocuted before and I'm happy to die without having had the pleasure. I step onto the X, but don't kneel. I know the second I kneel, the bored bureaucrat with the bolt gun will end me, and I'm still holding out hope that someone's going to burst in and announce that this whole pandemic has been an elaborate April Fool.

A seizure sends my arms waving, my chains rattling like Marley's ghost. At the same time, my left knee gives out, sending me into a lurching semi-fall that would have toppled me if the other leg hadn't refused to bend. Several muscles pull and I let out a moan, again like

Marley's ghost—no, who am I kidding? I'm a Romero zombie. The executioner titters.

My mother's face crumples like velvet. "Oh John, do we have to watch this?"

"Go outside," says my father softly. She clings to his arm, not wanting to leave alone. His eyes, for a fraction of a second, flit to the door, then back to my mother. I can tell he wants to go with her. But he shakes his head. "I have to see," he tells her, his voice so quiet only the echo off the walls renders it audible. "I need to make sure this—this *thing* is good and dead."

This is the final stake through my extracted heart.

I've suffered a lot of degradations since getting sick, things that have made me feel somewhat less than human, but this is the first time I've felt truly undead. My own father has rejected me, and now there's no one in my ear telling me to grant him some grace because it's not really *me* he's talking about, it's the mindless monster he thinks has stolen his son's body, but you know what? I wouldn't buy that anyway, because it is *me* he's talking about, whether he knows it or not, and how can he not? *How can he not look into my eyes and know in his soul it's his son in here?*

Rage surges in my veins for only a second, before the world turns to static. My hands fly to my ears, as if mere flesh could block the clamour in my brain.

It's like a million of us have woken up at once, are all chittering in each other's heads trying to make sense of it. Between the jail cells and the island and the undiscovered hiding places, I knew there were more of us than the government accounted for, but before this moment I had no idea there were *this* many.

I'm overcome by a sense of inevitability. The pandemic has reached a tipping point, the sickness spreading exponentially. They can kill us in the thousands and it won't matter; our population will be the supermajority in a matter of days.

This is the moment their world ends, and if I die knowing that, I'll be at peace.

Actually, fuck that, no I won't. If we're taking over the world, I don't want to die five minutes before.

I flex the fingers of my left hand, wriggling until my nails reach the top of the mitt. *No seizures, please.* Behind the cattle prod guard, my lawyer is back to her nervous tic.

The guard has let his guard down after my collapse, lowered his electric stick. He doesn't expect me to spring from my crouching position, lunge at him, and wait until he lifts the prod in his right hand before I duck to his left, pouncing on my lawyer. She shrieks, the echo against the concrete walls deafening, and we tumble to the ground.

I pin her with my knees and grope for the nail file, closing my hand around it as tightly as I can, despite the oven mitt. At the last second, she realizes what I'm about to do and tries to tighten her own grip, but too late; I wrench the file from her hand and raise it to my lips, slicing through the thin stitches.

It feels so good to have air on my tongue again.

The cattle prod's sparking, arcing towards me, but I'm on my feet before the guard completes his pivot, and this time it's really him I'm lurching for.

The executioner gets off his ass and fires the bolt gun without any pretense of aim, sending the bolt into the other guard's foot. He stumbles backwards, collapsing into the wall, leaving his colleague undefended.

I grab Cattle Prod by the neck, grin for the first time in ages, and bite. I don't enjoy the taste of him, but I pretend to.

* * *

THE EXECUTIONER IS the first to flee, then my lawyer, patting her face as if trying to remember whether I touched her or not. I didn't, but let her wonder. My parents escape next, my former father shaking Mom out of her stupor and pulling her out the door with him. That's okay.

None of them deserve to be one of us. Maybe they'll join the horde eventually, but it won't be my doing.

The two guards are dead. The first went pretty quickly; teeth to the jugular will do that. The second I strangled with my handcuff chain, the four inches of slack just enough to wrap around his throat.

The death chamber to myself, I set about removing my restraints. First, I break my right hand, crushing it until I can slide out of the cuff and mitt. This limits the dexterity of my fingers, but I'm able to wrest the keys from the dead guard's belt and unlock the rest of my shackles.

I stretch like a cat, smiling as the hive mind cheers me on. My nerves tingle with similar stories from across the country, my peers lashing out at their jailers, freeing themselves, setting each other loose upon a new world.

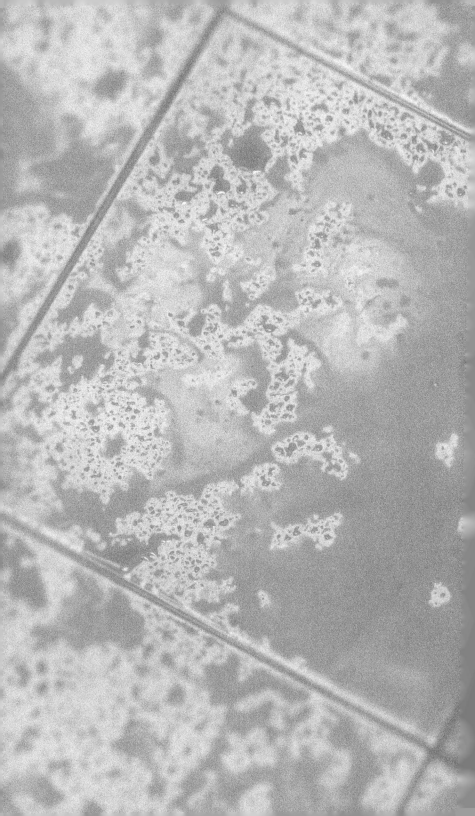

EYES OPEN, KNEES APART FOR THE END OF THE WORLD

RAE KNOWLES

Sarah was about to come when the apocalypse started.

Her abdomen clenched, mind finally free of unfolded laundry, the tone of that PR woman's email, the ingrown hair festering in her upper thigh. Her free hand gripped the blankets and her back raised from the mattress in a serpentine arch. Above the buzzing, one phrase echoed over and over in her mind: *You like that you dirty little—*

Then the shadow of a boom.

The first, they'd been told, in a series of explosions. Ringing bounced off every wall and the tile floor, or did it emanate from inside her own head? And just as the dust cloud rolled in, the mounting pressure in her core dissipated.

Her eyes shot open.

It wasn't fear that made her lurch upward to a sitting position. Sarah'd had weeks to process the looming end of days. She chucked the vibrator on the floor where it rattled around like a defunct toy, and her cheeks flushed—not with terror but with rage.

Just one more orgasm ruined by the ineptitude, the arrogance, the *audacity* of men.

One more in a long line of disappointments.

Outside, tires squealed. That bitch, Wendy—the neighbor who complained to the HOA about her driveway pavers, Sarah just knew it had been her—shrieked and ran past the bedroom window. Footsteps pounded up the path to the front door. A key scraped against the knob. *Todd. Goddammit, Todd.*

Sarah took a deep breath. Todd was to stay at the office. That was the plan. Jessica and Ashleigh (Sarah hated that spelling. *Hated* it. But Todd insisted) were to stay at school. There'd be no sense dying alone on the highway trying to get everyone home. Better to go on as normal until it wasn't. That's what they'd agreed on.

The front door creaked on its hinges.

"Honey?" Todd called from the foyer.

Sarah threw the blanket off her legs and managed to slide to the bathroom and lock herself in before Todd could make it down the hall. The vibrator still hopped around on the tile.

Buddap-buddap-bzz.

"Honey?"

Buddap-buddap-bzz.

Sarah pressed her back against the door, gathering her legs in a hug. Stubble pricked at the tender skin of her forearms.

"You in here?"

She'd considered shaving last night, but what was the point? To look sexy in her coffin? No, there'd be no coffin, no funeral. No one left to bury her.

Sarah had decided to die with hairy legs.

Buddap-buddap–

The vibrator clicked off. Sarah winced as she imagined it in Todd's meaty paws.

Beside her left eye, the knob jiggled.

"Don't come in," she said.

It jiggled harder. "Honey, what's going on? Are you alright?"

Sarah shifted, feeling the slickness between her thighs. She eyed the scissors on the bathroom counter.

"You okay? Let me in!"

Let me in. Let me in. How many times had Sarah heard that? Jessica or Ashleigh or both in chorus? How many times had she been asked, *You okay?* with a tone that said, *don't answer that.*

That bitch Wendy rounded the corner of her yard, a flash of red curls beyond the sheer curtain. She was still screaming, and the light that poured in from outside dimmed, choked by the roiling wave of dust they'd been warned was coming. Weeks of tweets and TikToks. Noise, noise, noise strangling her feeds.

"Sarah?"

Todd never used her name, not in years. At some point she'd been reduced to a pet name in exclusivity, in perpetuity, a change she never agreed to, but let pass, one of the million blinks that blended together into the long sleep that was her marriage.

"What are you doing here?" The words slipped out in place of what she'd intended, dripping with vitriol. On any other day she would've been milder, would've masked her displeasure. But not today. Not when she'd been so fucking *close*.

"I came home to..." The end of Todd's thought was replaced by an earnest thud against the door that made Sarah jump. She leapt to her feet, and wasn't sure what she was thinking when she grabbed the scissors and brandished them like a knife. Another thud knocked chips of paint from the door frame, and on the third, the hardware bent, the lock failed, and Todd came tumbling in, huffing.

Even with her back pressed to the window, Sarah knew the dust cloud had thickened from the darkness around her. Still, flecks of eggshell white speckled on Todd's alcohol-swollen cheeks, glittering in the remaining daylight. The whites of his eyes looked all the more jaundiced by comparison, and the sallow yellow bulbs widened when he noticed the weapon in Sarah's hand.

"What the fuck are you--"

"What are *you* doing?" Sarah's eyes darted to the scissors and back. Her hand was not shaking. It was perfectly still. "What are you doing here?"

"I came home to–"

"To what?!" Sarah was screaming now, but not the high pitched yelp she'd heard from Wendy, hers was a low, throaty sound.

"To catch you flicking your bean, I suppose." Todd barked a thoughtless laugh.

A beat passed. A moment in time measured by the shrinking pitch of Wendy's cries.

Sarah didn't know what she was thinking when she plunged the scissors into Todd's chest. They stayed right where she put them, those two shiny handles suspended in the air. The dark stain started small, then spread, painting Todd's baby-blue polo in a midnight winter color palette. Near-black indigo at the center bled into mulberry. Or maybe the shade was more like wine. They watched it bloom together, and the irony didn't escape Sarah that this might be the first thing they'd done as a couple since–

"What the fuck, Sarah?" Todd dropped to his knees, then let out a yowl. Old football injury, Sarah remembered. His knees were never good, and from the clapping sound they made against the faux marble tile…

"Was it too much to ask?" Sarah walked a semi circle around her sputtering husband. "To get a few goddamn hours of peace and quiet at the end of the fucking world?"

Todd's mouth opened. His tongue moved and his lips formed shapes. But no sound escaped, like an infant imitating mama.

From the doorway, Sarah spotted the vibrator: a teal stripe on the pilled, floral bedspread. "I think I want a divorce," she said without looking at him.

Todd sucked in a gurgling breath. "Crazy bitch." His too-thick hands floundered around the scissors in his chest, fingers dancing over the handles, like he thought it might be a good idea to remove them, then thought better of it, cycling over and over on repeat. Delicate flicks of his fingertips over the shiny steel, nearly a strumming motion, and Sarah had the strange thought that if Todd had been so tender with her in the bedroom, she might not have had to wait until he left to *take a quick piss* to finish herself off.

Sarah crossed the room, clutching the teal, body-safe silicone in her palm. It was heavy. When she first got it, Todd had joked she needed a license to operate that kind of heavy machinery. Sarah hadn't laughed.

When she turned back, Todd struggled to his feet. Bracing himself on the doorframe, he held himself erect. "So this is how you want it to end?" he asked, the wine-colored stain now stretching its tendrils, engulfing a good three quarters of the polo.

Sarah couldn't help but think of how many bottles of peroxide it would take to remove a stain like that. Three, at least. Her nails dug into the satiny finish of the toy. "No," she said.

Todd gestured weakly at his injury. "What do you *want?*"

"I wanted it to end in quiet."

Todd shook his head with an incredulous curl of his mouth.

"I want–" she started, but stopped when she realized that was it.

I want.

I want.

I want.

He stepped toward her.

Sarah didn't remember deciding to swing the fist holding the vibrator, but she must've, because she heard that crack of body-safe silicone against flesh, then the smack of a meaty paw against faux marble tile. She saw a teal blur, then a sliver of white bone against pink and red sinew.

Sarah didn't count how many times she hit him.

Wendy had long stopped screaming, or perhaps she was screaming still, but in someone else's yard. Sarah's shoulder got tired, and when she looked up, no more light pushed through the sheer curtain; the dust cloud brought an artificial night.

Sticky blood coated the vibrator's head, crowned by a film of gray particles that must have wriggled their way into the house through some imperceptible crack in a window. But she remembered from the packaging that it was water resistant. *Not waterproof, water resistant,* as she'd reminded herself so many times. Gingerly, she ran it beneath the faucet, digging her fingernails into the grooves until Todd's stain was thoroughly removed. Stepping over his body, she nestled herself back under the covers, her spot still warm.

Click.

More explosions were coming.

Buddap-buddap-bzz.

And Sarah let herself want.

You like that you dirty little...

You like that you dirty little...

You like that you dirty little...

ENDLESS POSSIBILITIES

RJ JOSEPH

I would hate for this to be the last thing I see if I die in my sleep.

Drea squeezed past the group taking pictures in the ship's narrow hallway, trying not to wrinkle her nose in distaste. She couldn't begrudge the tourists their desire to capture their trip in photos. What she hated with more passion than she thought she could muster at her advanced age was the gaudy, garish, glaring décor the ocean liner designers decided to foist on them all. She stumbled as the ship lurched from side to side, and lost her footing.

Even the ship was attacking her, now.

Loud colors that clashed with her sensibilities screamed from every inch of the ship. Glittery walls and accoutrements shone brightly, painfully, giving her a headache and a pain in her butt, all at once. She couldn't understand the design choices. Nothing was cohesive, and yet, nothing was purposefully abstract, either.

How could surroundings so boisterous promote relaxation? How could bulbous blobs of clownishly colored glass melded onto flat, icy glass backings promote warmth and safety? Except... she'd reached out to touch one of the blobs when they first got on the ship the previous day and it felt warm. Hot, even. Startled, she snatched her hand back when she thought it moved beneath her hand.

"Cedric? Do you see these?"

"What are you talking about?" Her husband was already walking far ahead of her, straight towards the bar in the middle of the entryway. She looked around at her fellow passengers. No one else was examining the decorations. They weren't touching the glass.

The glass wasn't touching them.

She dismissed the sensation, chalking it up to having been herded onto the trip in the first place by the man she already knew she no longer wanted to stay married to, despite their ongoing twenty-five-year marriage.

Not for much longer.

Drea ground her teeth and groaned. The incessant, unsettling hum she'd been hearing since boarding continued to plague her. It reminded her of electricity but louder and more grating. She'd always loved thunderstorms and felt invigorated by the electricity in the air. This hum didn't give her that same comfort.

It hurt.

She rubbed her temples. She'd ask a staff member about it as soon as she found one. The phone in their cabin didn't work and she needed to report that, as well. The vessel made another sudden pitch and her last meal threatened to move upwards from her stomach. The water had been rough since embarkation, and it was getting worse the further out they traveled. Drea had never been on a ship before, and she worried she'd never get her sea legs. Not that she wanted them if it meant more of this extraneous movement.

A resonant voice came over the loudspeaker as she tentatively made her way further along the hallway, holding on to the doorways for stability.

"This is your ship's captain speaking. The water is unexpectedly rough and we advise all passengers to safely and in an orderly manner, retire early to your cabins. We will expand the room service offerings, but request that you only place necessary orders, for the safety of our crew. We apologize for any inconvenience this may cause and are working with the cruise line to process vouchers for missed excursions tomorrow and an inconvenience restitution. We will keep you posted on travel conditions throughout the evening."

* * *

THAT CEDRIC WOULD CHOOSE SUCH a tacky and boisterous setting for what he was dramatically calling their "Reawakening as a Couple" was just like him. He held these grand ideas about everything and lived for drama and appearances. Their marriage was no different—all show, no substance. She'd bought into his charming showmanship when they were dating and during the early years of their marriage, back when she had been so in love. She would have followed him anywhere.

She literally had followed him anywhere—everywhere. When he'd declared he wanted to be an actor and that he had the magic formula to guaranteed success, she'd packed up their beloved Texas cottage and unpacked in the tiny apartment in Los Angeles that followed. He worked at becoming the next best thing in Hollywood for a whole two years. Then, a more earnest—according to Cedric—endeavor called to his soul from Wall Street in New York city. They picked up and moved again, that time to a drafty, old apartment half the size of the apartment in LA. It always smelled of tobacco and smoke from the cigar shop they lived two stories above.

Drea stayed in and out of the hospital, her asthma getting exponentially worse with the drafts and the smoke exacerbating it. Medical bills ate up most of the financial gains they could have made. But it didn't help that Cedric never brought in the kind of money he claimed was theirs for the taking. By then, she'd begun to question his plans for their family.

"When will we be settled, Cedric?"

"This ain't about you changing your mind about having a baby, is it?" He liked to answer her questions with questions of his own. It was an admirable trait for a finance guy or a salesperson or an entertainer. It was a terrible attribute for a husband.

"No, I still don't want kids. But do we have to have kids to be stable? To stay in one place long enough to put down real roots?" She had been hopeful then. Still loved her husband and the prospect of spending the rest of her life with him.

"Maybe we should have a kid. You can't get a job. I don't want you to work, anyway. Maybe you need something to do while I'm out hustling. I'm gonna hit it big. I know it."

"I have plenty to do with constantly packing and unpacking. What I need is a chance to make a real home for us."

For me.

"It'll come. Just stick with me." He brought her chin up so her eyes met his and placed a confident kiss on her lips.

That was the first time his kiss failed to warm her the way it always had. It wasn't the last.

Drea sighed. She'd stuck with him, always, up to then. They stayed in New York for three years, her health growing much worse before Cedric announced they were moving to Chicago. That lasted six years before he uprooted them yet again. They landed back in the South, in New Orleans. Drea fell in love with the row house he'd purchased for them. For the first time ever, she planted a garden and the citrus trees she'd always longed for. She hummed as she painted the walls and learned how to perform minor renovations. Driving up to their home after she returned from errands brought her immense pride.

Finally home.

Cedric seemed to lean into his role as the safety manager for one of the local chemical plants. He talked incessantly about his earning potential and what they'd do with all the money. She was happy for him. For them. As they passed year seven there, she'd begun to feel like she just might be able to love her husband again. Drea couldn't put her finger on when, exactly, she had fallen out of love and begun to stew in the resentment of being unheard and unattended-to for years. Maybe they would be okay after all.

Then Cedric flew into their wonderful little home with that unholy glisten in his eyes that she recognized as wanderlust. She tensed up on the couch where she sat, slamming her teacup down on the coffee table a bit harder than she'd planned.

Cedric didn't flinch. He was in his own little world, as always. "Babe, I have the best news!" He prattled on and on about Oregon, something. West coast, another thing. Before he stopped his animated soliloquy, Drea interrupted.

"I'm not moving again."

His lips continued to move until she yelled.

"I'm not moving!"

Cedric finally broke from his self-focused litany and looked at her then, as if she had sprouted an additional head. "What's wrong with you?"

His confusion might have been endearing if it hadn't been his default for the past few years. Cluelessness in a middle-aged man with responsibilities was ultimately a bad thing.

She stood up. "I'm sick and tired of you not listening to me. You never ask me what I want, what I need. You've done this our whole marriage and I'm over it."

They stood in the living room, staring at each other. Cedric finally lowered his gaze. She refused to back down. His shoulders slumped and he walked slowly to their bedroom. That night, she slept in the guest bedroom.

When she awakened the next morning, Cedric was gone. He left a note indicating he was moving to Oregon and they could have a long-distance marriage. He promised to continue paying the bills at their home and would visit every few months.

Drea accepted the arrangement for what it was. He wasn't abandoning her, but she was already one foot out the door on their marriage.

She used the time he spent away from home to enroll in law school. There weren't many jobs she could perform that her debilitating asthma would allow, but as a lawyer, she could set her own hours and still earn a living wage. She had also developed a burning desire to help women in divorce proceedings get fair outcomes. The training would provide useful for when she instigated her own divorce.

Drea understood Cedric's financial assistance could run out as soon as he got a wild hair to do something else with himself. She was under no delusions that he would ever come back to their home. And she was fine with that. But she couldn't yet support herself, so she worked extra hard to get done with her degree as quickly as possible.

The right time to tell Cedric about the divorce hadn't come in the three years since he'd moved away. She'd just graduated from the program and already had a job with a local firm lined up. She wanted to tell him, wanted to finally start her own life, her own way.

I will tell him soon.

Before she knew it, he'd breezed into town, pushed her to pack a suitcase and medications for a week, and gotten her into the car.

"We're going on a trip."

"This will be a new beginning for us."

"It'll only be a week."

"It'll be fun."

Drea went along with him. She hadn't been on a trip in years and she did want to celebrate her recent accomplishments, even if she wasn't yet ready to share them with Cedric. Until they pulled up at the port and parked, she'd entertained fleeting thoughts—wishes?—that he'd chosen somewhere fun, something she would enjoy, for them to do.

Then, reality hit. He had never taken her wants or needs into consideration before. The trip was more of the same old same.

* * *

NOW SHE WAS STUCK in the middle of the ocean with crowds of strangers, surrounded by dangerously rough waters and under quarantine. She had already gingerly made it to the main foyer on their floor and felt her way along the glass walls enclosing the elevators. Drea would follow the captain's orders and return to her room but she wanted to get a staff member and tell them about their phone first. She had asked Cedric to tell someone when he headed out earlier that evening, but she knew he wouldn't remember. She'd have to take care of it herself, like always.

Her stabilizing hand on the wall began to move. Drea used her other hand to place it against the same wall, to prevent her impending fall. Except she wasn't falling. She held her breath for the few seconds her impaired lungs would allow and tried to focus. How long had she been out of her room? Four minutes? Five? It seemed like forever and the pain inside her head grew until it throbbed in time with the pulsating blobs that covered every glass surface on the ship.

The ones underneath her hands grew warmer and melted until they ran down the glass, covering her palms. She wanted to scream but she couldn't. People swarmed around her, running back to their rooms. No one else touched the walls.

No one touched or looked at the ceilings, either, where more colored glass protrusions slid from their flat anchorings, dripping in her direction.

Drea staggered back towards her cabin, stabilized by the throngs of passengers congesting the small hallways. She shook her hands and the molten glass remained. Its counterparts continued their singular journey towards her.

"Help me. Please. Do you see this?" None of her fellow shipmates answered her. No one looked at her.

By the time she made it back to her room, she had to hold onto the bolted down furniture to keep from falling. The glass never left her palms, even when she slammed them against the wooden surfaces.

The hum grew louder until it was a low-timbered roar, reverberating deep in her belly. She watched the agitated waves cresting higher and higher alongside the ship, for as far away as she could see them.

Something is terribly and irrevocably wrong.

Drea made her way to the balcony door and used her knees to help her open the door that threatened to slam shut on her in the strong winds. The glass on her palms ran down her forearms, covering her skin in its warmth.

I don't want to die. I haven't lived yet.

She pressed herself against the balcony door, gripping the supporting posts to stand as straight as she could. Drea had lived her whole life being scared. Scared to trigger her asthma. Scared to decline Cedric's marriage proposal. Scared to leave when she no longer loved him.

I won't be afraid anymore.

She couldn't feel the tears on her face in the onslaught of saltwater splashing from the ocean, drenching everything. The colored glass soon covered her shoulders. She looked down at the floor of the balcony as other colors flowed onto her feet, up her legs. The warmth cocooned her, eased her breathing. Drea should have been wheezing with panic, but she'd never breathed more steadily in her life.

Underneath the waves, a large, luminous orb reflected the light of the full moon. Something gargantuan, something ancient, broke the hostile surface of the ocean and emerged, scale by scale, tentacles writhing; her mind had no reference for what she witnessed.

"You can remain." None of these discordant voices were her own. They were a sonorous chorus coming from the glass covering her body.

"Accept the one true god."

"You are chosen."

Drea met the emergent eye with her own gaze, the only thing left uncovered by the glass. The ship bucked, leaning almost horizontally in the water. The god held her stare. The roar faded out as her ears filled.

"Accept us."

"Live again."

"Live forever."

The body continued to rise from the ocean, turning the ship over yet again.

"I accept." Drea had previously accepted far less for herself. She embraced the offering of something that couldn't possibly be as restrictive as her life had been to that point.

Forever home.

Drea's last cognizant thought before the glass covered her eyes was relief at the exaltation her spirit engaged in with the substance and deity to whom she acquiesced. She rose, past the height of the divine being, past the full moon, past the stars—into the beyond of endless possibilities.

THE SMELL OF SUMMER

EMMA E. MURRAY

A stripe of sunlight wakes me, falling over my eyes and making me sneeze. My bladder is bursting. Stomach is rumbling. Time to get up. Time to run. Run, run, run upstairs to Mom and Dad's room. I whine at the door, scratch gently with my paw. Come on, come on. What's taking so long? I scratch again, just a little louder. Gotta be good.

Then, from under the door, a smell. I bend down, force my nose as far through the crack as I can, and sniff, sniff, sniff.

No.

My heart jumps and I jump with it, all feet off the ground for a second, banging my nose on the edge of the door as I pull it out abruptly.

No.

I bend down again, a whimper trembling through my whole body before traveling up and out my throat as a frightened bark. Bark, bark, bark! No, *that* smell. So much like the squirrel on the road, flattened by a truck, brains splattered across the pavement that I almost got to taste before Mom yanked me away. So much like the bird I caught in the yard and crunched between my jaws, hot blood leaking down my lips, mixing with strands of drool. Sister was so scared when she saw me, and Dad had forced it from my mouth with a stick. *That* smell. Dead, death, glazed eyes, still blood. *No.* Why does it smell like *that?*

I inhale again and again as my voice alternates between squeaky whines and my lowest bellowing bark, but they don't open the door. Their feet don't pad across the carpet. They don't snore. Not a single breath or heartbeat, even when I press my ear to the door as hard as I can. *No, can't be.* Gotta get Sister. She'll know what to do. She'll fix it.

I bound down the hall to her bedroom. The door's wide open, but she's not there. *Sister?* I bark and put my nose high in the air, lift my ears. No sound, but I catch a whiff of something and follow it to the bathroom. The same smell waits there, fetid and pungent. I rub my nose on the carpet and cover my eyes.

I scratch at the door. *Sister? Open up Sister. I want to see you even if you smell like dead things.* There's no answer. My heart is pounding. I don't know what to do.

I run to the backdoor and jump at the lever handle again and again. Gotta get out. Don't want to get in trouble with an accident. Mom doesn't like when I open the backdoor, but she hates accidents more. I want to make her happy. Make her proud of me. I rear up on my back feet and paw the handle. Come on! Please, please, please, I pant with every leap, and then I catch it just right and the door opens enough for me to push my snout through and get into the backyard.

Run, run, run.

I frantically sniff and then there's the spot. On the big tree in the corner. Ahh, relief. When I'm done, I scratch at the ground and snort, looking back at the quiet house. No lights on. Not a sound. Only that smell. That bad, bad smell. Don't want to think about it. No, not Mom and Dad. Not Sister. I love them. I bark at the house. *Wake up! Wake up!* But it won't work. I know from the squirrel and bird and other small deaths I've seen; you don't wake up. Though these are different. The sick scent lingers. There isn't the bright, violent smell of the others. My family stinks of a cold emptiness I've never smelled before, but still laced with sour death. I cower and a dribble of urine I didn't know was still in me runs down my leg, my tail pulled up under me. I bark again. I don't know what to do.

Then it hits me. The whole world is quiet. The morning sounds are disturbingly absent for the sun to be this high. No children laughing and screaming while they wait for the bus. No car doors closing and tires on the road. No babies crying so loud I hear them through their thick walls. No smell of simmering bacon and eggs and pancakes through open windows. No scent of packed lunches or aftershave or perfume or dirty socks shoved in leather shoes wafting through the air.

The only sounds are the morning birds, a few dogs barking in their yards, longing to go in to their families, and a few muffled sounds behind doors of dogs like me, needing to go out.

What is happening?

My stomach flips and I gag but nothing comes out. I haven't eaten since yesterday morning and my stomach is just a bag of air and acid. Mom and Dad were too sick to come downstairs and fill my bowl, or even make their own dinner, so there were no scraps given under the table from Dad and Sister's salty hands, licked clean while they smiled.

So hungry. Gotta eat.

I go back inside, pace the kitchen, but there's nothing I can get. It's all locked behind metal and wooden doors. I whine and roll on my back, tongue hanging over my lips as I salivate at the fridge door. There's a feast in there. Four-day-old meatloaf, a chunk of ground turkey, a soggy cardboard box of greasy noodles, carrots, chicken, and water chestnuts. I want it, I want it, *I want it*! But I stand up. There's no getting it. Not now, with *that* smell upstairs. I cry again, for myself and for Mom and Dad and Sister. *Wake up!* I shout up the stairs, but only silence answers me.

Back outside I run, run, run along the fence then I see the pile of loose dirt Dad lazily pushed back into the hole I dug. It's easy enough to dig it up again and squeeze, squeeze, squeeze through. The bottom of the fence drags along my back and digs into fur, but then I'm out.

I'm free. I look at the quiet house again. I miss them, but my stomach growls and commands I find food, so I reluctantly start down the sidewalk, the route I know by heart. I always walk here with Dad in the mornings and Mom at night.

The eerie quiet of the neighborhood brings a shudder down my spine but I shake it away. I raise my nose in the air and there's a wild wet in the air. Rain's on the way. I take in a deep breath, trying to find any clue of what's going on, but all I find is the faintest smell of death, human death, so many bodies, mixed together and carried on the wind. My lungs exhale in a long, painful whine. I pull my tail between my legs again and hurry along.

Something moves in a window and I turn to look. It's only a cat—but there's something on its face, smeared red and syrupy thick.

No. Not that.

I pick up my pace, sprinting along my usual route, avoiding the gaze of other cats in the windows as they stare out at me.

When I reach the end of the street, I stop. Wait. I'm not supposed to cross without permission. Three quick barks and a low whine, but there's no people to tell me it's okay. I hold my breath and run across as fast as I can, guilt boiling through me, sending waves of itching through my fur. I slow down, scratching and biting at my legs and over my shoulder, trying to find some relief. Then I hear something through the door of the house to my left.

Walking closer to investigate, I quickly recognize it as the high-pitched yammer of a small-breed, her voice softened and hoarse from barking for help for who knows how long. I answer and wag my tail despite knowing she can't see. She needs help. I can smell her desperation, frenzy, and puddle of stale, frightened urine creeping through the keyhole.

When she hears me, her tone turns to a yelp, the register so high it rings in my eardrums. I want her to stop. Jump, jump, jump, I bat at the door handle with my paws, but it's round and slippery. It won't budge.

I stand up high, dig my claws deep into the green paint and pull them down, leaving a long furrow down the door. I whimper, press my head against the door. I want to help her, but I don't know how. If only Mom was here. She'd let her out. Make sure she had food. Food for both of us. My stomach rumbles again, and I know I have to leave. There's nothing else I can do. I try my best to ignore her panicked yelps as I run away, but they follow after me to the end of the street, the ghost of them lodged in my ears even after she's well out of range.

The farther I go, the more I hear noises beyond the quiet. Dogs trapped in houses, trapped in yards, tied to stakes, chained to steadfast anchors, crying for help, food, freedom. This can't be real. I need Mom's warm lap. I need Dad's belly rubs. I need Sister's sneaked treats and a welcome scritch behind my ear.

Come back, I bark into the wind, to no one.

A few others have gotten loose like me, but they run as soon as they see me, skittish little ones mainly, so I ignore them, keep going. The more my stomach rumbles, the sharper my sense of smell becomes, and finally I pick up the scent of something edible. Something good.

But as I get closer to the smell, revealed to be a bag of garbage, torn open and strewn across the yard and street, another smell lingers just under it. I'm too hungry to care, ignoring the underscent and digging my face into the smorgasbord of discarded people food. Search and swallow, search and swallow, I repeat this until I've had my fill of jelly-smeared crusts, cheese rind, baked beans, and clumps of peach cobbler. I'm licking sauce from my chops when I notice the sickly underscent again.

No, no, no.

My skin crawls, but I have to investigate. It's so close and fully fragrant, like it's out in the open to be seen, nuzzled with a sad whine or ripped open like a trash bag. I shake that thought away.

There. An open car door. A hand, an arm. I approach, tail tucked and teeth bared. The growl is insuppressible, instinct ruling me just beyond curiosity. The man hangs out of the open car door, his skin waxy and eyes vacantly staring at me. I bark. He doesn't move.

Because he's dead. With a whine, I nudge his dangling hand but it doesn't respond. Only swings a little then hangs as still as before. A buzzard circles overhead, waiting for me to leave so he can find the tender bits, but I don't want to leave the man.

The people are gone. Dead. Death. Illness. I smell it on him, just like how Mom, Dad, and Sister smelled as they coughed and got sicker over the last many days. The smell of copper, decay, solidified vomit, sludge, mucous, death. I sit on my haunches and crane my neck, letting out the loudest, longest howl I can muster. A final funeral dirge for the people.

I loved them. I miss them.

I lay near the car, watching the sun move across the sky, the bird still circling above us, others joining in, all waiting for my exit. After a long time, I get up and leave.

I've never felt so lost in my life, wandering aimlessly down this street and that. *What will I do now?* I'm alone, scared, trembling, aching. My stomach churns with grief and I feel like giving up.

Then, there's a dog in the street ahead of me. A big dog, like me. Just standing in the open middle between cars parked along the curb, as if it wasn't against the rules. I stop. My tail wags tentatively, head cocks to the side, waiting to be acknowledged. He doesn't look up, he's too busy sniffing at a crumpled fast-food bag, nose deep in the fried smell. I bark, a quick, cheerful greeting, and he finally looks up. We stare for a moment then I see his tail move and his mouth open, tongue lolling out. He gestures to join him, and I hesitate. *What about Mom and Dad and Sister?* Then I remember the smell and shake my head, bringing it low and rubbing the pads of my paw over my left eye, trying to erase the olfactory memory burned into my brain.

He gestures again, leaps with a dancer's grace, and I can't resist any longer. I'm running with him, running down the road with no worries of cars or people. Something deep down calls to me, something that tumbles with abandon, bites and claws, pisses where it wants, and doesn't worry about any rules. We turn a corner and there's more dogs running together, six big, strong dogs just like us. We fly over the ground, catching up, joining them.

We'll soon be out of here and forget it all. I bark and they join me, running as hard and fast as we can, never to go home again. I'm not afraid anymore when we move as a pack down the road, following the smell of cattle, forests, wild rabbits, and deer on the wind.

MUERTE LUNA

V. CASTRO

I smelled the blood on their bodies and discharged weapons. We tracked the hunters this far then slaughtered them before leaving them for the others out for our pelts. They couldn't hide for long. Poor bastards didn't know how. But we did. Strobes of light zig-zagged across the sky above the trees.

It was the first day of all out war.

Schools and businesses closed. Hospitals were at capacity, many boarded up to prevent intruders and even those seeking treatment. Every building where they attempted to hide was burned to the ground. It could be sunrise or sunset with the brightness of the flames coloring the atmosphere.

Unlike them, we were fast, and strong. We could survive longer without food or water with highly evolved metabolisms. And we'd finally had enough.

For centuries, we tried to live peacefully with the humans. But no matter how hard we attempted to stay in the trees and reserved spaces, they wanted their trophies. Big game hunting was small-time compared to bagging the head of a wolf, or multiple wolves. Many clans were brought to the point of extinction. Little Red Riding Hood was the first known piece of propaganda.

Nelly, my best friend, was only half human at this point. Her fur and teeth had sprouted in reaction to seeing so many of us dead. This was the end of it all.

My lips were dry from over-feeding. As clan leader I told everyone we were only out for kills, no new transformations, yet. That would be Phase Two if any survived. "You alright, Nelly?"

She nodded ,her tongue running the length of her blood stained teeth. She couldn't speak words in this state, but she understood.

"We have to make it to city hall. This town will be officially declared ours when we pull down their flag and raise our own. Every city across the country will have the same outcome. No more living in fear. Now don't get fucking killed, bitch. Jorge should have cleared the entrance. Small towns are good for something."

My mind wandered to the news from the cities. Longer to take, but the would all fall. Humans had a penchant for their own destruction. We lit the match, they would keep the fire going as food ran low and desperation kicked in. Wolves would heel for the final days.

I cracked my neck with the flag tied around it. The flag would be ripped to shreds when I transformed if I tried to wrap it around my waist. This was better. I looked like a superhero with a cape. My chest hitched and the pain of a thousand needles injected all at once seared my skin. My hair grew longer as did the muscle and sinew around my bones, joints popping out of their sockets. But the pain was nothing compared to the freedom I felt in my natural state. I dropped to the dirt and howled. Those already at city hall howled back. It was time.

Nelly and I ran at full speed through the trees that would lead to the most dangerous point, the streets. Many times Nelly and I walked through here in our human forms, eating ice cream as we plotted this night. How would we avoid getting shot? Where could we go for cover? How long would it take us to do this running as man eating wolves? On the coldest and typically darkest night of the year, when we were sure most people would be inside, we practiced. Five minutes. We had to run for five minutes with the sole purpose to make it to city hall. There would be others to make sure it was no longer fortified and we could break in with ease. But we couldn't guarantee anything. We would be prepared.

Nelly and I weaved around abandoned cars. Shots rang out as we suspected. No time to look or stop. Just run. But I knew is this world of fear had come to end. We stopped thinking of the world we hoped for and decided to make it so.

That meant an absolute end to humankind as we knew it.

To my left, growls and a yelp. Human screams mixed with snarls echoed. We were being followed in the shadows.

I would forever be grateful to those who fought with valor.

The ice cream shop was in sight which meant city hall was not far off. Police cars burned. Bodies stank of early decay. Jorge did his job. All humans left alive locked themselves in when the alarm rang, including the mayor. The police and the few loyal citizens trying to protect it lay dead in pools of their own blood.

We slowed our approach. I could smell my clan. The City Hall parking lot looked like an abattoir of both wolf and human. We knew there would be heavy casualties. All wars have a price. So did the end of one world before another began.

We burst through the chained doors and slinked through the front hall on all fours. A photo hung on the wall of Mayor Deane standing next to a dead wolf strung up by his feet. Nelly growled. He would be next and probably knew it by now.

I stopped and allowed my heart to slow. I focused on my human form, vocal chords, thoughts of hot dogs and popcorn. Muscles shrank and joints popped into place.

What would these pearl clutchers think of my nudity with a very large Nelly in her true wolf form? I stroked her fur.

"Time to take it all."

We made our way down the long corridor. The stench of human sweat filled my nostrils. Some of them cried, others tried their phones, hoping to reach loved ones. A radio played the news on low volume. It was a recorded message of what to do. No, we didn't die from silver, so forks and knives were indeed useless for stabbing.

I looked at Nelly, "1…2…3!"

She ran full speed and knocked open the double doors of the main conference room. Furniture piled high against the doors flew in all directions, hitting a few of those sat in the center.

The Mayor at the back of the room held a shotgun. "Stay back, dogs!"

"No." I said with a calm smile. Nobody else had a gun or attempted to fight back. They looked like a cowering litter of pups.

He pulled the trigger, but his heart rate had already alerted me he was about to move. My legs carried me faster than his shaky aim. The ten other humans screamed. He fired again, but Nelly and I ran circles around him until he was out of ammunition. He threw the gun down and put his hands up. With brutal honesty in his eyes he asked, "Why?"

Ignorance truly is bliss.

"Why did you hunt us?" I threw back.

His eyes glanced over at Nelly, then ran the length of my body. "You're unnatural. Not real humans. And you eat us."

"Control. But tonight will forever be known as Muerte Luna." I growled.

Nelly let out a howl. With a deafening crash, our clan burst through the windows. Glass sprayed across the room like blood from a dying man's neck. They wasted no time devouring the remaining humans.

I walked outside again feeling a deep sense of relief and stood before the flagpole. Years I'd waited for this moment. My dreams and future hinged on the success of this plan because there was no telling when my world would end.

I'd live near the coast after this. Something I always wanted.

Without care, I took down one flag and replaced it with another. A white background with the image of a full moon was our signal for the end. Followed by a beginning. It looked wonderful. It didn't mean allegiance to one party or group or even country. It meant victory over our pain and perseverance to survive. Something universal, but humans wanted homogeny, everyone to be the same without dissent. That was unnatural. Felt bad for them. We didn't hate humans or even want to kill them all. Yet, they wanted that for us.

B we knew in our souls—the souls they said we didn't have—that this day would come. We built our numbers and our ranks. Those from loyal families raised their young to live mostly human lives and infiltrate the human world in the highest places. Those in board rooms, presidential offices, the military, leaders across governments were all changing, leaving no survivors.

It wouldn't happen overnight, or beneath a single full moon, but the end of the world of humans had come.

Praise be Muerte Luna and her bloody gift of transformation.

LOST TIME

EÓIN MURPHY

You're sitting at your desk. The office is quiet—it is a Saturday afternoon after all. There's a couple of junior consultants at the back of the room, talking to each other when they should be catching up with work, but you remember what it was like when you were that age. There was always more time.

Noise echoes from around the corner, a murmuration of accountants working through papers as the tax year draws to a close.

You can't hear any of this. You have earphones in, the familiar roar of heavy metal from a lifetime ago drowning out the silence of the office. The scream of the music brings you back to when you were young and had all your hair, when your back didn't ache from even thinking about venturing into a mosh pit.

For a moment the spreadsheet wavers, a little wobble from eyes that have been fixed on one thing for too long. There is a slight pulse of pain in the middle of your head, a promise of the headache that will come later in the day, probably strong enough to steal whatever sleep the stress was happy to leave you with. More time to get the report done, you think, almost happy with the thought of having more time to work.

Cassie won't be pleased but you have leave coming up at the end of the month and you can all head away for a few days. The only work you'll have to do then will be playing with the kids and trying not to spend all your time sleeping. You might even get a couple of hours free to work on the Knockdoman tender. Cassie won't mind. And if anything comes up there won't be any need to go into the office, they can always get you on your phone.

But still. You know you're getting tired and that it's time for a break. Go to the toilet, get a coffee and another chocolate bar from the vending machine. Take five minutes to regroup and then another burst of work should see the report ready to go up the line for approval no later than five or six. Then you can head home, have dinner and maybe spend an hour or two reading through the juniors' work to make sure they've got everything covered.

You stand, a hollow ache running down your lower back that almost has you moan in pain. You pop out the headphones, leaving your phone on the desk and locking your desktop screen. A dull glow filters into the office, the third floor not high enough to do anything but catch glimpses of light from outside, the other buildings greedily eating it in for themselves, leaving the lower floors in shadow. You can't see the ground from where you stand, just red bricks and grey cladding. Light reflections from the windows opposite are such that the vague shadow of desks might be its interior or a reflection of this one. You think you can see a figure in the other building, some other office thrall in on their day off in order to catch up with work that will never end. You raise your hand and give them a slow wave but it's too dark to see if they respond, their torso cut off into darkness so all you can see is their legs.

You smile at your own silliness and go to the bathroom. When you come out, looking at your watch and calculating how much time you need to add to your charge sheet, you see that the juniors are gone, stale cups of coffee still sitting on their desks, and papers scattered across the surface. You sigh. The younger ones don't grasp the concept of information security, or even what a clean desk policy is. You make a mental note to bring it up with them tomorrow, as well as the need to show clear dedication to the company. Yes, they need to work long hours, but do it for long enough and you'll be recognised and promoted. Get your own office and your own staff, the grind of working at weekends replaced with dinners with clients and trips to international offices where you can focus on the strategies and policies, not the minutiae of cash flows and net present costs.

You push down the little traitorous voice that points out you've been there ten years and all you have for it is a promise that in the next promotion phase they'll consider you for senior consultant.

The kitchen is a mess. The accountants have clearly not bothered cleaning up after themselves and when you stick your head into their section you see that most of them have bolted, the only people still there a couple who have their heads together, clutching at each other.

You think about saying something, that this is not the place for trysts, it's an office, but then you check yourself and find you just don't care. Then you realise that the couple is Sam and Monica, two women that you know for a fact are married to other people and that Sam is at least two pay grades above you. Monica is crying, her shoulders heaving even as they kiss. Your self-preservation kicks in and you walk away, filing the sight away as something you can share at the next Christmas party, a little bit of gossip to hand out or hold in reserve, just in case you need it. So you get yourself a chocolate bar and a coffee and return to your desk.

Before you unlock your computer you take a quick look at your phone.

When you got in this morning at ten you set it to Do Not Disturb, put on your favourites list and then placed it face down, so even the flash of a notification on the screen wouldn't distract you.

Giving in to the temptation you lift it and unlock the screen. There are a deluge of messages and missed calls.

Your stomach twists, your first thought that something has

happened with the draft you sent through earlier today, that Thompson had found a massive error and was ringing to bawl you out. That instead of getting home at six it would be another all nighter of fixing problems that don't really exist but which gave Thompson that little bit of power that he loves to wield.

But it's not. The calls are from Cassie, your mother, your brother in Essex, one of the kids has even rung you. Text messages fill the screen, and over it all is a notification telling you to take shelter.

You click on it and it tells you, in a bland and matter of fact way, that a launch has been detected. That the missiles will hit in twenty minutes. But the message is ten minutes old and now you only have ten minutes left.

It can't be true though. This isn't the nineteen eighties, with public service films terrifying you about what to do if missiles are fired, and iodine tablets sent through the post, little booklets showing you how to build a shelter with doors and mattresses.

Yes there were problems in Eastern Europe, and there was that whole Taiwan thing the news kept going on about, but no one was stupid enough to launch nukes these days, were they?

There's a voice mail from Cassie. She's crying, demanding that you pick up, that the kids are scared, get home, now! That she loves you, that she's sorry, that she'll see you soon. In the background you can hear Abbey asking when is Dad coming home and the soft wail of Alex crying, the baby complaining to the world that he was hungry, or tired or bored.

Then texts, where are you? I LOVE YOU. this can't be real. COME HOME. Shelter in place. It's another hoax, isn't it? Call MUM!!

You ring Cassie. The phone bleeps a dead tone, the network gone, the signal lost. It's eleven minutes since the warning.

You stand, packing your laptop and grabbing papers and shoving them into your bag. You have to get home, the laptop sits weird and you shove at it, its stuck on a cable and you know home is an hour away on the train and that you didn't drive today because its such a faff, and fuel prices are so high and you know you're not going to make it and why the hell have you packed your laptop, you hate this fucking thing, you hate this job, you only started because you couldn't think of anything else to do and ten years later your body aches and your hair is gone and your head hurts ALL THE DAMN TIME. And you know Cassie loves you and you love her and the kids but you've seen that look in her eye that makes you think that maybe she's tired of the late evenings and the missed events and that soon, maybe not this year or next but that she'll give you an ultimatum and you're afraid that you'll pick the wrong answer because you've given up so much how could you give up on the job now?

A wail starts outside in the street as you rip the laptop from the bag and hurl it against the glass. The window spiderwebs and the laptop hits the ground, not even damaged and you stop, chest heaving, tears in your eyes.

You place your hand to your face and sob.

It's too far to get home. You could go downstairs, to the basement, but you're in a major city and you know it'll take a direct hit, they said as much on the news the other week, one of the few broadcasts you were able to catch, Cassie pulling Abby closer to her and giving you a fearful look. You said it would be fine, remember? That it would never come to that, but they were just words and it was not that you didn't believe them or just saying them to comfort her. They were automatic, you didn't even think as you spoke, more concerned with responding to an email from Thompson about some numbers that didn't add up.

You go and stand by the window, phone held in your hand and look down at the street. The glass is thick and soundproofed so you can't hear the panic but you can see it. Cars have rammed each other in the street and people run everywhere. The homeless man that sits in the theatre alcove each day until it opens watches the panic with confusion, making himself small and tucked in against the wall to avoid the fleeing masses.

A woman falls near him and he goes to help her up but in seconds she is gone, trampled by a scattering of shop workers. When they pass by you can see she's still alive and the man goes to her, pulling her into the alcove and talking to her.

Families charge back and forth, their big trip to the city for shopping and a nice lunch gone in a moment, parents desperate to find somewhere safe.

But there is nowhere safe.

You slump to the floor, still not sure this is real, that it's just a joke or a mistake and that soon another message will come through to say that the first one was sent in error, but there are three minutes left and no sign of anything. You rock back and forth, taking deep breaths and thinking about how you should have just stayed in bed this morning, wrapped in the duvet, with your spouse beside you and the kids burbling away downstairs. But you got up instead, in to do some work, all so that in the future you could carve out some time for them.

The seconds pass, each one precious, a little moment to be savoured of what was before what is to come. You remember those pamphlets from when you were a child, reading them with a sort of delighted horror. You know there's no point in running. If one hits the city, and it will, then you're dead. Even if you go to the basement, you'll just be killed by rubble or radiation, the wall of fire that will inevitably come, burning you away in seconds.

You push the thought away but you know. They're fifteen miles away. The blast won't kill them, and if they hide inside and cover their eyes and stay away from windows, they shouldn't be blinded by the blast or hit by debris. They'll live. But then the fallout will come, clouds of radioactive dust. Tomorrow was shopping day, there isn't much food in the house, so Cassie will have to go out or face starving. The radiation will be everywhere. Toxic dust that gets into your lungs and eyes and ears. The burnt up remnants of cities and people.

As it reaches the final minute you stand and face the window, knowing that you have the small mercy of a quick death and you lie to yourself that they'll be fine. The blast won't reach them, the fallout won't be that bad and after a few weeks of hardship the government will rescue them and the kids will grow up and Cassie will find someone who will treat her right and you won't have to be guilty.

As the world flashes into white, in the moment before the glass shatters and you turn to ash, you give up on the lie, at last, and let the guilt consume you, that you, having spent so long ignoring your family, will have the good death.

And that they will not.

ALL THE DEAD ASTRONAUTS

J.A.W. MCCARTHY

When the news first breaks, Kira stands with the tongs in her hand for a full thirty seconds. She doesn't hear the customer's words go from concerned to irate. She doesn't flinch when he grabs the donut dangling from the tongs going slack in her grip. The morning anchor's words throb inside her head: "Asteroid. Cataclysmic." The anchor starts to sob, but no one in the bakery is looking at the TV overhead. Customers make frustrated grunts and throw up their hands when Kira finally regains control of her body and walks out from behind the counter, leaving the pastry case open and the lattes unmade. Someone barks an annoyed "hey!" as she goes to grab her leather jacket—the one she saved up for for nearly a year—but she pivots towards the door instead. It's no longer an *if* or a *when?* She's nothing like our father, who was always the last to leave the office. She's nothing like our mother, who would've made sure everyone was fed and happy before she tended to her own needs. Kira's always been more like me.

"You saw?" she says to me once we meet on the sidewalk. "Did you know?"

"I only know what you know." I fall into her rhythm as she marches ahead. She's always been a fast walker. "I swear," I add when she raises an eyebrow. "I'm not privy to stuff like this. They don't tell us ahead of time."

"They didn't tell you it's about to get real fucking crowded up there?" She laughs wryly. "Unless there really is a hell?"

We cut through the busy street, throngs of people hurrying to work, focused on their phones and their coffees like any other day. Cars obey traffic signals. Jaywalkers scurry towards bus stops and coffee shops. Only one young man stops abruptly in the middle of the sidewalk, eyes wide as he stares at his phone screen. Up ahead, two women hold each other, crying. Then, as we get closer to our home, a middle-aged man sits in his parked car, face buried in his hands. After that, chaos unfurls. Crying, screaming, phones waving as strangers turn to each other in fear and disbelief. They're like dominoes, a wobble in the beginning, a person-by-person shift as the news spreads, then an all-at-once collapse of humanity as the news sinks in.

Belief and acceptance burst through the usual propriety, leaving behind leather jackets and donuts and responsibilities and reputations. Like Kira, we all want to be at home in our sweatpants, barricaded behind the safety of the people and things we love.

"They said twenty-four hours, maybe less," she says, sweeping into the apartment. Her fingers twitch with the urge to turn the lock, but she stops herself. Instead, she heads to the kitchen, grabs a pint of chocolate peanut butter ice cream, unfastens her jeans, and plops down on the couch. "Fuck me. Why didn't I tell Mr. Evans to fuck himself? Why did I waste my time—my fucking *life*—on that stupid job? I'll never see Paris or Tokyo," she mumbles through a fistful of ice cream. "Fuck, I've never even been to Vancouver."

I join her on the couch and place what is supposed to be a comforting hand on her knee, even though she can't feel me. "You didn't know. No one knew for sure. They kept saying scientists were working on it, that they were gonna save the world."

"Well, they failed. Should've known better." She tosses the carton aside and wipes her sticky hands on her jeans. When we were kids and I used her as my napkin, she would cry to our mother until she learned she could pinch as hard as I could. She used to worry about stains on her clothes, spills on the rug. Just an hour ago, a drop of melted ice cream on the floor would've sent her into a cleaning frenzy, not from a fear of ants or our parents' scorn, but to prove that she was organized, careful, successful—an adult. Now, she's crass, sticky, reckless. My favorite kind of Kira.

"You'll be there, right? When it's over?" She leans back, her head drooping towards where my shoulder should be. "You'll be the first thing I see?"

"Of course."

She nods and closes her eyes. "Tell me it doesn't hurt."

More than anything, I want that to be true. I want to assure her it will happen so fast she won't have time to feel it. If only I could put my arms around her, hold her, be the one to absorb the blow when the asteroid breaks her into pieces too small to recognize. I want everything I've told her about death to be not just empty comfort. I want the heaven I promised to be there, waiting for her.

WHEN I FIRST CAME TO Kira, I couldn't speak. Time was different for me then; while she had just returned from my memorial, the last thing I remembered was the dry sear of the seatbelt slicing through my throat. I knew I was dead, but the real fear came as I realized she could see but not hear me. She interpreted my struggle to communicate as a different kind of panic, my hand-waving and pantomiming as a sign that I was stuck on some horrible plane, unable to follow the light to paradise.

So Kira bought books and crystals and learned the difference between banishing and freeing. She attempted to release me in a flurry of white sage and incantations. When I came back, she thought she'd failed, so she tried new herbs, new blessings, new prayers. What she achieved on her subsequent attempts was to give me back my voice, or thinned the veil enough to finally hear me. The first thing I told her was I'm okay, I'm here by choice. When she asked about our parents, who had died in the early days of the pandemic—Had I seen them? Were they okay? Why hadn't they visited her like I did?—I lied. I told her there is no hell and the dead have choices about how they spend the afterlife. Mom and Dad welcomed me in a magnificent beam of light, young again and even more beautiful than we remembered them, pulling me into an embrace that felt like reunion and paradise and home. Peace. They chose to remain in heaven, but I told Kira I wanted to stay on this earth to be with her. I told her death has shown me an earth that is always beautiful, always perfect. This is what I see, and being near her is my idea of heaven.

Really, I never saw our parents. I was in my car one moment—all that metal crushing my legs, my chest, glass slicing me open and tearing me apart so I'd never be put back together again—then I was in Kira's living room. I've never seen our parents, or any other ghosts. No one except Kira has acknowledged my presence. If there is a heaven or hell, no one's filled me in. I walk the streets when she doesn't want me around, alone as a person or ghost can be. I see it all: the dead creatures in the grass, the garbage where flowers once grew, the vulnerable stripped of their security, agency and dignity—every facet of human depravity on display. It's not the idealistic fantasy of a parallel utopia I created to comfort her. I can't tell my sister the truth when she's so worried about my peace and happiness. Not when I abandoned her as brutally and abruptly as our parents had.

Now the world's ending and she'll learn there is no heaven, not for us, anyway. There's no teleporting to the Eiffel Tower or the pyramids of Giza. Chocolate mousse and the best Pad Thai we've ever eaten are distant memories, fading every day. I don't remember the feel of kitten fur or warm hands on my back. All I have is loneliness and envy, the bitter film of being eternally trapped as a photocopy of myself in a world that has no place for me. Kira will learn that I've never been at peace—there is no peace—that all I've done this last year is wander and worry. The only comfort I've had is the hope that when she dies she'll join me and we'll walk this earth together. We'll have each other.

But now there's an asteroid big enough to obliterate this planet and everything on it. With the earth gone, what happens to us? What happens to a ghost when she no longer has an earth to walk?

* * *

THE "MAYBE LESS" of the scientists' twenty-four-hours-remaining prediction hits hard. It also gives Kira a second wind. Though she lost her appetite while that donut was still dangling from her tongs, she plans a feast for her final meal. The staff has abandoned our local market, so I accompany her as she joins the frenzied mob of our neighbors in filling her basket with crabmeat, eclairs, those expensive frozen salmon puffs we had at a party once. We lament that the sushi station has already been pillaged.

A man smashes the glass case where they keep the fancy liquor and passes bottles into the crowd. With his big beard and jolly sing-song-ing of "for you! and you!", he's a doomsday Santa Claus. He hands Kira a beautiful blue bottle of the tequila I used to admire when I was alive.

Back at home, her loot piled on the kitchen counter, she shifts to deciding her final outfit. Time ticking down makes her scattered, bouncing from her closet to the laundry hamper as she lays out various choices ranging from Sunday sweats to a dress she bought for New Year's but never got to wear. "Do I die comfortable, or beautiful?" she muses, unzipping the garment bag to reveal black lace and mauve tulle. "No one's gonna see it, but I guess it matters because this is what I'll be wearing for all eternity, right?" She surveys me in my hoodie and jeans. At least we've both been spared the bloodstains, the piss, the smears of various bodily fluids that marred my clothes in life.

After more back-and-forth, she comes to a compromise: New Year's dress, hair down, no makeup, her favorite beat up old Converse. She gets to work on her feast, swigging tequila out of the bottle, eating crabmeat with one hand and an eclair in the other while the oven heats up. Pastry cream drips onto the bodice of her dress and she licks it off. She wipes her fingers on the tulle. This is how I want to remember her; not the frenzy and indecision, but splayed on the couch, chocolate smeared around her mouth and her feet on the coffee table.

Remember her. As if being dead somehow exempts me from getting sucked into the black void of nothing.

"Oh god, Kimberly," Kira sighs, licking chocolate from her fingers. "I wish you could taste this. No, what am I saying? It's even better in heaven, right?"

"Better than you can imagine," I say.

Watching my sister gorge herself on these small pleasures, I feel envy. For the food—the textures on her tongue, between her molars—but mostly because she knows when her end will come. If I'd known mine ahead of time, I wouldn't have skipped breakfast. I would've had wine with lunch. I would've worn my nicest underwear, the ones I was stupidly saving for the right guy. I would've told all the wrong guys to fuck themselves. All that time I wouldn't have wasted.

And, for the first time, I feel guilt, too. The lies still come too easy They brought me as much comfort as they did her.

By the time the salmon puffs are done, Kira's too sick to eat them She's too anxious to keep even water down.

"Why am I so scared?" she moans, kneeling in front of the toilet hands gripping the bowl. A ribbon of her long brown hair dangles past the seat, dangerously close to dipping into the swirling miasma o undigested crab, pastry and bile. I long to hold back her hair like used to when we were teens trying to hide her hangover from ou parents. "I mean, I know it's natural to be scared—we're all going t fucking die—but I have you," she says. "I have an advantage ove everyone else because you know—you've been through it. You'r proof that there's an afterlife where everything is going to be okay Better than okay. I should be excited, right? I mean, those cult peopl kill themselves trying to get to this. I'll never have to deal wit another rude customer again. I'll never get scalded by the espress machine. I'll never have another man grab my ass or call me a bitch. I'll never lose another person I love. I mean, what was so great about this life anyway? I should be celebrating. I'll be fucking free, right? I'll finally get to be with everyone I love."

My hand hovers over her back, making a circular rubbing motion. It's habit, muscle memory. Even though she can't feel it, I want her to know I'm here, not just ears to listen but *fully* here for her. When I first came back, we tried all kinds of things, but my hand always passed through hers to no discernible effect. She's never felt my breath in her face, the squeeze I feel in my own embrace even though my body is a phantom even to myself. None of that has ever stopped me from going through the motions.

"Mom and Dad are waiting for us," I tell her. "And Hoot and Holler. Did I tell you I just saw them? Remember how they used to climb up our legs when we got home from school?"

That calms Kira. As she's reminiscing about our childhood cats, I'm thinking about the man in the market, the Santa Claus handing out the liquor. In all that fear and frenzy, he was joyous, celebrating. Like he was finally heading home. Did he know something I don't? Or does he have a ghost too, one who's a liar like me?

* * *

KIRA WANTS to take a shower and she wants to be alone, so I leave. Last time she'll shower, brush her teeth, put on clean underwear. Every action carries so much weight, like even putting on deodorant should be a ceremony. Last time I leave this apartment, last time I walk these streets. Last time being alone—or conscious of being alone, anyway—if there really is nowhere for us to go.

The streets are quiet, despite the end-of-the-world frenzy. Now most people are cocooned in their safe spaces with the people they love, eating their favorite foods and listening to their favorite music. Windows are lit up, the people inside creating compelling tableaus: a living room full of friends dancing, hoisting champagne glasses, wet faces split with laughter; a cozy bedroom cradling a woman and two young children curled together on the bed; a kitchen with an elderly couple holding hands across the table; another kitchen with a man sorting piles of cash and various guns spread on the counters. A surprising number of people fuck against the glass in a variety of positions. Some sit on porch swings, ready for the last sunset. A man throws a ball to a dog in his front yard while using his t-shirt to dab away the tears. I know they're afraid, and I know that no matter how hard they try, they can't smother that fear in pursuit of these perfect moments.

Joy is not a choice. I don't care what people say. I've tried, and all that's been presented to me in the afterlife are faded images, things I once knew—good and bad—that I can't touch or taste and can barely remember. The good things—Kira laughing, cats purring, birthday cake—are a cruel tease, a reminder of what I can never have again even if I did appreciate them in life. The bad things, though as dulled and indistinct as the good, stubbornly remain, lest I forget that death is not an escape.

Despite this, I haven't been afraid since adjusting to the afterlife. Not for myself anyway. Once I learned that when I closed my eyes I wouldn't slip into some hellscape or black void, that my sister would always be there, I've felt as at home as a ghost can be. My fear has always been for Kira. I can keep her safe—warn her about the oncoming car, the strange man in the dark alley—but I worry about her happiness. I've always had the comfort of knowing that when she died she'd join me and we'd walk the earth together. We could make each other laugh, keep each other company like we did when we were alive, for all eternity.

When I was a kid, I used to look up at the night sky and imagine all the astronauts up there. Not the ones working on space stations or those who set foot on the moon, but the ones who are still up there dead in their suits, corpses drifting through the cold expanse of space where they're forever preserved in their last moment of terror as they realized that forever is black and silent nothingness. How long did it take them to run out of oxygen? How many hours did they have to stare into that endless nothing without angels or even demons as proof of a life beyond our mortal ones? I can't imagine anything worse.

That scared Kira too, but she always looked to me as her older sister and there was power in that. Because I experienced most things first, I could be her guide, prove to her that if I survived, she could too. But now? There comes a point when even the most well-intentioned of lies becomes a cruelty. You're blissfully secure until that moment you find yourself soft-bellied naked on a stage.

I have to tell her the truth. I owe my sister that.

WHEN I GET BACK, Kira's sitting on the couch wearing only a bath towel. Her New Year's dress sits in a sticky heap on the floor. She's staring out the window, empty, oblivious to the sun-burnt sky, the swirling birds, the guy perched on the ledge of the building across the street. I know she smells like lavender because that's the shampoo she's used since we were teens.

That's another thing I miss: smells. Like everything else from my corporeal life, the scents of things have faded beyond a wisp of memory. I've lingered in the bakery every day Kira's worked, seen the buttery flakes of pastry gathered on the trays, the steam rising from the coffee, but all I know are the words to describe them, and those words are now meaningless to me. A donut might as well be a plastic model, unfathomable to my nose, on my tongue, between my teeth. I miss the smell of butter being worked into dough. I miss the cheesy popcorn odor of Kira's scalp. Hell, I even miss her B.O. Kira says I have no smell, not to her. My favorite perfume doesn't precede my entrance into a room. I don't leave sulfur in my wake, like a demon. It's like I've already been practicing for the nothingness that awaits.

And Kira knows, doesn't she? She's sitting there in her towel, too defeated to dress herself, because there is nothing. There is no point.

"We could do something fun," I suggest. "Something dumb. Hey, haven't you always wanted to burn money?"

Kira glances at her bag on the kitchen counter. "I thought about that, then I thought, what if the scientists are wrong and the world doesn't end? Then I'll have no money." She laughs. "Isn't that stupid? The world is ending and I'm still worrying about fucking money."

"Then how about that guy, the one who groped you on that date," I try. "You could slit his throat, or stab him—whatever. No consequences."

"But if I do that, won't that mean I won't get into heaven?"

"You'll be a ghost with me," I assure her. "You don't have to worry about hell."

She looks down at the bills spread on the coffee table. I know that look, when the overwhelmingness of it all blurs problems into unidentifiable, unfathomable urgency. "But there won't be an earth anymore. Where do we go? The only thing left is heaven, right?" She turns her attention back to me. "So what happens if I can't get in?"

This is it. The way she's looking at me, those big dark eyes exaggerating that little sister naivety, a lure to catch me in my lie. That was her go-to trick with our parents when she wanted ice cream, or her hand held, or some gentleness. This is my chance to tell her, to not fall into the trap where the gentleness I intended will end up being so much more bitter than sweet.

"They let me in," I say, forcing a laugh.

Kira's brow creases. I hate the lines her features make, the slow shame she instills in me. "Kimberly, just stop. I know, okay? You really think I still believe in heaven and hell? You proved me wrong with the ghost thing, but I'm supposed to believe that you're here because you like it, because you'd rather be with me in this shitty world than in paradise?"

I open my mouth, but she cuts me off.

"No, I mean it. Stop it. I don't want to spend my last hours debating the definition of heaven and the afterlife. You remember those astronauts, floating dead up there in space for all eternity?

That's what it is, isn't it? Just be honest with me. That's what's going to happen to us."

It's a fist through my core, enough to awaken an ache I'd long forgotten. If, instead of being obliterated with this earth, we somehow land as ghosts in space, that will be worse. Nothing to see beyond each other's faces, and that's if we are very lucky. The sights, sounds, smells, tastes, textures we remembered from life will fade until they are abstract concepts lost as quickly as high school algebra. If we still have voices, we'll have nothing to reminisce about. We'll wander with no destination, no agency, no home.

I join her on the couch. My ghost still finds the shapes I used to make, even if I no longer remember. "I'll be with you when it happens," I promise. "Wherever we go, we'll go together."

"Tell me it won't hurt," she says, tilting her head towards my shoulder.

I slide my phantom arm around her and she leans into me as if she can feel it. Out the window, I see the man on the ledge has now been joined by another man who's holding his hand. I think about the people in the grocery store, feasting and puking and crying. I think about the people fucking in windows, all those orgasms nothing more than dying gasps. The people enjoying one last celebration, one last game of catch, one last embrace. What heavy moments to carry into a void that doesn't fucking care.

I brush what used to be my lips against Kira's forehead. "I promise, it won't hurt."

CONTENT WARNINGS

See below for warnings regarding the content of the stories in this book. If you do not see a story listed, it's because the editor did not see a need to include any warnings for that story.

COMING EARTHSIDE BY TARYN MARTINEZ

- Childbirth

A EULOGY FOR THE FIFTH WORLD BY CARSON WINTER

- Sexual content

ESTRANGEMENTS BY D. MATTHEW URBAN

- Mariticide

THE HUNT BY ALEX FOX

- Ommetaphobia

NO MORE MEATLOAF MONDAY BY ANGELA SYLVAINE

- Implied child death

BONNIE'S ABLUTION BY M. LOPES DA SILVA

- Child neglect
- Implied child death

THE DOOR IN THE BASEMENT BY RUTH ANNA EVANS

- Sexual content

TUESDAY BY BRITTANY JOHNSTON

- Implied attempted sexual assault
- Implied child death

DIRT AND BLOOD AND SILENCE BY ELOU CAROLL

- Implied attempted kidnapping
- Implied attempted sexual assault
- Spouse death

TEN TOTALLY FREE PLACES TO WATCH THE END OF THE WORLD BY NICHOLAS BOUCHARD

- Sexual coercion
- Religious themes

ANYMORE BY L. MARIE WOOD

- Sexual Assault

THE END IS VERY FUCKING NIGH BY W. DALE JORDAN

- Homophobia
- Religious themes

WHEN THE HORIZON BURNS BY ELFORD ALLEY

- Infanticide
- Suicide

EYES OPEN, KNEES APART FOR THE END OF THE WORLD BY RAE KNOWLES

- Sexual content
- Mariticide

THE SMELL OF SUMMER BY EMMA E. MURRAY

- Animal endangerment (dog)

ABOUT THE AUTHORS

TARYN MARTINEZ || "COMING EARTHSIDE"

Taryn Martinez is a Mexican-American mother of two (one human, one dog) who has been a New York City public school science teacher for the past 10 years Her fiction has been published by Dark Fire Fiction and Dark Horses Magazine and won her an Academy for Teachers Bread Loaf Scholarship. She lives in Queens with her husband and children. You can find her on Instagram @taryn-martinezwrites.

ARSON WINTER || "A EULOGY FOR THE FIFTH WORLD"

Arson Winter is an author, punker, and raw nerve. His fiction has been featured in Apex, Vastarien, and Tales to Terrify. "The Guts of Myth" was published in volume one of Dread Stone Press' Split Scream series. His novella, Soft Targets, is out now from Tenebrous Press. He lives in the Pacific Northwest.

D. MATTHEW URBAN || "ESTRANGEMENTS"

D. Matthew Urban hails from Texas and lives in Queens, New York, where he reads weird books, watches weird movies, and writes weird fiction. His stories have appeared or are forthcoming in *Ooze: Little Bursts of Body Horror, No Trouble at All,* and *Split Scream* Volume 4, among other venues. He can be found on Twitter @breathinghead or on the web at https://dmatthewurban.com.

SARA TANTLINGER || "THE VIRIDESCENT DARK"

Sara Tantlinger is the author of the Bram Stoker Award-winning *The Devil's Dreamland: Poetry Inspired by H.H. Holmes,* and the Stoker-nominated works *To Be Devoured* and *Cradleland of Parasites.* She has also edited *Not All Monsters* and *Chromophobia.* She is an active HWA member and also participates in the HWA Pittsburgh Chapter. She embraces all things macabre and can be found lurking in graveyards or on Twitter @SaraTantlinger, at saratantlinger.com and on Instagram @inkychaotics

ALEX FOX || "THE HUNT"

Alex Fox hails from the wintry Northeast, USA. She has words in Podcastle, Martian Magazine, Apex's Strange Libations, and Grende Press. You can find her on twitter @afoxwrites and maybe one day a afoxwrites.com.

TIFFANY MICHELLE BROWN || "RED ROVER, RED ROVER"

Tiffany Michelle Brown is a California-based writer who once had conversation with a ghost over a pumpkin beer. She is the author c the collection How Lovely To Be a Woman: Stories and Poems an cohost of the Horror in the Margins podcast. Her fiction and poetr has been featured in publications by Black Spot Books, Dread Ston

Press, Death Knell Press, Cemetery Gates Media, and the NoSleep Podcast. Tiffany lives near the beach with her husband Bryan, their pup Zen, and their combined collections of books, board games, and general geekery.

ANGELA SYLVAINE || "NO MORE MEATLOAF MONDAY"

Angela Sylvaine is a self-proclaimed cheerful goth who writes horror fiction and poetry. Her debut novel, *Frost Bite*, and her debut collection, *The Dead Spot: Stories of Lost Girls*, are forthcoming from Dark Matter INK. Her short fiction and poetry have appeared in/on over forty anthologies, magazines, and podcasts, including *Southwest Review*, *Apex Magazine*, and *The NoSleep Podcast*. You can find her online angelasylvaine.com.

M. LOPES DA SILVA || "BONNIE'S ABLUTION"

M. Lopes da Silva (he/they/she) is a non-binary trans masc author and artist from Los Angeles. He writes pulp and poetry. Previously he's been employed as a sex worker, an art and film critic, and an educator.

In 2020 Unnerving Magazine published his novella *Hooker*: a pro-queer, pro-sex work, feminist retrowave pulp thriller about a bisexual sex worker hunting a serial killer active during 1980s Los Angeles using hooks as her weapons of choice. Dread Stone Press recently published his first novelette *What Ate the Angels* - a queer vore sludgefest that travels beneath the streets of Los Angeles starring a non-binary ASMR artist and their vore-loving girlfriend - in Volume Two of the *Split Scream* series. His poetry can be found in Eye to the Telescope, The Dread Machine, and Electric Literature. You can find him on Instagram @authormlopesdasilva or on Twitter @_MLopes-daSilva

ANDREW CULL || "THE SCREAM"

Andrew Cull is an award-winning writer and horror director. His story collection Bones has been described as "a masterclass in emotional cinematic horror fiction." His debut novel Remains was shortlisted for the Best Horror Novel Aurealis Award. Andrew lives in Melbourne, Australia. He loves horror and Hitchcock and, like you, he's not easily scared. Follow Andy on Twitter @andrewcull

RUTH ANNA EVANS || "THE DOOR IN THE BASEMENT"

Ruth Anna Evans is a writer of short horror fiction who lives in the heart of all that is sinister: the American Midwest. She has been composing prose of all types since childhood but finds something truly delightful in putting her nightmares on the page. She edited and published Ooze, an anthology of short body horror, has written and published a short story collection and two novellas, and has a story coming out in Dark Town, an anthology of revenge stories from D&T publishing. She also has a story in We're Here, an LGBTQ horror anthology out in June 2023. You can find Ruth Anna on Twitter @ruthannaevans, on Facebook as Ruth Anna Evans, or visit her website, ruthannaevans.com.

WENDY N. WAGNER || "SILVER ALERT"

Wendy N. Wagner's longer works include the forthcoming *The Creek Girl* (Tor Nightfire, 2025), *The Secret Skin*, *The Deer Kings* and *An Oath of Dogs*. Her more than seventy published pieces of short fiction, essays, and poetry range from horror to environmental literature, The Locus award-nominated editor-in-chief of *Nightmare Magazine* Wagner lives, works, and hikes in the Pacific Northwest. Keep up with her at winniewoohoo.com.

GWENDOLYN KISTE || "A SWEET SOIREE ON THE LAST NIGHT OF THE WORLD"

Gwendolyn Kiste is the three-time Bram Stoker Award-winning author of The Rust Maidens, Reluctant Immortals, And Her Smile Will Untether the Universe, Pretty Marys All in a Row, The Invention of Ghosts, and Boneset & Feathers. Her short fiction and nonfiction have appeared in outlets including Lit Hub, Nightmare, Tor Nightfire, Titan Books, Vastarien, Best American Science Fiction and Fantasy, and The Dark among others. She's a Lambda Literary Award finalist, and her fiction has also received the This Is Horror award for Novel of the Year as well as nominations for the Premios Kelvin and Ignotus awards.

Originally from Ohio, she now resides on an abandoned horse farm outside of Pittsburgh with her husband, their calico cat, and not nearly enough ghosts. You can find her online at gwendolynkiste.com and at Facebook and Instagram.

OLEN CROWE || "THE BOY WHO PRAYED FOR THE WORLD TO END"

Olen lives in the Appalachian foothills of North Carolina. Besides reading and writing, he likes to hike, watch cheesy, B-horror movies, and study linguistics. Check out more at www.olencrowe.com or talk to him on Twitter @olencrowe.

BRITTANY JOHNSTON || "TUESDAY"

Brittany (Britt) Johnston is a horror writer based in California with a passion for things twisted and raw. She aims to produce and consume art that explores both the lovely and unpalatable facets of human nature, the shifting picture of the self, and the endlessly complicated relationships we form with one another. She can currently be found on Twitter at @sadboyarc and hopes to soon launch a website for her work.

ELOU CARROLL || "DIRT AND BLOOD AND SILENCE"

Elou Carroll is a graphic designer and freelance photographer who writes. Her work appears or is forthcoming in The Deadlands, Baffling Magazine, If There's Anyone Left (Volume 3), In Somnio: A Collection of Modern Gothic Horror (Tenebrous Press), Spirit Machine (Air and Nothingness Press), Ghostlore (Alternative Stories Podcast) and others. When she's not whispering with ghosts, she can be found editing Crow & Cross Keys, publishing all things dark and lovely, and spending far too much time on twitter (@keychild). She keeps a catalogue of her weird little wordcreatures on www.eloucarroll.com.

NICK BOUCHARD || "TEN TOTALLY FREE PLACES TO WATCH THE END OF THE WORLD"

Nick is an award-winning copywriter and undecorated father of four. He enjoys writing when there's time and thinking about it when there's not. His work has appeared in anthologies from Darkhouse Books, Dream of Shadows, and most recently "Stone's Blood" in Mother: Tales of Love and Terror from Weird Little Worlds. He can be found online @nicktionary19

L. MARIE WOOD || "ANYMORE"

L. Marie Wood is a two-time Bram Stoker Award® and Rhysling nominated author, screenwriter, essayist, and poet. She writes high concept fiction that includes elements of psychological horror, mystery, dark fantasy, and romance. She won the Golden Stake Award for her novel The Promise Keeper. She is a recipient of the MICO Award and has won Best Horror, Best Action, Best Afrofuturism/Horror/Sci-Fi, and Best Short Screenplay awards in both national and international film festivals. She is also part of the 2022 Bookfest Book Award winning poetry anthology, *Under Her Skin*. Wood has penned short fiction that has been published in ground-breaking works, including the anthologies like *Sycorax's Daughters* and *Slay: Stories of the Vampire Noire*. Her academic writing has been published by Nightmare Magazine and the cross-curricular text, *Conjuring Worlds: An Afrofuturist Textbook*. She is the founder of the Speculative Fiction Academy, an English and Creative Writing professor, a horror scholar, and a frequent speaker in the genre convention space. Learn more about L. Marie Wood at www.lmariewood.com.

V. DALE JORDAN || "THE END IS VERY FUCKING NIGH"

V. Dale Jordan is an out and proud gay author living with his husband in the wilds of East Texas. His imagination was always just a little too big for him growing up, and it often spilled onto the page. Today, he splits his time between running Off Limits Press and writing his own fiction. He is a big believer that representation in media is vital to equity in the real world and incorporates those ideas into his writing whether it's a scary creature feature or a fantasy tale like those he loved growing up.

LFORD ALLEY || "WHEN THE HORIZON BURNS"

lford Alley is a horror writer and disgraced paranormal investigator from Texas, currently exiled to Oklahoma. He recently released his horror-comedy novel *Apartment 239*. His stories have appeared in the anthologies *Campfire Macabre*, *Paranormal Contact*, *Something Bad Happened*, and *A Compendium of Creeps*. You can find his horror story collections and novellas, *We Will Find a Place for You*, *The Last Night in the Damned House*, *Ash and Bone*, *Find Us*, and *In Search of the Nobility*, X Wildman on Amazon and through this website.

CHRIS MASON || "ALICE"

Chris Mason is an award-winning author who lives on Peramangk land in the Adelaide Hills of South Australia. Her stories have appeared in numerous publications, including the *Things in the Well* anthologies, and the Australian Horror Writers Association's magazine *Midnight Echo*. Chris is a Shirley Jackson finalist, has won Aurealis Awards for Best Horror Short Story and Best Horror Novella, and also received the Australian Shadows Paul Haines Award for long fiction. You can visit Chris at: facebook.com/chrismasonhorrorwriter or on twitter @Chris_A_Mason.

MATTHEW M. BARTLETT || "SMASH HIT"

Matthew M. Bartlett was born in Hartford, Connecticut in 1970. At an early age he was given as a gift the novelization of The Omen; not long after that, he inherited a worn copy of Christine by Stephen King. He fell deeply in love with horror: with the Universal monsters, with Hammer films, with the rented videos from the horror section of that almost-gone artifact known as the Video Rental Store. He began writing poetry while in the English program at Central Connecticut State University. An abiding interest in horror fiction led him to start a Livejournal page whose posts were his first forays into fiction: bite sized tales accompanied by doctored daguerreotypes and his own photographs taken in Leeds and Northampton, Massachusetts. These posts centered around a long-dead coven using radio waves to broadcast disturbing and dangerous transmissions from the dark woods of Western Massachusetts. His inspirations are varied and the foremost are certainly not atypical for the genre: H.P. Lovecraft, Thomas Ligotti, Robert Aickman, T.E.D. Klein. Other authors he admires include Donald E. Westlake, Richard Yates, J.D. Salinger, and Hunter S. Thompson. He also draws inspiration from the radio monologues and shows of Joe Frank; the poetry of Philip Larkin, of Mark Strand, of Stephen Crane; the movies of Wes Anderson, of Ben Wheatley, of the Coen Brothers. He continues to write dark and strange fiction at his home in Western Massachusetts, where he lives with his wife Katie and an unknown number of cats.

MADISON MCSWEENEY || "I AM THE VANITY MIRROR SHAPED LIKE A SKULL"

Madison McSweeney is the author of the horror comedy *The Doom That Came to Mellonville* (Filthy Loot) and the heavy metal/folk horror novelette *The Forest Dreams With Teeth* (Demain Publishing). Her gothic poetry chapbook *Fringewood* was released by Alien Buddha Press in 2022.

She lives in Ottawa, Canada, tweets from @MMcSw13 and blogs at www.madisonmcsweeney.com.

RAE KNOWLES || "EYES OPEN, KNEES APART FOR THE END OF THE WORLD"

Rae Knowles (she/her) is a queer woman with multiple works from Brigids Gate Press. Her debut novel, The Stradivarius, released May 23, her sapphic horror novella, Merciless Waters, is due out winter 23, and her collaboration with April Yates, Lies That Bind, in early 24. A number of her short stories have been published or are forthcoming from publications like Dark Matter Ink, Nightmare, Seize the Press, Taco Bell Quarterly, and Nosetouch Press. Recent updates on her work can be found at RaeKnowles.com and you can follow her on twitter @_Rae_Knowles

RJ JOSEPH || "ENDLESS POSSIBILITIES"

Rhonda Jackson Garcia, AKA RJ Joseph, is a Stoker Award(TM) nominated, Texas based academic and creative writer/professor whose writing regularly focuses on the intersections of gender and race in the horror and romance genres and popular culture. She has had works published in various applauded venues, including the 2020 Halloween issue of Southwest Review and The Streaming of Hill House: Essays on the Haunting Netflix Series. Rhonda is also an instructor at the Speculative Fiction academy.When she isn't writing, reading, or teaching, she can usually be found wrangling her huge blended family of one husband, four adult sprouts, seven teenaged sproutlings, four grandboo seedlings, and one furry hellbeast who sometimes pretends to be a dog. She occasionally peeks out on Twitter @rjacksonjoseph or at www.rhondajacksonjoseph.com

EMMA E. MURRAY || "THE SMELL OF SUMMER"

Emma E. Murray writes horror and dark speculative fiction. Her stories have appeared, or are forthcoming, in anthologies like What One Wouldn't Do and Obsolescence, as well as magazines such as Vastarien, Pyre, and If There's Anyone Left. To read more, you can visit her website EmmaEMurray.com or follow her on Twitter @EMurrayAuthor

V. CASTRO || "MUERTE LUNA"

V. Castro is a two time Bram Stoker award nominated writer born in San Antonio, Texas, to Mexican American parents. She's been writing horror stories since she was a child, always fascinated by Mexican folklore and the urban legends of Texas. Castro now lives in the United Kingdom with her family, writing and traveling with her children.

EÓIN MURPHY || "LOST TIME"

Eóin Murphy has been writing horror stories ever since he was no allowed to go to the cinema to see The Monster Squad so he wrote his own version. He still maintains his version was better. Eóin lives in Northern Ireland with his fantastic wife, awesome son and occasion ally energetic cat. His work has previously been published in Phantasmagoria, The Twisted Book of Shadows, Uncertainties Volume 5 and The Best Horror of the Year Volume 14. He can be found lurking on Twitter as @Ragemonki.

J.A.W. MCCARTHY || "ALL THE DEAD ASTRONAUTS"

J.A.W. McCarthy is the Bram Stoker Award and Shirley Jackson Award nominated author of Sometimes We're Cruel and Other Stories (Cemetery Gates Media, 2021) and Sleep Alone (Off Limits Press, 2023). Her short fiction has appeared in numerous publications, including Vastarien, PseudoPod, LampLight, Apparition Lit, Tales to Terrify, and The Best Horror of the Year Vol 13 (ed. Ellen Datlow). She is Thai American and lives with her husband and assistant cats in the Pacific Northwest. You can call her Jen on Twitter @JAWMcCarthy, and find out more at www.jawmccarthy.com.

ABOUT THE EDITOR

Brandon Applegate lives and writes in a parched suburban hellscape near Austin, Texas, with his wife and two daughters who have so far failed to eat him. His debut collection, "Those We Left Behind: And Other Sacrifices" is available now on Amazon and here on bapplegate.com. More work appears in "Shredded" (Cursed Morsels Press), "Theater Phantasmagoria" (Night Terror Novels), Frost Zone Zine, and Crow & Cross Keys. He is the EIC at Hungry Shadow Press, where he edited "It Was All A Dream: An Anthology of Bad Horror Tropes Done Right".